SHADOW TRAFFIC

Johns Hopkins: Poetry and Fiction
John T. Irwin, General Editor

SHADOW

TRAFFIC

Stories by Richard Burgin

The Johns Hopkins University Press
Baltimore

This book has been brought to publication with the generous
assistance of the G. Harry Pouder Fund.

Printed in the United States of America on acid-free paper
2 4 6 8 9 7 5 3 1

The Johns Hopkins University Press
2715 North Charles Street
Baltimore, Maryland 21218-4363
www.press.jhu.edu

Library of Congress Cataloging-in-Publication Data

Burgin, Richard.
Shadow traffic / Richard Burgin.
p.   cm.
ISBN-13: 978-1-4214-0273-4 (alk. paper)
ISBN-10: 1-4214-0273-4 (alk. paper)
I. Title.
PS3552.U717S53 2011
813'.54—dc22   2011004502

A catalog record for this book is available from the British Library.

*Special discounts are available for bulk purchases of this book. For more
information, please contact Special Sales at 410-516-6936 or
specialsales@press.jhu.edu.*

The Johns Hopkins University Press uses environmentally friendly
book materials, including recycled text paper that is composed of at
least 30 percent post-consumer waste, whenever possible.

For John T. Irwin

CONTENTS

SHADOW TRAFFIC

Caesar

He leaned back and looked briefly at the Christmas lights on Kingshighway, then at the oddly shaped planetarium, which looked like an alien spaceship that had landed on the outskirts of Forest Park. Some piano pieces by Ravel were playing—not the usual thing you heard on the radio.

"Is the music bothering you, sir?" the driver said.

"No, I like it. That's Debussy, isn't it?"

"No, sir. I think it's Ravel."

"That's right, of course, Ravel. How angry it would have made them to be confused with each other. Anyway, it's a great relief not to hear any more Christmas carols for a while. Those Christmas carols are like zombies, aren't they? They never die. I mean it's almost New Year's Eve, isn't it, and they're still playing Christmas music everywhere, and the Christmas decorations are still up because somehow it all still goes on." Onward Christian Shoppers, he thought to himself, but didn't say it lest he possibly offend the driver. He'd realized for some time now that St. Louis was a conservative town where young men like the driver were just as likely to be religious as people his age.

But the driver was laughing or making some kind of equivalent sound. "I feel the same way, sir," the driver said.

Was he a kindred spirit? Maybe it was worth a try to continue talking. The alternative was twenty minutes more of his dark thinking and staring at the half-dark highway.

"Do you like Ravel?"

"Very much."

"Of course you do or you wouldn't be listening to it. What other composers do you like?"

"Oh, quite a number."

The driver rattled off a list, including Beethoven and Mozart, of course, but also Bartók and Prokofiev and one or two he hadn't heard of. When he asked him if he ever studied music, the driver said, "Yes, sir, I studied piano for a number of years."

"Really?" So they were both musicians, though he was pretty sure he'd never worked as hard at it as the driver had. "You know, I enjoy talking with you but I wish you'd stop calling me 'sir.' I'm beginning to feel like an institution of some sort."

"Sorry about that."

"I remember the first time someone called me sir—it was like the beginning of death—like my death watch began from that moment on."

The driver laughed. It was a youngish laugh that made him think he might still be in his twenties. "Of course I haven't given you an alternative, have I? I haven't told you my name."

"No, you haven't."

"There's a good reason for that. My name is Caesar."

"Mine's Chris."

"How appropriate for the season—a real Chris. I, myself, wanted to be a great dictator like Julius Caesar, that's probably what my father had in mind, too, when he named me, but instead I merely repeated the second part of Julius's life and got stabbed quite a few times in the back. So I should call myself Caesar the Second, I guess."

The driver laughed again, probably out of politeness, he thought, but maybe not.

"The truth is Caesar is actually my middle name. My real first name is Malcolm—that's right, I'm a Malcolm. Ever know a Malcolm?"

"Sure."

"Ever like one?"

Again, the driver laughed.

"You all right? Everything OK tonight?"

"You just make me laugh, that's all. You're very funny, Malcolm."

"There you said it. You know a Malcolm. Now, I'm afraid there's no going back."

More laughter, definitely slightly forced this time. Then as quickly as they talked, they fell silent. It was as if there were a certain number of potential subjects they could discuss, like a little school of fireflies all lit up and waiting to be picked, but then just as quickly as they arrived their lights went out and they disappeared. He didn't like that. If it continued, he'd have to try to control his thoughts, while looking at the highway or the driver's neck. He'd seen far too many necks lately—in cabs and planes and in theaters and in lines at the bank. It had become a world of necks, they'd taken over almost everything, it seemed.

He was going to ask Chris how good a pianist he was—though he sensed he'd hear a tragic story if he did—when Chris suddenly surprised him with a question of his own.

"Are you going somewhere special tonight?"

"Moi? Why do you ask?"

3

"You look pretty dressed up like you might be going out somewhere. That's a nice evening coat you're wearing."

"Thank you but no, I'm not doing anything I'd consider special."

"I thought, because you're going to the Ritz they might be having some kind of event."

"I am going to the Ritz but my plan was to go to their lobby and sit there with a drink and try to feel rich."

"I hear you."

"Actually, I am kind of rich. Not Donald Trump rich, but I came into some money recently."

"Congratulations."

"There's really nothing to congratulate me for—I didn't do anything to deserve it. As they say, 'I did it the old-fashioned way, I inherited it.' You're laughing but it's true. Strange the way money is so often connected with death, isn't it?"

"I hadn't really thought of that before."

"Of course you haven't. That's one of the fringe benefits of being young, you don't have to think about it. No one's even called you 'sir' yet, have they?"

"It's happened once or twice."

"That you were 'sir'ed' with your subpoena? I'm surprised. But they were probably joking. I mean I've seen young children called 'sir' by people who think it's cute. I think calling the wrong people sir is a national sport, it's like Christmas, it will never go away. People flagellate the aging with it in the name of respect, and embarrass the young with it in the name of humor. You can see that I really do need to have a drink, don't I?"

"Everyone feels that way sometimes."

"You, too?"

"Sure, sometimes."

"But you can't do anything about it while you're driving your cab, can you?"

"No, not while I'm driving."

"Not supposed to anyway. I thought that after I finally got my money the number of occasions when I'd need a drink would decrease. Instead the opposite has proven to be true. You would have thought I'd know better."

"So what's it like to get all that money? Changed your life, I guess."

He paused as if he were making an intricate calculation. "I would say it's changed my life five to ten percent, no more than that."

"Must be nice to be able to buy whatever you want, though."

"The things I bought made less than one percent difference to me, so far, if that."

"Really? Well, still it must be nice not to have to worry about money anymore."

"You get a different set of worries instead. Actually, I'd say my biggest surprise is how little I'm able to use my money to actually *change* anything in my life in any fundamental way. Maybe if I got it when I was younger, say at your age, it might have been different. I wanted to be, for example, at one time—well, not exactly a composer, but I wanted to be a songwriter. I wanted to write theater music though I wound up working in an office. But if I'd had my money then, it might have helped me chase my dream. Do you see? For me to get the money now at my time of life—well, it's kind of an ironic gift, wouldn't you say?"

"But you're not old, Malcolm. I mean, you could still do whatever you want, couldn't you?"

"Call me Caesar," he said with a laugh.

"You look good, Caesar. You don't look old at all."

"Well thank you. That's the kindest thing anyone's said to me since—well, since I got my money."

He looked out the window and realized they were already on Clayton Road. They'd be at the Ritz soon and he felt strangely anxious.

"So, why did you stop studying piano?"

"That's a long story . . . it just got to be impractical."

"Do you still play, I hope?"

"No, not really anymore."

"But you could, you don't forget something like that, I imagine."

"No, you don't forget, not completely."

He could see the Ritz already looming above them like the brick castle of St. Louis.

"I really do enjoy talking with you. Why don't you join me for a drink, my treat?"

"I'd like to but I couldn't have a drink on the job."

"You can drink a ginger ale then, and just keep the meter running."

"How could I do that?"

"Good point. Well, call in and tell your dispatcher you're waiting for me, that I'm making another stop and I'll more than pay you for whatever time we spend. Surely you can do that."

Chris turned to face him. He was so young that Malcolm felt a sense of shock.

"Come on," Malcolm continued, "here's something for a deposit," he said, handing him two fifties. "You can do this. It's New Year's Eve, after all."

"That's tomorrow."

"It's the eve before New Year's Eve then. That's still a holiday in my book."

"OK, sure. Thanks very much," he said, putting the money in his pocket.

· · ·

There was a large Christmas tree in the Ritz, fully decorated, with a lot of tinsel and a star on top, but the lobby was so big the tree merely blended into the room instead of dominating it. In the approximate center of the lobby a pianist and saxophonist were playing "Someone to Watch over Me." A few middle-aged couples and one elderly couple were dancing on the relatively small dance floor.

Chris and he sat on a green sofa in a corner of the room waiting for their drinks. He'd forgotten that there was sometimes live music at the Ritz. That made it more difficult to talk, of course, and he sensed Chris was feeling awkward. They sat through a somewhat jazzy version of "Have Yourself a Merry Little Christmas" in something close to silence, then, after some tepid applause, the musicians took a break just as their drinks mercifully arrived.

"Not exactly Debussy *or* Ravel," Malcolm said, with a smile.

Chris smiled. "No, not exactly."

"The pianist had pretty good chops, though, what'd you think?"

"He played all the notes, but I couldn't really evaluate him as a musician," Chris said, "'cause they make them water down the music so much so people can dance to it."

"Elevator music, we used to call it."

"Yeah, I know. I used to have a gig like this once."

"Really?"

"Not at the Ritz but at the Adams Mark."

"Still, that's a pretty good hotel."

"It was a good gig, moneywise, the best I ever had."

"So you really were at a professional level?"

Chris shrugged, then took a large swallow of his tequila sunrise, and Malcolm followed, fugue-like, with his.

"Why did you stop?"

"I was studying to be a classical pianist till that got too expensive. Then I tried to do something with jazz, but I didn't really have the nerve and I never had the money."

Malcolm finished his drink and ordered another round from one of the waitresses who were pouncing on tables every ten minutes like leopards to solicit more drinks. "I wish I'd known you then. I might have been able to help you. When did you stop studying?"

"Maybe four or five years ago."

"Before I came into my big money, but I still had enough where I could have helped."

Chris gave him a strange look and then began his new drink.

"It's so rare that we meet the right person at the right time," Malcolm said, "or that we realize who the right person is in time. It makes you wonder sometimes why we've lived at all if we only realize things when it's too late to do anything about them."

He looked at Chris for a response, but he was busy finishing his new drink.

"There's a poem by T. S. Eliot," Malcolm continued, "I hope I'm not confusing him with W. H. Auden, no seriously, it *is* from Eliot. Anyway, he wrote 'we had the experience but missed the meaning.' Do you identify with any of this?"

Chris shrugged moodily again with his eyes averted, and Malcolm felt the same sense of panic he'd felt earlier—like a buzzing in his brain, easier to hear now that the music had stopped. Then

Chris finally answered and the buzzing sound went away as if it too merely had the endurance of a firefly.

"Sure, that's happened to me, I've realized things too late. But other times you do know what you should do, you realize the path you should take but just can't afford it. I was once in the Curtis School of Music in Philadelphia."

"Wow," Malcolm said, "pretty good school."

"Yah, but I had to take care of my father because he'd had a heart attack, and support myself, and I couldn't do all three, so I just had to leave school before I got my degree."

"That's a shame. I feel very badly for you. That's different from what I'm saying really—that's definitely a different kind of tragedy."

Chris nodded. "I've had the other kind, too, especially with my last girlfriend," he said, suddenly turning his head and staring directly into Malcolm's eyes.

Had Chris emphasized the word "girlfriend" or had he imagined that? He heard the buzzing again and finished his next drink quickly, as if to drown it.

"You want another?" he said, holding his glass up in the air.

"No, thanks, I've got to get back to my cab now."

"What? You've hardly spent any time here at all," Malcolm said, withdrawing a couple of fifties from his pocket and holding them out above the table as if he were about to throw food to a fish or duck.

"No, no, I really can't."

"But I . . ."

"Please put your money away, sir," Chris said, rising from the table almost as if he were going to fight him. "My . . . time isn't for sale like that."

"Oh my God, I know what you're thinking, oh this is funny, sad mainly, of course, but also funny how you've gotten the wrong idea. Should I say what I think your idea is?"

"I don't have any ideas, sir."

"I thought you were an intelligent, very intelligent and interesting guy and you told me about your musical career and I felt badly for you and wanted to see if I could help you out and you thought or think, that . . ."

"Don't tell me what I think," Chris said, gritting his teeth. "You don't know me, or what's happened to me. Your money doesn't buy you that kind of power."

"You've misunderstood."

"Weren't you quoting from that poem about experience? Well I've had the experience and I don't miss the meaning and I'm going to learn from my experiences, OK? I don't know what gives you rich guys the right to think you can treat a person as if you've discovered some great truth about them and what they really need and then insult them with it just because you think they're sad or alone and poor."

Malcolm looked up at him and saw that his face was getting red.

"No, not at all, Chris, you've really misunderstood."

"I haven't misunderstood," he said, pounding his fist on the table. A number of people looked up from their seats at them and Malcolm lowered his head. "*You've* misunderstood, Caesar," he said, hissing his name sarcastically.

Then he walked away from the table in a few quick, imperious strides. Malcolm was afraid to look around now, knowing that he was still being watched. He knew he should put one of the fifties on the table and go, yet he felt frozen, as if rooted to his chair.

The leopard waitress picked that moment to pounce. "Would you like another drink, sir?"

"Yes, another," he said. He had reached the point where he was afraid not to drink. Otherwise, the memories would come back, swarming and silent and no two alike, like snowflakes he supposed. Many of them would melt on contact, he told himself, but all the while more were accumulating then melting, and even now he knew Chris would be part of that memory snow that would stick. That was the price of human contact, or, in his case, the attempt at some. Would he never learn his lesson?

The waitress was back with his drink. They were unfailingly dependable when collecting money was involved. Yet how could he blame them, or even Chris, who'd walked off with his hundred dollars. He hadn't been any different when he was young. He was more selfish than any of them. Of course, he'd been at a tremendous disadvantage having to live with all his secrets weighing him down like a backpack of snow. Yes, he'd lived a life full of secrets, and the worst part of that was he never knew who knew and who didn't, not even with his own parents, from whom he was now rich. It was as if they'd rewarded him from beyond the grave for keeping his secret and sparing them the pain of hearing it. That was irrational, he knew, but memories eventually made you irrational, burying your rationality under an avalanche of snow.

It was odd how the beautiful memories hurt more than the painful ones. At least with him it worked that way. Even when it involved the relatively few men he'd been with. He could feel himself tearing up when he thought of them, or before them if he thought of his sled rides with his father down the hill across from the house where he grew up. Their laughter in the snow.

He finished his new drink and looked up for the leopard but

saw a man walking toward him instead. It reminded him of the car accident he was in a few years ago, the way the man approached him as if in slow motion.

"Hi there," the man said. He was probably around his age although Malcolm hoped he looked a few years younger. The man was well dressed too, in a navy blue blazer and light blue cashmere sweater. He could tell by his half-ironic, half-pitying smile that he'd witnessed Chris's dramatic exit—how could he not have?

"Hello and Happy New Year. I'm just on my way out," Malcolm wanted to say but instead only managed a muted "hello."

"I'm Gene," the man said, still standing in front of his sofa, which in a way was worse than if he'd sat down next to him uninvited. He rose from the sofa and said, "I'm Malcolm," then right on cue Gene extended his hand and they shook.

"Are you having a happy holiday?" Gene said, in a half-ironic voice.

"I was having a reasonably happy holiday until a little while ago."

"Oh?" Gene said, raising his eyebrows until he managed to form a completely convincing quizzical expression. He was a good-looking man somewhere in his late fifties, perhaps he'd once done some modeling or acting, Malcolm thought, the way he'd just maneuvered his face so adroitly.

"I'm sure you must have witnessed the unpleasant scene here a few minutes ago. I'm sure the whole room saw it."

"I saw something. I'm sorry that it was unpleasant for you. What was that youngster in such a snit about? Oh, well, why don't we have a drink and make things more pleasant?" he asked politely enough, yet it seemed more a statement of policy than a request. Here was his chance to start the exit process back to his house in Clayton, where he could recover from Chris, but instead he said, "Sure, sit down."

Gene sat in a chair, not exactly opposite him but not next to him either. The furniture here was arranged like a museum of odd angles, Malcolm thought.

Then a leopard, who was probably watching this entire encounter, pounced in front of them and Gene ordered drinks, putting twenty dollars on the small circular table in front of them.

"Well . . . you're looking good, Malcolm."

"Thank you," he said, vaguely aware that he should return the compliment. "By the way, many people call me by my middle name, Caesar. Do you like that name more?"

"Malcolm is just fine."

"You like it better than Caesar?"

"Caesar is maybe a bit militaristic. I vote for Malcolm," he said, smiling.

"Oh, OK, then Malcolm it is."

That was the way their conversation began. It was long on smiles, of one kind or another, but short on wit. Yet, at the same time, it seemed orchestrated by Gene, as if he was keeping his intelligence in reserve, knowing it was a weapon he could use later, whenever he felt the time was appropriate.

"Do you remember the term 'generation gap'?" Gene said, arching his eyebrows meaningfully.

"Sure, of course. It was the national buzz word once and old buzz words never die, they just grow older."

"Exactly. So this young man who landed a hard left hook on the table—was it, in retrospect, really more of a generational thing than anything else?"

Malcolm paused and found himself seriously thinking about Gene's question, painful though it was to think of Chris again.

"In a certain sense, I suppose it was."

"I'm just curious."

"But in a certain sense isn't everything partially true? Isn't that why we find ourselves in such a wonderfully clear and lucid world?"

"Oh, oh. You're being sarcastic. This can't be good."

"I read somewhere that sarcasm is the protest of the weak, so I suppose that's true."

"Are you weak, then?"

"In certain ways I'm afraid I am."

Gene smiled and looked at him closely.

"Well, I didn't mean to cut you off before when you had a point to make about, how did you put it?—'everything being partially true.' Is there a point in my asking for an example?"

"Oh, let's say you have a possessive mother, as I actually did, who tried to keep you away from your father and from your friends because of her own need for you. You could easily enough say she was selfish, but it's also partially true that she loved you in the only way she knew how. You couldn't really say she didn't love her child at all, could you?"

"No, you couldn't. And I'm sure she did," Gene said, smiling earnestly. For a moment he looked like a cat, but a kind he'd never seen before. My mind is working strangely tonight, Malcolm thought, I definitely need another drink.

. . .

Life rewards vigilance, he knew that, but no one could be vigilant every moment, could they? He was walking down a hallway in the Ritz, following a step or two behind Gene, the way he used to follow after his father, because Gene wanted to show him his suite at the Ritz. Talk about wanting to feel rich. At least he hadn't told Gene about his own money, he didn't think. He'd been vigilant enough not to do that, but of course, he did wonder now about what might happen with Gene, and perhaps, more to the point, why he'd agreed to go with him? Was it just because Gene had listened to him babble about his parents then listened further to some of his ideas that were little more than bitterness-induced truisms? Did one derive such power from the mere fact of listening?

He tried to recall the moment of transition when Gene had suggested they go to his room—but couldn't remember exactly. It must have happened when Gene noticed that he'd dropped his guard for a few seconds, and now he was following an essential stranger, and a strange stranger at that, to his room, ostensibly so they could smoke some pot. Finally Gene stopped and withdrew his plastic key while Malcolm leaned slightly against the wall to help steady himself.

It wasn't a room that gave away much about its occupant, other than that he kept it tidy. Gene pointed him to a sofa, a smaller version of what they had downstairs, then disappeared into the bathroom. If there was such a thing as a generic, expensive hotel room, Malcolm thought, this would be it. In musical terms it reminded him of a clean, long-lined but quirkily dissonant melody of Hindemith. Odd how, in his own way, Hindemith could be more terrifying than Bartók.

Gene returned with a lit candle in one hand, a pipe, and some other drug paraphernalia, which he set down on the coffee table between his chair and the sofa on which Malcolm sat uneasily.

"Are we really going to do this?" Malcolm said, realizing that this was something other than pot.

"Why not?" Gene said, smiling just enough to reveal a few teeth.

Malcolm wished he hadn't asked him that way. It made him seem like a child.

"But aren't we both pretty high already?" he said. He was still sounding childish. He was a rich man now, couldn't he finally put an end to these infantile posturings?

"This will take us to a different place, one that I'm sure you'll like."

How do you know I'll like it, Malcolm wanted to say. How do you know I even want to be in this hotel room?

"Here," Gene said, handing him the lit pipe. "Inhale slowly but steadily."

He inhaled, then noticed that Gene had changed his clothes while in the bathroom and was now all dressed in black.

"What did you say you do?" Malcolm asked, as he handed the pipe back to Gene.

"I didn't." He inhaled, then handed it back to Malcolm. "I don't mean to be secretive or rude but I find it so . . . limiting to talk about money. Can I get away with saying that I'm in a financial situation where I no longer have to work?"

"Yes, you can." I am, too, Malcolm wanted to say but was afraid to. It was paradoxical—Gene was good-looking but wasn't younger than him or bigger either. He didn't even color all his hair, which was silver in places, yet he seemed to dominate everything. Malcolm inhaled once more, coughing a little this time.

"Do you really live here?"

"I do tonight."

"You're very mysterious." Gene raised his eyebrows and smiled a little but he was also studying him.

"Why do you think I'm mysterious?"

"You're just a big black bird of mystery," Malcolm blurted,

laughing as the high moved throughout his body. "A black leather bird, too, for the most part," he said (looking at his clothes), which for some reason made him laugh still harder.

"Why you're just a little boy, aren't you?" Gene said, looking at him intently. "Fortunately I like little-boy men, very much."

It was what he thought, then, but he didn't want it. He was still thinking of Chris, missing him so much. All his life there'd been a Chris, of one kind or another, just out of reach. It was the Chris principle, he supposed. Because he suddenly had a lot of money now wasn't going to change that. People speak of free will and the unpredictability of life to console themselves, the same way they speak of heaven, but he knew it wasn't true. There *was* an element of unpredictability, of course, just enough to create a surface illusion or diversion, but he knew that undergirding everything were certain patterns of events and behaviors and people one was attracted to and these patterns kept repeating themselves throughout your life. It was true for him, at least, he knew it in his bones.

"Why the sad face?" Gene said. "You don't want to be sad now."

He saw what Gene was doing, treating him like a will-less child, but he merely shrugged in response.

"You can tell me anything, you know. There's very little I can't deal with."

"Just feeling sorry for myself, is all. Probably the drugs are intensifying it . . ."

"Sorry for yourself? That won't do. You're a good-looking man, judging by your clothes you must make a decent living, and you're with me, so what's there to be sorry about?"

"I was just thinking about the past."

"Well, don't do that. *Ever*," Gene said, as if it were a command.

"I try not to, but when I do, well, I'm forced to see things."

"What things?"

"You know the line from Beckett—'Do you believe in the life to come? Mine was always that.'"

"Well, I've had a great life," Gene said, moving a little closer and staring into his eyes again, "and it's getting greater all the time."

"How did you do that?"

"It's all about attitude, isn't it? Well, not *all*. It does help to have some natural attributes. Good looks and some money never hurt anyone, did they?" Gene said, with a little laugh.

"OK. So what's the secret, can you tell me?"

"You have to create your own world. Where your dreams do come true."

"And how do you do that?"

"With desire and will and awareness, of course. Of the three, I think awareness is the most important."

"Awareness?"

"Knowing what you want. I *know* what I want and I know what you want, too."

"How can you be so sure what I want?"

Gene smiled. "You don't believe me? Why are we in this room getting high together? Why did you even let me sit at your table and buy you a drink?"

"You knew I'd say yes?"

"Yes, Malcolm, I did."

He wondered briefly if it was true. "So you know everything I want?"

Gene smiled at him.

"Tell me what I want then."

"I'll do better than that, I'll show you. When I used to take creative writing courses in college they told us to show things instead of just telling them. If you sit still for a minute, I'll show you what you want, OK?"

"All right," he said.

"Just sit still," Gene said, walking to a desk Malcolm hadn't noticed before by the bureau. Since he wasn't told not to look, Malcolm watched him remove a small safe deposit box from the desk, then begin to fiddle with the combination. When the safe opened, Gene seemed to cover it like Dracula raising his black, winglike cape and Malcolm looked away, in fact, turned his head in a different direction.

"Be patient, I'm almost ready," Gene said, finally walking toward him.

"Now have a look," he said, handing him an envelope stuffed with photographs.

There were pictures of hooded men in chains doing forbidden things to their master, who was holding a whip and who was masked in some photographs, although it soon became apparent in others that it was Gene or a younger version of him. In still others, the slaves were dressed like children and were attempting to simulate their size by being photographed on their knees.

Malcolm stared at the pictures, frightened and appalled. Then the photographs began to feel like little snakes in his hands, but he forced himself to handle them and not say anything, told himself the drugs were causing it and that Gene mustn't know how stoned he was.

"What's it like looking at the future, little boy?"

"These pictures are really something," he heard himself say. "Very powerful."

Gene's smile was self-satisfied and slightly contemptuous now. "I need to use the bathroom for a few minutes, but I'll be back with some things for you. Stay here," he added, before he closed the bathroom door.

Malcolm got up from the sofa immediately and tiptoed as quickly as he could toward the door, though the carpet was so thick he realized he probably could have just run on it and not be heard. Then he undid the locks and left the room, walking rapidly to the nearest exit. He ran down two flights of stairs to the ninth floor, where he briefly considered taking the elevator before continuing to run down the remaining stairs to the lobby.

Music was playing in the brightly lit lobby. A jazzy version of "Auld Lang Syne." He thought of asking the concierge to call him a cab but didn't want to risk encountering Gene so headed for the street exit instead, turning once and seeing the star on top of the Ritz Christmas tree just before he left the hotel.

Outside it had started to snow and the wind had picked up. The streets were icy, it would be difficult to walk. There were a number of taxis in front of the hotel but they were all filled with passengers. If only Chris hadn't left. He not only could have gotten a ride home—where he longed to be—but he could have avoided that whole hellish time in Gene's room. Why couldn't Chris understand that all he expected was a warm, intelligent conversation? But how could the young man know that at a certain age that was often quite enough?

It was irrational, he supposed, but he felt nervous standing in front of the hotel, lest Gene come outside and make some kind of scene. A pervert and predator like him was capable of anything.

"Would you like a ride, sir?"

He turned and looked at a bellhop, half expecting him to be Gene in disguise.

"Yes, thank you, I would," he said, climbing into the taxi and shutting the door before the bellhop could.

...

He felt unusually tired in the taxi and weak, as if he'd left three-fourths of his strength at the Ritz. He wondered briefly if he should ask the driver if he knew Chris, then sat back closing his eyes, fully expecting a "thought essay" to begin. That was his term for it. Often when he was traveling alone he selected a topic then proceeded to examine or empty out his thoughts on it as if he were writing an essay on an exam. Tonight's topic was "The Futility of Human Effort," but no thoughts emerged, not even the opening line. He looked out the window, where it was snowing harder, closed his eyes again and dozed off for a minute or two.

"Sir, sir," the driver said, waking him up when they'd reached his house.

He paid the driver, tipping him generously.

"Thank you very much, sir. You have a safe and wonderful new year."

"I will, thank you."

He often overtipped now, he realized, because he enjoyed the enthusiastic responses he got. That was one good thing about his money.

He began walking very slowly through the snow and wind. He was being careful. The driver even waited for him till he reached the sidewalk before pulling away. He watched the taxi turn the corner and disappear, then immediately thought he heard something unusual, like the high-pitched cry of a bird. He turned his head, heard a fainter version of the crying sound as if it were its echo, then started looking around frantically in the snow, wondering if he were imagining it or not.

Ah, it was true enough! An elderly woman was lying on the sidewalk a few doors from his house. He didn't recognize her (though he wasn't really aware of any of his neighbors, so she could well turn out to be one of them).

"Stay still, don't try to move," he yelled. "I'm coming to help you."

Could he even be heard through this wind? At least the woman had stopped trying to move. Her eyes were gray and shocked looking, as if she'd just been electrocuted.

"Can you help me?" she said.

"Of course, I'll help you." He looked at her. She was at least in her late seventies. "I think it's best if I just pick you up and carry you."

"Can you do that?"

Though she looked frail, he wasn't sure that he could.

"Yes, ma'am. I can," he said, bending down and lifting from his knees so he wouldn't strain his back as he'd done several years ago when he foolishly tried to help move his piano.

"One, two, three," he said, as he lifted her from the snow.

"Thank you. You're very kind."

"You're very welcome. Now, where can I take you? Do you live around here?"

"Just a few houses down on the left. I was visiting my son. You can put me down now. I'm much too heavy for you, I'm sure."

"Not at all. As long as you don't mind a slow pace, I think it's much safer this way."

He carried her through the snow, slowly but steadily. He

didn't think he could, but the fact that he'd said he could helped him do it.

Then he carefully shifted her as he rang the bell with his right hand. Soon her son appeared, with a startled expression as they explained what happened.

"This man picked me up from the snow, Donny. He was so kind to me," the woman said.

"Thank you so much. I'm Don Porter, your neighbor. That was very kind of you."

"I'm Caesar," he said, shaking his hand. He received a final thanks as he walked toward the sidewalk. It felt good, he had to admit, in a peaceful sort of way, like sitting next to a fireplace would feel, he imagined, where your thoughts finally settle and slowly melt. It would not be quite so bad to go home now, he thought. Not so bad at all. Life was funny that way.

The Dealer

The dealer is a giant with a body like a bear's. I'm a good-sized man but the dealer is taller and substantially heavier than me. Big as he is, his voice is even bigger and compels you to listen to it. There's something else that's special about his voice. When he talks you believe what he's saying, at least initially, which gives him a tremendous advantage. It's a voice of absolute confidence.

I met him at the regular basketball game on the playground in Center City. At first he was just one of the players. On the playground the dealer told lots of jokes, mostly dirty ones about women, which made the other players laugh. I laughed too, but mine was forced. The dealer claimed he used to be a radio DJ in Boston, where he knew lots of famous people in the entertainment and sports worlds, and was now the lead singer in a local rock band. He had one of those lives where you never knew what was true and what wasn't. It was just one strange thing after another—like a parade of strangeness—but the rock band part I knew was true. The dealer had a good singing voice, actually, and would often show it off in the most incongruous places. It was something I could never do.

His whole approach to basketball was different from mine,

too. I pass, hustle on defense, scrap for every loose ball, but the dealer was only interested in scoring. When we played on the same team he would shoot too much, especially from long range. He was a streak shooter, but he shot as if he thought he was always hot. I had to hide my irritation that he didn't pass the ball to me enough, which made me nervous, but worse still was when we played on different teams and I had to cover him. He'd use his strength to camp out in the key and when he got the ball, back me down till he got a lay-up. Sometimes, it was too much for me, and I had to call a three-second violation on him, which he didn't like. More often than not, I tried to cover someone else.

When we introduced ourselves he said his name was "Dash." He told me his stage name but never his real one. I was pretty stressed when I met him, having just broken up with my girlfriend. I'd also recently been transferred to a new division of my company that allowed me to work almost exclusively at home in my new condo. I thought I wanted that (I was making more money at this new position, as well), but after my ex left, being alone so much began to weigh on me. I didn't have use of my driver's license either (which is a long story), and Dash used to drive me home to West Philly. That was nice of him, I know, but during the rides he'd often sing '80s rock songs at the top of his lungs or talk right-wing political stuff (Bill O'Reilly and Rush Limbaugh were two of his heroes), always trying to convert me but never succeeding, or else talk about all the women he'd had sex with. One time I told him I wasn't doing well with drinking and wished I knew a way to get pot. I explained that I hadn't been in Philly for a long time and didn't know who to ask. The dealer said maybe he could help, and that's how it all began.

Whenever I'd ask him how his music gigs went the dealer would say, "Primo, great," something like that, yet he never seemed to have any money. Then I learned that he wanted to be paid in free pot from the stash I bought rather than in cash, which might explain, in part, why he was so hard up financially. As far as the pot went it worked this way. I'd give him the money (eighty to a hundred dollars up front) then wait for him to come back from his source. Then I'd give him about a third of the pot outside in his car, then run back to my place with the remainder. The good part about this method was that I got to stay home. The bad part was he almost always took two to three times longer than he said he would.

During my wait I'd become hyperconscious of time, staring at my watch dozens of times till I'd get his call. It wasn't so much that I was craving pot as that I feared Dash would just run off with my money and never return. I'd have to give up basketball as well as pot then. It would be too humiliating to face him on the playground if he stole my money.

One time, he didn't call me until four hours after he said he would. He explained that something had come up but that he had my stuff and would call me the next day to arrange a drop off. Turns out five days passed before he finally gave it to me after basketball, admitting he'd already smoked a little of it himself. During those days while I kept wondering if he'd call me or not, I became ultrasensitive to the sounds in my condo as well. I was on the ground floor and had rarely heard the elderly lady with bright red hair who lived directly above me and who I'd nicknamed Birdwoman to myself because she was thin and talked very rapidly, as if she were always being chased by someone. But during those waiting days I started hearing every step she took as she'd walk from room to room, restless bird that she was. Bottom line—I had a lot of trouble sleeping and had to waste some of the pot I did have left just to finally knock myself out.

Next time we talked, I told Dash I wanted to ride with him on his drug runs, which meant getting dropped at a gas station / carwash that had a convenience store as well, until he came back with the stuff. (He'd never bring me to the source, of course.) I thought this would make it harder for him to take off with my money, but it had its drawbacks too. Sometimes Dash would return empty-handed, saying the source wasn't there. Once I said, "Why don't you call him before you drive over to be sure he's home?" "I do, brother," he said, "but he doesn't always answer his phone." He went on to explain that the source (who was an electrician) generally didn't do much once he got home from work, but sometimes he got emergency calls to fix something. "Then he's gotta split right away in his car. . . . On the road again," Dash suddenly sang, but more like Freddy Mercury than Willie Nelson.

Waiting at the gas station for him to return was nothing I enjoyed. It was like a mini-mall for the unsavory. A number of times I saw some hookers hanging around there, sometimes with their pimps, other times I thought I saw drug deals going down. Worse still, about a third of the times I'd see parked police cars. The bottom line is waiting there I often found myself worrying about getting mugged or getting busted.

The dealer worried a lot too. He'd been arrested before and once had to wear a wire for the FBI as part of his deal to stay out of prison. He'd had some really harrowing experiences as a result of that wire—one that involved sending his ex-wife to jail and her lover into a gunfight with the cops, who "blew his brains out then scattered them in all four directions," as the dealer put it, looking me right in the eye. He worried more about getting caught than anyone I'd ever bought from, which wasn't a bad thing really because it made him careful in lots of ways, like never mentioning what we were doing on the phone, or never using anyone's real name. It made me feel better about our odds of not getting caught. But it's also true there's a thin line between productive worrying and paranoia that the dealer sometimes crossed. For instance, his always wanting me to smoke while we were together, even in his little blue convertible. I thought it was reckless and said I didn't want to do it. The next time we went out riding (it was in the afternoon after basketball this time) he asked me again, and I told him I didn't want to get messed up in the middle of the day, 'cause I had work to do and I wanted to save my stuff for when I really needed it. It wasn't until the time after that (which was only a few days later) that I finally understood. We were driving toward the source when he suddenly said, "Are you a cop, Jeff?" looking me straight in the eye again in that dramatic way he had, like he was a detective on a TV show interrogating me.

"You're kidding, right?" I said, half laughing.

"Do I look like I'm kidding?"

"Why would you think that? You've known me for months, you've been to my place. You know what my job is."

"You never smoke in front of me, OK? If you smoked in front of me I'd know you weren't a cop."

Next thing I knew he produced a joint and somehow lit it while he drove.

"Come on, brother," he said, "you have to smoke this now."

No man likes to hear the words "have to" from another man. But he was my only link to pot and the other drugs I was also sometimes taking, so I gave in and smoked.

Things went along all right for a while but then the dealer began having trouble with his girlfriend, Maryann. He lived with her in a pretty nifty apartment in Center City, which I saw one time. She was a good-looking woman with an excellent body, but she was almost fifty, nearly fifteen years older than him, and the dealer liked younger women. Maryann had some pretty serious bucks, though, and he was living with her for free. He claimed he loved her and bragged that he was being "almost faithful" to her. I thought, when you're economically dependent on someone things can get confusing and it's hard to separate love from money, but I kept that opinion to myself.

As things got worse with Maryann I could see he was getting worried. She didn't want him smoking for one thing. She probably also sensed he could never be monogamous. Soon he began calling me to do dope runs every three or four days. Even though more than half the time the source wasn't there, I was still buying too much pot, and keeping so much in my apartment was making me nervous. I knew that if you got busted your punishment was determined by how much pot you had in your possession. "One or two small bags probably won't get you put in jail," Dash had said. But I had a lot more than two bags. As a result I began smoking more so I'd have less in my possession if I were ever caught—which seemed logical at the time. As a result of that, however, I was spending too much on it and told myself I'd have to just stop answering his calls for a while and skip basketball for a while too—which would hurt—or else just say no to him on the phone and risk getting him angry, maybe so angry that he'd stop buying for me. The dealer was already saying from time to time that he was gonna quit soon. "You better start buying more 'cause I'm gonna stop doing this soon, it's just not worth it," he'd say, though I never fully believed him.

Just as all this was reaching a crisis point the dealer went away for a while. He'd gotten a minitour for his group—three or four gigs in small towns in Missouri and Wisconsin. It was like the sudden removal of a loud, relentless noise and my first reaction after he left was, paradoxically, to feel disoriented, nervous. But after a jittery first day, my normal sense of time returned, then my normal sense of hearing, though I could still hear Birdwoman puttering around. It was as if once I started hearing her a few weeks ago I would always hear her. But with the dealer gone it was comforting, in a way, to know she was there to potentially talk to, if only I could, like the dealer, take more of the initiative.

For the first time I found myself wondering about Birdwoman's life. So far we'd talked mainly about condo issues (there were only the two of us in the building), like where to put recycled trash, or about the condo fees I'd forget to pay. A couple of times she'd met me in the hallway outside my condo and helped me install a new fuse she gave me. It felt good to have someone do something for me without paying them. My mother was maybe the last person I'd experienced that with, but she was far away now, so it was really nice.

Soon I found myself wondering what Birdwoman was doing upstairs, how she spent her time. I knew she didn't work and had once been a professor. I think the real estate agent told me she was a painter to reassure me that her noise level would be low. Once when I gave her a copy of my keys I stepped inside her place for a minute or two and was dazzled by its elegance—at least in comparison to mine. I remember she had lots of paintings on the walls and that many of them were hers and were very good as far as I could tell. I wished I'd told her so then, when I had the chance, but not wanting to reveal that I didn't know anything about photography, I said nothing. I did compliment her place but didn't think that would matter much to an artist who put so much of herself into her work.

I was disappointed in myself, at how stingy I was to her, especially considering her age (probably late sixties to early seventies) and how few times she would probably ever hear her work praised again. I promised myself to tell her how much I liked her work but so far I hadn't found the right time. Unfortunately, that's the way I am. I often know what I want to do but aren't able to struggle enough to be able to do it. It was like my relationship with the dealer, who, like a magician, had suddenly appeared again.

"I'm baack," Dash said to me on my cell phone, sounding in his clowning way like Jack Nicholson in *The Shining*.

"Hey, how'd the gig go?" I said, trying to sound lighthearted.

"Fabulous, primo. They loved us."

I congratulated him. I was suddenly full of congratulations, like Santa Claus with his bag of toys.

"I'm going over there now, you wanna come? It's no biggie to me if you do or not but I'm only gonna do this one or two more times, so if you do it, you have to buy in quantity."

"Is one hundred OK?"

"One hundred's OK. I'll be over in fifteen minutes, then we'll take a ride together."

I wanted to ask him if he'd actually spoken to the source first but I held my tongue. While he was away I'd secretly worried whether I'd ever hear from him again, being afraid he might move to the Midwest or else truly have his much-threatened change of heart about dealing, and now that I finally had him on the phone I didn't want to aggravate him.

Meanwhile, Dash was telling me more information about our trip. "We're gonna go straight there, I just have to stop at a Kinko's to check my e-mail—unless you have a computer I could use at your place. Do you?"

Reluctantly, I said yes. The dealer had only been in my condo once before and even that was over my protests. Instinctively, I didn't want to ever have him over. The first time I did he commented on how big my place was and asked me what the rent was, not understanding that I owned it. I told him it was five hundred a month less than it would have been if it were an apartment and he believed me. In some ways the dealer was naïve (like the way he believed everything Bill O'Reilly said). This time he said almost the same things as before.

"Look how long the hallway is," he gushed, as he lumbered bear-like toward my computer room. "Look how big the rooms are. How much money you make anyway?"

I could feel my heart beat as I mumbled something incoherent.

"Turn left for the computer room," I finally said, and then quickly changed the subject. Fortunately, it was easy to do that with Dash, who I think had ADD or something close to it. He also seemed to have a belief that socializing was something he had to do in business, even the cut and dried business of dealing. That's why he kept me waiting so long when he was with the source. He felt he had to chat up the electrician, and, to a lesser degree, he did it with me too.

"This won't take long, brother," he said as he sat in front of my computer. "I just need to go through my mail while I was gone. . . . Hey, how 'bout those Red Sox?" Dash added. "Isn't it a drag how they blew that last game?"

"Yeah, tell me about it."

"You watched it, right?"

"Of course. I felt like committing suicide afterward."

"Oh well, if we hadn't traded Manny, we would have won it, right?"

The dealer and I were both native New Englanders. I'm from Brookline, which borders Boston, and he's from Stowe, Connecticut, so we're both Red Sox and Celtics fans. He'd use this connection relentlessly when we talked, but a part of me enjoyed it, I have to admit. It isn't easy to leave your hometown, especially when you're over thirty-five, as I was, and then find yourself in a new, bigger city like Philly that doesn't even know you exist. In spite of what he was doing, the dealer was a naturally friendly guy, which I appreciated.

Predictably, with all our talking plus his insisting I check out the pictures taken from his latest gigs on the Internet, it took much longer than he said it would before we hit the road. During our trip the dealer made one call after another on his cell. Between the calls I realized that he'd been ripped off in his Missouri gig. Basically, the promoter claimed 251 people showed up at the concert and offered him a check based on that number, while Dash said it was more like 600 people, at least, and rejected their offer. Just before he dropped me at the gas station I said, "So you didn't get any money at all for your concert?"

"Don't worry, I will. I'm gonna sue their ass and get twice what they owe me."

He pulled to a stop by the convenience store and I got out.

"I'll call you if I have to stay a long time," he said before driving away.

It was cold out and already getting dark. I didn't want to look around at the dealers or cops, and kept my eyes straight ahead like a soldier while I paced. My ex used to make fun of my pacing. She made fun of my worrying too. "What's a big guy like you worry about so much?" she'd say in the friendly, sexy way she used to tease me during our first few months. Then, toward the end of our relationship, her tone of voice completely changed as she'd run through my defects. Also, it suddenly became a much longer list. Of course, those kinds of changes always happen when things go bad. I was shocked when she left me, yet I'd always worried that she would, that I wasn't enough for her. I used to smoke pot to help feel confident with her. Then I got her to smoke with me while we made love and it was out of this world sweet. But when we started to argue (I never trusted her with men) the pot made us paranoid at times and we'd have to take 'ludes to calm down. That reminded me that I forgot to give Dash the money for Quaaludes, forgot to even remind him to ask for some from the source.

"Shit," I muttered, then looked up and saw Dash's car, back already.

"Get in," Dash said. "He wasn't home." I wanted to make him promise right then to never drive me there again unless he talked to the source first. That just because you wanted someone to be home didn't mean they would be, but I held back. The dealer's depression was obvious. He made more cell phone calls in the car, obsessively going over the details of how he was cheated. Then, a block from my condominium, he asked me if he could use my computer again and I said OK.

"I've been a real pill to be with today, brother," Dash suddenly said as he parked. "First I take you for a ride, then I make all those phone calls and barely talk to you at all and now I need to use your computer again."

"Don't worry about it, that's nothing," I said.

"Thanks, bro," he said, as he disappeared into the little room that seemed barely big enough to contain him. "I'll only be about five minutes."

I paced the hallway while he used my computer, periodically looking at my watch. When seven minutes passed I ducked into the room and asked him how things were coming.

"Check this out," he said, indicating the screen that was full of photographs of women. "I've already boned two of them on this screen alone."

"Who are they?" I blurted, trying to hide my irritation.

"They're from Match.com. They're a gold mine of pussy, man, you should check it out."

"Yuh," I said softly, thinking of my own experiences with Internet dating, which was full of much less happy stories. "So how are things with Maryann?"

"It's all over," he said, as he flicked to another screen full of young women.

"I'm sorry."

"We're still best friends but I'm not doing her anymore. Yeah, I've already moved out of her place."

"So are you staying in your office?"

"No, there's mold there now. The last storm it got flooded and now there's mold. Hey, you've got a lot of space, you want to rent me a room, Jeff?" he said, turning in my swivel chair to face me with a big, hopeful smile on his face.

I looked down at the floor for a moment. It was what I always feared.

"No, that wouldn't work. I've got a new girlfriend now who's coming over tonight so . . ."

I let it trail away as if what I were saying were so obvious it didn't need to be spelled out. But I felt he didn't believe me. Though he congratulated me, I thought he knew I was lying.

"I'll have to go on Priceline, then," he said, turning back to my computer. "I can get a hotel on Priceline for fifty bucks but it's gonna take me fifteen minutes. No more than fifteen and I'll find one, OK, bro?"

"No problem," I said, feeling temporarily relieved as I stepped into the hall and resumed my pacing.

Twenty minutes passed, then forty-five. I asked him how things were going with Priceline and he told me he couldn't find a thing but was still trying. I looked at the computer and saw that he was really looking at hotels this time and not women. It had gotten dark out. It was mid-November, and I could feel it getting colder. I thought I'd maybe drop a 'lude and watch some TV but I stayed in the room and watched him in silence.

"Jeff," he said after another five or ten minutes, "Are you sure I can't crash here just for a night? I promise I'll flush the toilet and clean up after myself, ha ha, cause it's looking like your place or my car, OK? I'll pay for the time I stay, I promise."

. . .

When you take drugs they produce the drama in your life so your dramas are very short and controlled, lasting only as long as the high does. But people who take drugs, myself included, like or maybe need it that way. We crave excitement as long as it's part of a routine. With Dash in my house I tried to adjust by accepting new routines as long as I could know their results in advance. Here are some of the things I knew would happen that did happen after I let Dash stay that night.

1. He stayed longer than one night.
2. He never paid me any money, nor did I ask him to.
3. He increased the number of drug runs that we took.
4. I hid my cash, credit card, and drugs that I used to keep in my bureau drawer deep in my hallway closet and found myself

checking them all four to five times a day. (As far as I know he never stole anything from me.)

5. He asked to smoke with me every night and sometimes during the day and more often than not I agreed and never charged him.

6. He monopolized my computer.

But things I didn't know would happen happened too. I hadn't shared a place with a man since I was in college, so there were bound to be surprises. One night he called me from a bar. I didn't answer the first time, but as usual he started repeat calling me as if he knew I was just pretending to be away from my phone until I finally answered.

"Hey bro, I'm at my favorite pussy bar and I just scored a really hot one. You don't care if I bring her over, do you?"

For some reason my mind went blank and I heard myself say, "It's OK, you can use my room."

"Thanks, bro. I'll be over in ten minutes."

I dropped my cell after I hung up. Then I paced around my place looking into my rooms as if half expecting that they'd disappeared or were radically rearranged. Finally, I stopped to take a Quaalude. Then I rehid my money and drugs in a new place, went into the living room and, anticipating that there'd be noise coming out of my bedroom soon for the first time since my ex left three months ago, turned on the TV.

I was watching a political talk show—one of those where the host keeps interrupting the guest as if he's really interviewing himself—when I heard my door open and only then remembered that a few days ago I'd let Dash talk me into giving him a key. I could already hear them laughing and talking, so I turned up my TV and shut off the lights.

Then I heard the door shut. Don't come into the living room, I said to myself, not wanting to see who he'd picked up. Just take her straight to my room.

"Hey, brother," the dealer said, in a voice that sounded more drunk that stoned, "come out and meet my girl."

I ignored him. Maybe he'd think I was asleep.

"Come on, bro, I want you to meet my girl," he repeated.

I knew if I didn't get out of my La-Z-Boy he'd bring his trophy into the living room and show her off to me there, but I still stayed in my chair. I didn't want to walk out there where it was lighter and have to stand next to him like his little brother and have her see how much bigger than me he was.

"Bro, come on, say hello to your new houseguest." This last time there was a little edge to his voice so I hit the remote, went forward in my La-Z-Boy, finger combed my hair and checked my fly in the dark as I walked out to the living room.

"Jeff, this is Maggie, named after the Dylan song, right? But I'll tell you, bro, Dylan was wrong about her 'cause I'll work on Maggie's farm any day. Yah, I'll plow that farm *anytime*."

The dealer was cracking himself up, only louder than usual because he was drunk.

"Shut up," Maggie said, laughing a little herself, as she mock punched him in the shoulder. She was wearing a short black leather skirt and stockings and a black shirt with the top two buttons open. Her body was about as good as I figured. (Though he was overweight, the dealer had to have women who weren't.) It was harder to evaluate her face because she wore so much makeup and a lot of it seemed to be smeared around, giving her a kind of blurry look. "You keep making those jokes, I'm gonna change my fuckin' name to Margo."

"Hey, that's not nice," Dash said, spanking her pretty hard on her bottom, then looking at me to check my reaction.

"What was that for? That hurt a little, Bubba."

"That's for using a bad word."

"What? What'd I say?"

"Women shouldn't use the 'f' word in public . . ."

Maggie looked profoundly confused for a moment. She was pretty drunk too, I figured.

"I'm just kidding," Dash said, "Geez, I really had you going there."

Except I knew, right-wing nut that he was, he was only half kidding.

"So what do you think of my brother Jeff's place? Pretty nice, huh? Yah, he's got some serious bucks. Works for a big company that's very impressive. Plays good basketball too."

She looked at me with a bit more interest now. "It's very nice . . . lots of space," she added as vaguely as if she were talking about the sky.

"OK, time to mosey over to the bedroom," Dash said smiling, then winking at me as he put his thick arm around her while tapping her bottom a couple of times. "Say goodbye to brother Jeff," he said, as they started walking down my hall.

"Goodbye," she said, turning to wave.

I walked back in the half dark to my La-Z-Boy. A few seconds later I turned the TV on pretty loud, hoping of course to drown them out, at least for most of the time (though I imagined his orgasm would sound like a whale bellowing during a tsunami), while hoping I wouldn't wake up Birdwoman upstairs.

My TV, and the acoustics of my condo, did succeed in blocking them out for the most part, and therefore in helping to keep me from thinking about or visualizing what they were doing.

Oddly, I kept thinking about what Birdwoman was doing instead. How *did* she pass her time up there, flitting from room to room by herself in what looked like an art gallery more than a condominium. She'd mentioned once that she had a daughter, but I gathered that she lived pretty far away and in any case I'd never seen her. In fact, in the eight months that I'd lived here I'd only seen three or four people going into or out of her place.

I knew she used to be a professor, the real estate agent told me that. I knew from looking at her mail, which was often mixed in with mine on the floor that she subscribed to a variety of art and other cultural publications. So she must keep herself informed, yet I never heard her TV or radio, not even once, nor a note of music. She was trim and very active, which were good indicators about the quality of her life, yet her rapid-fire high-anxiety speech patter made me think she didn't have much peace of mind.

Generally I'd see her, albeit only for a few seconds, almost every day. Sometimes I'd see her picking up her morning newspapers from the front lawn (one *Philadelphia Inquirer*, one *New York Times*) like a bird gathering its birdseed, then climbing up the flight of stairs to her home. I'd feel bad then, more often than not, and wondered if I shouldn't bring the papers up to her doorway myself. It didn't seem like much of a sacrifice to make for a nice older woman, but I hadn't yet done it.

Finally I did start to hear laughter mixed in with sex sounds coming from my bedroom, but luckily it was after my Quaalude kicked in and in a little while I was asleep. It was a short dreamless sleep. When I woke (and it was probably what *did* wake me up) I heard the heavy strides of the dealer walking toward me until he stopped two feet in front of my chair.

"Hey, bro, you awake?" he said.

"Kind of. What's up?"

"Come with me now and I think she'll do you too."

"What are you talking about?"

"Maggie. I got her all sexed up and doing whatever I say and I told her to suck your dick and she said she would. How's that for sharing the wealth, Dash style? Better than Obama, huh? Ha ha. Come on, we'll end up banging her together. It'll rock."

"Thanks, but I don't think so. I'm really tired and I took a lot of pills to sleep."

"Are you sure?" he said, in an incredulous tone of voice I'd never heard from him before.

"Yeah, I'm sure."

"Wow, you just blew it, bro."

"Just enjoy her yourself." I said. "I really need to get to sleep. I've gotta work tomorrow morning."

"OK, bro, your call. Don't say I never did anything for you, though. She's got an incredible bod."

Then he walked away. In the silence I soon began to wonder why I didn't do it. I could certainly use the release, but I knew I couldn't bear to perform in front of him, couldn't stand to have him see me naked (I was convinced by now he must be very well endowed) while I tried to come. It all felt like a setup somehow.

The sex noise came back a few minutes later but mercifully I fell asleep. When I woke up it was the next morning and Dash and Co. were quiet—either asleep or gone.

I tiptoed over the hardwood floor and pulled open the Venetian blinds in my living room. A light snow almost as transparent as dew was falling on our little front lawn. It was early for it to snow, which reminded me that the whole summer and especially fall had seemed colder this year. But didn't that contradict the global warming theory that I'd argued about with Dash? Then I remembered seeing someone on TV who explained the reason for it but I couldn't quite recall what he said. I had to realize that it was just another thing I didn't understand, any more than I understood how television itself worked, or how my own brain worked that chose to watch television and why it made the decisions it made, such as last night about Dash and Maggie, or why, for that matter, I kept acting in a way that I knew would drive my ex away even though I thought I wanted her to always be with me.

I started thinking about Quaaludes again. (I certainly couldn't smoke if Dash was still home or he'd immediately smell it with his supersensitive nose and then find a way to join me, after first talking with me about the Celtics or how cool Cape Cod used to be.) I had more or less decided to take a 'lude when I saw Birdwoman, in a sweater and jeans, walking in her hopping sort of way to pick up her morning papers. I raced back to the living room, put on my bathrobe and slippers, and met her in the yard a few feet from the door. She had her typical, hypervigilant birdlike expression, maybe a smidgen more startled than usual since I'd never gone out of my way to greet her before. It was an expression that all but demanded to know what I was doing outside like this, as she clutched her newspapers to her tiny, palpitating bosom.

"What do you think of this snow?" I blurted, trying to cover up my embarrassing lack of purpose. She produced no words in response, but did nod her head rapidly a couple of times.

"I was going to bring your newspapers up for you."

"There's no need to do that," she said, clutching her papers more closely to her birdlike breast. "I like the exercise."

Of course you do, I thought. The worst thing you can do to

a bird is to make it stay still. She even looked slightly hurt that I should doubt her capacity to gather up her papers, and I felt myself start to panic.

"By the way, I wanted to tell you how much I admired your paintings. I really think they're . . . superb" was the word that finally emerged.

"Thank you, Jeff," she said, smiling so widely I could see her teeth. Yet I had to admit she looked very pretty while she smiled.

That was my magic moment in the snow with Birdwoman. I don't remember the few more words we said. Her smile really said it all and I reentered my condo temporarily oblivious to the two lovebirds who were still, as it turns out, nesting in my bedroom.

. . .

Eventually I figured out that the real reason I didn't join the dealer and Maggie in a threesome was that I was afraid he'd want Maggie to live with us too and that he'd try to addict me to her sexually to achieve his goal. But like so much else in the world I was apparently wrong about this as well. Late the next afternoon after Dash took Maggie home and perhaps checked into his office, or perhaps not (he'd admitted to me that during his days with Maryann one of the chief functions of his office was to hide his stash and more often than not to smoke it, but now he had my place to use for both of those functions), he walked into the computer room where I was trying to work and started talking. That wasn't surprising but what he said was.

"Hey, bro, you were a prince last night, I gotta thank you for being such a prince among men."

I checked his voice for sarcasm but couldn't detect any.

"What?" was all I could finally manage.

"I'm talking about last night when I asked you to join us in bed and you turned me down. You knew I was bombed outta my skull."

"I suspected something like that," I said with a smile.

"Yah, you knew and you protected me from myself. I mean I never would have said it if I wasn't on pot, booze, and a little E too."

"Ecstasy?"

"Yah, bro, E rocks. And by the way, no offense, but she never would have done it with you if she wasn't just as high as me. She feels embarrassed about it now, 'cause she knows I told you she wanted to."

"Of course," I said, "I knew that."

"Ask me why this matters? Ask me why I'm talking about this to you now?"

"Why?"

"Because I just had the most fuckin' beautiful day of my life with her and I don't just mean sexually, bro. I mean beautiful. Yah, Maggie really touched my heart—really, truly, deep in my heart, and we're both crazy in love man, it's true."

"Wow, that's great," I said, trying to sound as earnest as possible and not remind him that his whole day had, of course, been completely created by drugs. I even wondered if he'd still feel any real enthusiasm for her a couple hours from now when more of his high would wear off.

I remember talking easily with the dealer that day. We talked about the Celtics, about women, a little about politics, too, during which the dealer surprised me by saying, "I'm going to respect Obama, you know, because he's our President and that's what we should do." We also talked about our families, he about his big one, me about my small.

"I love all my brothers," he said, "all my sisters, too. Love 'em to death."

There was a passion and a kind of laughter in his eyes when he said it and I knew it was true.

"My father was a helluva guy. I only wish he were still alive."

I said I felt the same way about my parents and that I was lucky they were both in good health. I told him I only had one sister, who I sometimes heard from, who lived in a small country town in western Massachusetts. Sure enough the dealer had been there. "I love Massachusetts almost as much as Connecticut. I've traveled in Massachusetts a lot." That remark led to a conversation about towns in Massachusetts where we'd both spent time, from Falmouth and West Harwichport in the Cape, to Lenox and Lee in the Berkshires.

We talked about a lot of things that day and I didn't mind not using the computer much, though it meant falling further behind at work. I remember wanting to tell him about Birdwoman and how I'd finally told her I liked her paintings and was planning maybe to try and buy one from her, but I didn't. Just didn't get around to talking about it, but I could have.

Dash made a lot of calls on his cell later that day, all about his lawsuit over the gig in Missouri, but he kept his voice under control and he washed the dishes after his usual dinner of cheese ravioli. I was even going to suggest we fire one up and smoke together when he walked back into the living room and said, "I'm going to Maggie's."

She has a place? I almost said.

"I've been missing her real bad and I need to be there. Don't wait up for me or anything. I'll probably end up staying there."

"OK, bro," I said.

· · ·

Dealers are probably the most vulnerable people on earth. I had trouble sleeping that night while I waited for Dash. Somewhere around 2 a.m. I realized he wasn't coming back. Nor did he return the next two days. I tried to keep from worrying about him but I couldn't help it, the way he threw himself at her, or at what he imagined her to be. He was like a child that way, always chasing his dream. Whether it was imagining he was a better ballplayer than he was or that Maggie was a better person than she was, a person with whom he would finally find love. It's not like I didn't do the same thing to a degree, but I already was thinking a lot less about my ex (who I now realized I no longer wanted back) and saw myself quitting drugs in the near future, whereas Dash was the type who would always "love" someone and never give up and so would need to take drugs forever.

On the third day he came back in his old electric blue convertible to take his things. He was moving in with her. "I've never loved anyone like this," he said.

"How big is her place?" I asked.

"We only need room for a bed," he said, laughing. Then he told me a couple of dirty jokes—he never ran out of jokes. When he said goodbye, he said, "Don't worry. I'll see you at basketball and we'll still take our trips together"—meaning to the electrician's. "I'll always be grateful, bro. Your decision that night saved my relationship with Maggie, probably our friendship too. You're a wise man, Jeff."

It was the first time anyone had ever called me wise, and then he left. I returned to the silence of my condominium. I watched it get dark and it started to hurt. I thought how I'd let a dangerous person stay at my home, but it turned out that after he left it felt more dangerous than before. Then I thought about going upstairs to visit Birdwoman but didn't have the will. I was gonna take a 'lude but I didn't want to wait thirty minutes for the high so I smoked a joint instead, put on TV, ate my food, fell asleep. My usual pattern. Only I didn't sleep for very long. I had a crazy dream that I had a different body. It was me but I was taller and stronger and strode around the playground like a giant. I saw the dealer shooting baskets at the other end of the court and began walking toward him wanting to see if I was as tall as him, when I woke up.

For the longest time (though it was probably only a minute or two of marijuana time) I couldn't shake the feeling that my body really had changed. It made me sad and happy at the same time as if I'd finally found the reason for my life being the way it was. I thought about seeing Birdwoman but worried I might scare her to death if she saw me in my new body. Anyway, she wasn't someone I could talk to about it, but Dash was. It's strange what you end up missing about people. You could talk to Dash about almost anything. I'll give him that.

Memorial Day

There's a lot to admire about Grandfather Pool. Even though he's close to a hundred and moves very slowly, he walks by himself—doesn't even use a walker. And even though his skin hangs on him like paper, you can see the outline of an excellent physique underneath. It's as if his bones were playing hide-and-seek and temporarily chose a semitransparent place to hide. Still, I admit, I'd rather not get too near him (he's not *my* grandfather, after all). I don't want to listen to him in the hot tub, where we were both headed until I saw him, if he should try to talk to me as he has before. He likes to talk a lot when he gets the chance, as old people do, and old-man talk makes me uncomfortable and sometimes sad.

It's odd how as men get older they slowly become more like women. The only man I know who handled his age really well was my father. He used to take me to this pool all the time, especially on weekends and holidays when I was around nine or ten (including a number of Memorial Days, which it is again today), until I thought I'd outgrown it, fool that I was.

I was addicted to the slide then. I liked the Lazy River and the whirlpool, but I spent half my time on the water slide. I loved it when he went on the slide with me, but when he got tired he'd still stand in the water and watch me every time I slid down. He said I always arrived with a smile.

Just as Grandfather Pool finally gets settled in the tub, I see a group of three men with walkers moving toward the kids' pool, of all places, slowly and stealthily as if returning to the scene of their crime. I guess it makes sense because at the entrance to the kids' pool the water's only a few inches deep and they couldn't handle anything much deeper. I notice they've got a lifeguard helping them walk and kind of sealing them off from the general public. The lifeguard is really ripped. He's got lots of muscles, but his face is almost comically blank and completely disinterested in what he has to do. When you're that young you live half in the present, half in the future, generally speaking. You can't imagine the way the past invades the present when you get older any more than you can imagine a world without sex.

My father was a monogamous man. You could say he was the product of a different era when it was easier or more expected to be a faithful husband than it is today, but he was honest in other ways as well. When my mother got sick for a number of years, he took exemplary care of her, never missed a beat. Of course such behavior meant the premature death of his sex life, but that was never a consideration for him. I doubt it was ever more than a fleeting thought. He was honest in his business, too. I worked for him, so I know. I wish I'd never left his business, but thought I'd outgrown that, too. (The song "Young and Foolish" didn't come from nothing.) Still, of all his forms of honesty, I'm most impressed by his lifelong fidelity—especially to a woman as difficult as my mother could sometimes be. He set too high a standard for me there. I knew even as a fairly young child, or certainly by my mid-teens, that I could never live up to it. Of course, once realized, I went a bit more than I needed to in the other direction and learned to say whatever I had to say to get women to go to bed with me since that was the way of the rest of the world, as I understood it.

It was a great shock when my father died nearly thirty years ago. It would have been a shock no matter how he died, even if it were from a slow-acting cancer. Still, it was a special kind of shock his having a fatal heart attack when he was only fifty-seven, not too far from the age I am now. As an orphan and only child (my mother had died six years earlier), I inherited a bit of money. I should have invested it or saved it or some ingenious combination of the two. Instead I traveled. I wanted to flee the country, especially the middle of it where I lived, in St. Louis, yet I also feared traveling (though my father had taken me to Europe as a child, then later as a teenager). I panicked at the thought of living among people whose language I couldn't speak. As a compromise, I went to London.

It was undoubtedly too soon after his death to travel such a great distance. A part of me knew this. Although I had no siblings or lover of any consequence at the time, I did have a friend or two, especially Phil, who warned me about my trip to London; yet I turned a deaf ear. I was determined to go there, so I made arrangements quickly, even paying in advance for the first week at my hotel in Princes Square. In an effort to divert myself, I went to the usual tourist attractions and was by no means disappointed. Not by the attractions themselves, that is, which were pretty much what they were cracked up to be. But the routine of the ubiquitous guided tours and especially the commercialization of it all began to irritate me. I remember it bothered me in particular that you had to pay to visit the so-called holy Westminster Abbey. It also bothered me that all these places had gift or snack shops attached to them, like mosquitoes to skin.

No doubt, my father's recent death contributed a little to my bitter reaction. I soon stopped going to the tourist attractions and began just walking around Hyde Park in the daytime and then at night getting pretty soused at one of the local pubs on Queensway before returning to my hotel room to sleep it off. It was on one of my evening trips to a pub that a quite attractive, if slightly waifish, young woman approached me with a troubled look on her face. She was a little shorter than average, with very white skin and dark shoulder-length hair, and wore a flower print dress that hid her figure more than revealing it.

Not really hearing what she first said to me, in part because she spoke with an accent, in part because she spoke quickly, I assumed she wanted money (everyone else did), so I fished out the change in my pocket and gave her a couple of pounds. Her troubled look quickly turned ironic.

"This man just gave me money, he thinks I want money," she said, addressing the empty space around her, as far as I could see.

"I'm sorry I misunderstood," I said, walking toward her. But she was walking away from me now with my money in her hand.

"Oh, I guess you do need the money, after all," I said, laughing a little now myself.

"No, I don't want your money," she said, turning and walking after me and soon giving me a different combination of coins of her own.

"I'm sorry. I guess I didn't hear you before. What did you want?"

"I asked you if you knew where the Spiritual Church is?"

"No, I'm sorry, I'm not from around here," I said, once more walking slowly away.

"I probably gave you more money back than you gave me," she noted.

That stopped me in my tracks, made me turn and walk back to her again.

"Obviously neither of us works in a bank. Why don't you let me buy you something to eat or at least a drink," I said, surprised by my sudden invitation as I pointed to the pub across the street. "My name's Gerry."

She uttered some pleasantry in return, but I could see she was nervous. She had one of those transparent faces that clearly revealed when she was thinking something over, as she was then, registering all the pros and cons of accepting my invitation.

"I was trying to get to the church, but I've only been there once before and now I've lost my way and no one seems to know where it is. I suppose I'll miss the service anyway by now. My name's Paulette," she said, extending her delicate white hand to shake.

"If I go to a pub with you, will you expect me to have an alcoholic drink?" she asked a moment later.

"I won't have any expectations one way or another. It's just a place where we could talk," I said, rather smoothly, I thought, again to my surprise. A car approached us then, which finally convinced her to get off the street, fortunately on the same sidewalk that I'd chosen.

"Is this something you do quite often?" she said.

"What?"

"Ask women you've just met to go to pubs with you?"

"No, I don't have a pattern. Why do women always assume that men have a pattern?"

"They do, you know, behave in patterns. It's merely a question of when the woman is able to unearth it."

"You make it sound like women are all archaeologists. Is there some kind of school where they get their training, I hope?"

Finally she laughed.

"OK, then, since you've made me laugh I suppose I can go to your pub with you."

"Fine," I said, wondering myself why her decision pleased me to the extent it did.

Once in the pub my veneer of self-confidence didn't last long. There are so many awkward things involved when you eat a meal with someone you've just met. I think Paulette felt the same thing. She became quiet most of the time, then laughed excessively at others. I quickly had two drinks, and before I was halfway through the first she changed her mind and had a beer herself.

I'd been drinking almost every night since my father died and hoped I wouldn't start in about him and end up losing it. But I needn't have worried because Paulette soon began talking about the man who'd just left her.

"It wasn't just the time I lost," she said, her earnest dark eyes tearing up, "I'm young enough to have more of that. It was what he did to my trust that I'll never get over, I don't think, what he did to my heart."

That made me think of my father, for some reason, and I struggled to keep my own emotions under control. "Do you want to tell me what happened?" I said, hoping for a variety of reasons that she wouldn't.

"Men don't like to hear those things."

True enough, I thought, thinking I was temporarily off the

hook. Of course, I pretended to want to know, realizing I was already starting to like her.

"He betrayed me is what it amounts to. He left me for another bird. The details don't really matter, do they?"

I nodded quickly to acknowledge her point.

"I'm sorry it happened to you," I said, wondering if she'd been drinking herself through her crisis, too.

"That's why I've started going to this new church I'd heard about, I suppose, to help me get through it . . ."

"The Spiritual Church," I said, quasi-embarrassed to pronounce its absurd-sounding name.

"It's not as daft as it may sound. It's a very liberal, modern church. Its members all share their different stories with each other. It was very comforting the first night I went, but somehow I got lost tonight and couldn't find it."

"I'm sorry I thought you wanted money."

"Am I really that shabbily dressed?"

"Not at all," I said, before I realized she was joking.

The rest of the dinner went more smoothly. We talked about the usual things—movies, the Beatles (who everyone still talked about then), our families, a bit about our jobs. I told her that my plans were uncertain as to how long I'd stay in London, which I rationalized could be technically true. I just didn't add that my return ticket to St. Louis was in five days and that there was no chance I wouldn't take it, as I had to get back to my job.

She asked me about the States, of course, and why it was I was considering not returning. It was in that context that I told her my father had recently died and saw the same look in her liquid eyes she had when she told me the story of her lover's betrayal.

Shortly after that we left the restaurant. She lived only ten minutes or so from my hotel, but the last few blocks were walked in silence. Finally I said, "Is there any way I can see you tomorrow?"

"Really?"

"Yes, really."

"You think we're well suited for each other, then?"

"I think I'm going to miss you after you go," I blurted, which was about as much as I'd ever said to any woman, being the cool, intentionally detached, idiotic type I was then.

"All right, if you really think so. I feel I was such a burden to you all night going on and on about my problems."

I assured her she wasn't.

She smiled, with a trace of a blush. "Well, then, can you come by tomorrow around seven?" she asked, very softly.

I was surprised how much I thought of her the next day. I figured it was because I hadn't had sex since my father died but sensed I liked her, too. Either way, waiting was a part of the seduction process I had little patience for in my twenties, though not succeeding at all would be still worse, of course. With Paulette I sensed I'd have to wait to succeed, although I couldn't wait too long since I had to fly back to the States in five days.

Instead of a pub, we met at a Japanese restaurant on Queensway Road. She'd dressed up more this time, wearing a conservative navy blue dress that screamed priggishness. It looked like a flight attendant's uniform, I thought, or something a middle-aged librarian from St. Louis would wear. Meanwhile, I was dressed all in black, which I thought was cool at the time, though I now see I must have looked like a priest or a funeral home director.

Conversation was not as easy this time. We spoke in brief, halting sentences about nothing in particular, as if it were taboo to talk about anything that mattered to us. I'd just finished ordering another sake to try to rectify the situation when she suddenly started talking. "Obviously I've been a big disappointment to you tonight."

"What are you talking about?" I said, trying to say the words as if I meant them.

"You can barely bring yourself to look at me, much less talk to me."

I knew women were more emotionally open than men by and large (though not so with my mother and father), but she was carrying her honesty to an uncomfortable degree. I protested but she cut me off.

"Don't tell me you've enjoyed it," she said. "That's what you said last time, but it couldn't possibly be true now because tonight I've had about as much personality as a slug, I'd say, you can't deny it."

"I think we're both a little nervous, that's all."

"Do you? That's a more hopeful way to look at it. Is it too awful that I'm so blunt? Wouldn't it be better if I were a smidgen more diplomatic?"

I shrugged reflexively.

"Don't bother to respond, I already know the answer."

At last my new drink came, which I made short work of. I noticed she was making progress on hers, too, and I felt a flicker of hope.

"Are you wondering what you're doing taking this crazy British bird to a restaurant and listening to her adolescent prattle all night?"

I laughed, then said, "You're way too hard on yourself."

"Am I?"

"You've been through a lot lately. So have I."

"You mean with your father?"

I nodded.

She asked me to talk about him and for a while I did. The same few friends, especially Phil, who'd told me not to go to London so soon after my father died, also advised me to talk to a therapist about him, but I didn't listen to that advice either, so this was the first time I'd really talked about him to anyone. When I stopped, Paulette's face was flushed with emotion. It's strange how something that would have embarrassed me was so appealing when it happened to her. Our eyes locked, and she slid her arm across the table and held my free hand. I don't know if my face flushed too, but other, unseen parts of me definitely did.

I don't remember what we said during the rest of our dinner, only that she continued to hold my hand for several minutes. On the street after dinner, we stopped touching and talking as well. My inhibition frustrated me. What was the point of drinking if it ultimately kept me shy and silent? I realized vaguely, while I was walking her home, that I was behaving a bit like my father or how I imagined he'd behave. It was almost as if he were living through me, like a kind of ghost.

When we reached her block, she turned to me and said, "Are you feeling sad now?"

I shrugged. "I'll miss you again, a lot."

"Would you like to come up to my flat and talk a bit more? I don't have much to offer you. Just tea and some chocolates," she said, as if my decision would be based on the quality of the food she had. I said yes, I'd like that and followed her up the stairs, feeling my true self already returning.

Her place was small and had a somewhat disheveled look that reminded me of my own apartment in St. Louis. It had the look of a place whose occupant stopped caring about it several days before, which fit her story.

"Of course I'm horribly embarrassed by my flat."

"Shouldn't be. It's much neater than mine."

"Do you mean your place in London or St. Louis?"

"Both," I said, lying fairly convincingly, I thought. "Every place I live in starts to look like every other place I've been in after a week or so."

"Well, you're a man, and that's to be expected, but I have no excuse."

I let that remark pass as I followed her into her kitchen, not wanting to risk her focusing on her recent romantic tragedy again. She opened her tiny refrigerator to remove some candy, and I thought I saw the top of a bottle of beer.

"Shall I fix you some tea?"

"Was that beer I spotted in your fridge?" I said.

"Oh, is that what you want, then?"

"If it's all right."

"You have a way of asking for things that makes it hard to refuse," she said, removing the bottle and pouring it into two glasses.

I took a generous swallow, unable to think of a toast (one more thing my father was good at that I wasn't) or even to look her in the eye. Instead, I said, "You say that as if it makes you sad."

"The last one was like that, too. I gave in to him and look what happened."

We both drank a little more. I was trying to deal with a flash of jealousy, which startled me.

"Let's agree not to concentrate on what hurt us in the past, OK?" I said.

"How do we do that?"

I moved closer to her and gently stroked the left side of her face. Then we kissed.

"That shouldn't have happened," she said.

"Why not?"

"I'm making myself too easily available to you."

"I don't think so," I said, and we kissed again. Several more times, in fact.

"Now I'm doomed," she half muttered.

I was too excited to know who was doomed and who wasn't. I rose from the table and sort of pulled her up with me so we could fully embrace while we continued kissing. Finally, we started moving toward her tiny bedroom. An image of my father's disapproving face suddenly popped into my head, as if he were saying, "You're taking her under false pretenses," so I reached back and took the bottle of beer from the table and drank some more of it while we undressed in her room.

Afterward, I felt her vibrating softly against me, and I realized how oddly beautiful everything with her had been. Then I realized she was crying, albeit very softly.

"I'm going straight to hell for this," she said between half-muted sobs.

"It's OK," I said.

"No, it's not."

"What we did is happening millions of times all over the earth this very moment."

"So is murdering."

"I hope you see a distinction between the two."

I thought I heard her chuckle a little. At any rate the sobbing soon stopped, and feeling encouraged I continued talking. "I thought you weren't a Catholic any longer. I thought you'd joined the Spiritual Church, which doesn't believe in an afterlife."

"I don't know what I am anymore, other than confused."

I put my arm around her and held her against me. Eventually she closed her eyes and began breathing more easily. Outside it had begun raining. I could hear it through her thin, dark windows.

"I love the rain, don't you?" she suddenly said.

"Sometimes."

I wondered how long it would last, then if it were raining back in St. Louis on my father's grave. I remember one day we drove to the lake in Creve Coeur. He always loved to be in any kind of water, while my mother usually considered it too much of a fuss. I was somewhere around eighteen, and he was walking with me along the water's edge in bare feet. My first girlfriend of any consequence had recently left me, and I'd confided in him about it.

"Did you love her, Gerry? Did you feel that you did?"

It was the first time I'd really considered that question. "I don't know," I said.

"You want to feel that you do before you have sex with a woman. I know you can't always tell, but you should try to know if you can," he said, looking straight at me, "and then be sure to tell her you do. It works out best that way for everyone."

A minute or so later I whispered the words that would have pleased my father, if they were true. But I decided they were close enough to "truth," given the wide latitude he allowed for individual confusion. Paulette said nothing after my short speech that ended with the "l" word. When I checked, I couldn't tell if she'd fallen asleep or not. A little later I rolled over on my side and fell asleep myself.

In the morning when I woke up, I was alone. It was the kind of thing I'd done myself more than a few times after a one-night stand, right down to the letter that she'd left for me on the kitchen table, where we'd gotten high. I remember that I didn't pick the letter up right away. I was still excited by her passion from last night and didn't want that to end. Then I realized that it could say anything, that it might even be a torrid love letter praising my sexual performance to the skies.

Dear Gerry (it began conventionally enough),

Last night some time after we made love you mentioned, in a barely audible voice, that you loved me. You said it very softly, but you said it, and, dumbfounded, I didn't respond and actually pretended I was asleep, for which I apologize. Your real sleep soon followed but, because of your words, I couldn't sleep a wink. Instead I wrote you this letter and now plan to take a long walk in Hyde Park, from where I'll eventually leave for work. By the way, you are free to feed yourself from whatever edible crumbs you can find in my kitchen (I do have a bag of crisps that I think might appeal to you) before letting yourself out. Had I any inkling before our evening started that you'd end up being my guest I would have provided more food. At any rate, eat whatever you want and just let yourself out. The door will lock automatically.

Obviously, I'm not much of a writer and this letter is especially hard to write, so I'll just get to the point of it. You know from listening to me as patiently as you did how vulnerable I am right now and why. And you also know that when people are vulnerable they often make poor decisions that they shouldn't have made. I, for instance, would not have done what I did with you last night were I not so vulnerable myself. I won't deny that I'm attracted to you and that you struck a deep chord in my heart, but even so, it would not have happened so quickly. But it did and now you've said you love me—a poor, lost girl who couldn't even find the church she wanted to go to for comfort. Yet, somehow, for some reason, you said those words to me. Of course sometimes people say things they don't really mean and wish they hadn't. By pretending to be asleep I deprived you of the chance to take your words back.

Now I find that I need to know if you meant them or not. If you did mean what you said, please call me tonight so we can plan our next meeting. I'd also like to know, straight up, what the odds really are that you're staying in London permanently and if not, just how long you are staying—a year, six months, two months?

If, on the other hand, you didn't mean your words, do me the favor of not seeing or calling me again as I cannot tolerate another great disappointment right now. I will be home tonight hoping for your call.

Paulette

I read the letter a number of times before I dressed and left without eating—looking around myself several times while heading for my hotel. Once there, I thought I could finally relax, only to continue reading the letter in my hotel room as well. I'd never received a letter that demanded an answer by a set time. That kind of pressure was anathema to me. Why was she acting this way, I wondered, even though part of me knew.

I went to the Victoria and Albert Museum to try to distract myself, and then took a cruise on the Thames but found little relief. I was excruciatingly aware of time. Soon Paulette would be waiting by the phone with only one answer she could accept. She was proud and demanded to be taken with the utmost seriousness, or not at all. I was in awe of her strength of soul even as it tormented me. I didn't know a woman could take such a stand or believe in principles so fiercely. God knows I wanted to keep seeing her and sleep with her again, but to do it I'd have to lie much worse than I already had. Even if I told her that I loved her or knew I could, the mere admission that I was leaving London in four days would shatter the little trust she might still have in me.

And so the hours ticked on, and predictably I went to a pub quite a distance from Queensway and tried to drink away the picture of her by her phone that I was convinced was now planted in my mind forever.

It's odd what our brains choose to remember. I recall vividly the day when I had to make my decision, but not the next four. (The letter I remember verbatim because I took it with me back to the States, where I read it many more times over the years.) Those days all ran together in a blur of anxious tourism and alcohol, until eventually I was back in St. Louis, probably back in this pool again, too.

I thought it would be easier to stop thinking about her once I was home. I thought I'd go back to mourning my father until that slowly lessened, while Paulette would vanish in a matter of weeks if not days. Instead, my memory of her (aided by her letter) made her more vivid, as if I were seeing her on a daily basis. Paradoxically, the main relief I got from Paulette was thinking about my father. It was as if he was still helping me out once again from his grave.

...

My thoughts are interrupted by a splashing fight that's broken out near me between two ten-year-old boys. They look somewhat alike—maybe they're brothers—and splash each other with equal ferocity. To get out of their range, I walk over to the kids' pool, where the old men with their walkers sit dangling their toes in the water, their lifeguard hovering behind them. I sit on the ledge looking at them, at Grandfather Pool in his hot tub, then at the giant clock on the wall, where I'm surprised it's as late as it is in the afternoon.

After a few months it got much better about Paulette, and she might have become one of those occasional twinges of guilt we all learn to put up with but for another letter she suddenly sent me.

Dear Gerry,

Are you surprised to hear from me? It was much easier than I expected to get your address, but I did wrestle with the decision of whether to write to you or not and though a lot of me didn't want to, because of my conscience, I ultimately decided to write.

Your one-night stand with me had more consequences than you might imagine, at least for me. A few weeks after our time together I found out I was pregnant and then had to decide what to do about it. I thought of writing or calling you then, but since you'd already chosen not to contact me it seemed rather futile.

Ultimately, after much agonizing, I decided to have an abortion, which happened a few days ago. I guess I'm not much of a Catholic after all. I'm telling you this without expecting or wanting any kind of reply simply because I think people ought to know that they can create life when they do (in your case it was apparently quite easy), and ought to know when they're involved, albeit indirectly, in decisions involving what happens to that life. Anyway, I won't bother you again. I've handled things very badly, although you did trick me along the way. Still, I hope one day you do find someone you can love and respect enough to marry and start a family of your own with. My church says, "Children are the meaning of life." T. S. Eliot says, "We had the experience but missed the meaning."

Paulette

"She's lying, don't fall for it," said Phil, who'd originally advised me not to go to London.

"How do you know that?" I said, waving the letter in my hand.

"All right, I don't know it, but she probably never got pregnant, and anyway you'll never know one way or the other. It sounds like a scam to me to guilt some money out of you."

"She didn't ask for any money. She's the most honest woman I've ever known."

"Then why would she write you? It might make some sense to write when she was pregnant and didn't know what to do. Why not write you then? By the way, if she had, what would you have done?"

"I don't know."

"OK. But since she says she went ahead and got the abortion on her own, her only motive could be to hurt you, which she's already done, or to eventually get some money out of you."

I listened, I nodded, but in the end I wrote Paulette a shortish letter expressing my sympathy and regret, and including a check for two hundred dollars, which I told her I'd heard from asking around should cover the operation.

A week or so later she returned my check, torn in half without comment. I still remember how I stared at it, stunned by my clear sense of the person it now revealed, a person I'd chosen to let go without knowing why, other than I judged myself incapable of handling the situation. Yes, I could have acted very differently. I had a job and some money and no dependents. I could have stayed longer, then offered to support her and live together in the States.

66

When you're young, you think most of what you want for yourself will eventually happen, as if some secret cosmic force is guiding you toward it. It's only much later that you discover you're not going to win the Nobel Prize, or become a multimillionaire, or live for the rest of time with the love of your life. I was young enough to believe in the possibility of that ultimately benign universe, but I was also an orphan who'd just lost his father, and I already wasn't so sure about having any guarantees. I only knew I hated the way things had turned out with Paulette. What force made me lie to her and walk away from someone I really wanted?

I began writing her, but my letters were never answered. The next thing I tried was the telephone. Fortunately, there was no caller ID then, and after a few days I was finally able to get her on the phone.

"It's me, Gerry," I finally said.

There was a silence, which I quickly tried to fill by asking if she'd gotten my recent letters.

"I did get them," she said tersely. "I got them but I don't know why you sent them."

"I was hoping you'd forgive me, and would let me see you again. I think about you all the time. I . . . "

"Please don't say that."

"I know I made a terrible mistake," I said soberly.

"Kind of a revealing one, wouldn't you say?"

"I panicked, I admit, but this had never happened to me before."

"You never took advantage of a girl before?"

"No, I meant I never loved one before. But it was just one mistake."

"It may have been one mistake, but it had multiple consequences, so it really was probably more than one mistake."

"What do you mean?" I blurted.

"You want me to rattle them all off? OK. You lied to me about
living here. You lied about loving me. You deserted me in my
hour of need, and as a result *I* panicked and did the last thing in
the world I ever wanted to do, which has scarred me for the rest
of my life. Does that answer your question sufficiently?"

"It's scarred me, too. I did lie about living in London and I
did panic about calling you that day because I didn't want you
to find out that I couldn't stay in London, but I didn't lie about
loving you." Then I told her she was the only person in the world
I did love or would ever want to have a child with, realizing after
I said it that it was true.

"It's too late, Gerry. It's much too late."

"It doesn't have to be," I protested.

"I'm sorry. I've made mistakes in this, too. Many mistakes. I
forgive you for yours and I wish you well, but please respect what
I need and don't call me again. Goodbye, Gerry," she said in a
tone just ambiguous enough to allow me to rationalize calling her
again. In fact, I called her five more times in the next month. In
each case I drank first, the last time quite a bit. Her response was
always the same, except she ended the last call more quickly than
she had the others, and yet enough of her normal self emerged in
each conversation to make me yearn for her and to realize more
acutely each time the immensity of my mistake.

There was only one thing left to do: go to London (without
telling her) and propose to her. It would be difficult to arrange at
my job and might get me fired, but I didn't hesitate. I didn't even
tell Phil about it, knowing what he'd say anyway.

I remember that I didn't say a word to anyone during the

flight and barely looked out the window. I didn't read or watch either of the in-flight movies. I simply thought or, more accurately, let my mind run where it would. I did take three short naps. The first nap was dreamless, but in the next one I dreamed about making love to Paulette in my St. Louis apartment. She was trying to get pregnant and in the dream we somehow knew she had. That dream seemed straightforward enough to me, but it was followed by one during my last nap that was much more mysterious, in which I dreamed I was playing hide-and-seek with my father. It began in the country, or at least on land more rustic than the neighborhood I grew up in near St. Louis. We were laughing as I ran after him, but soon he was out of sight. I was running by myself, occasionally calling out his name, but now in a different setting, where it was twilight by a lake. I was feeling anxious as I turned a corner and saw a cave. Still, I ran into it calling his name. The cave seemed to expand as I ran through it, as if it were made of elastic. I ducked my head, crossed another dark passageway then saw him suddenly, in an illuminated corner. He was smiling as I ran to him. When we hugged, I seemed to disappear into him. He was left standing alone, yet I was happy to have merged with him.

I woke up amazed by my dream. In ten minutes we'd be landing at Heathrow. I remember I spent almost no time at all in my hotel, stopping only to brush or wash a few key places. Then I was out in the London dusk, where it was chilly and purplish gray. I had only her face in my mind as I set off toward her apartment. I remember passing by the street where we first met, then past the pub where we went shortly after meeting, and then, like a stop on a tour, the Japanese restaurant where I took her to dinner on Queensway Road. I'd retraced in my mind the route we took so many times (even before I made the decision to go back to London) that I wasn't surprised that I only made one minor mistake before finding her place.

Except that it wasn't her place. She didn't answer her buzzer, which I tried intermittently for ten minutes or so. Finally someone asked me who I wished to see? It was a clear-eyed, dowdily dressed woman of fifty who identified herself as the building's manager.

"Paulette," I said. "I came to see Paulette."

"She moved out, I'm afraid."

"What?"

"Yes, she cleared out two weeks ago."

I looked at the buzzer and saw the name card had been replaced by that of a man (a man whose face I still sketchily recall, as I hung around after the landlady left, eventually knocked on the door, and looked into his uncomprehending eyes when he answered that he didn't know anyone named Paulette).

"Do you know where? Did she leave any forwarding address?" I asked the landlady.

She shook her head like a metronome. "I remember she said she was leaving London. I think she said she was going out of the country or maybe she said to the country. I really couldn't say. Out of London for sure, with no forwarding address, I'm afraid."

Of course I tried the operator, but there was no listing for her in London or in a number of other towns I tried. It was years before the Internet, when you couldn't track people down and you had to rely instead on your memory and its infinite limitations.

It was, of course, obvious that she didn't want to see or hear from me again. There was no ambiguity now. Everything she said and did was honest and sincere. That was the shocking beauty of it. I paid a lot of extra money to leave London the next day.

...

The old men in the pool are making noises—new, disturbingly high-pitched noises, like a cross between a violin and the whirring of mosquitoes. Maybe it's because it's raining now, and one can even hear some distant rumblings of thunder. In any case I start moving toward the hot tub, where Grandfather Pool has staked out his temporary home. Sitting there in the steamy part of the pool, his face seems slightly out of focus, as if I'm seeing it underwater. But I move toward it nonetheless, preferring the threat of his conversation to the reality of those weird, high-pitched noises from the old men in the kids' pool.

There are certain people you never recover completely from losing, and Paulette was one of mine. My father, of course, was another. Or maybe it's life itself we spend all our time trying to adapt to or recover from. And yet we do recover, partially, at least, as most of us choose to go on. Eventually I laughed again. I made progress in my work that brought me some satisfaction. I aged reasonably well. In time I went on to new women, a couple of whom even lived with me for a year or so. But it's also true I never got married or had a child, though these last few years I often find myself wishing I had. Those of us who can't love adults in a lasting way often turn toward children for their solace, and I wish now that I had acted on this tardy knowledge earlier. I think that even my father felt something like that in his decision to have a child, although I can't be sure.

I've entered the tub now where men shut their eyes to forget their lives for a while. I'm sitting opposite Grandfather Pool, wondering if he still remembers my father, when he used to come here with me. In the dreamlike light of the pool, whose windows seem to turn the sunlight gray, I can almost see my father's face in his. I wouldn't mind if he talked now, but Grandfather Pool is being as quiet as an angel. Perhaps there'll be no old-man talk today, after all, though I wouldn't really mind if there were. No, I really wouldn't mind that at all.

Memo and Oblivion

Although he was now taking Memo on a regular basis it was sometimes hard to remember the moment when he'd decided to become a member. He did remember how he'd first learned about it. It was through an ad in a literary quarterly, of all places, called *The Galaxy Review.* "Is Your Memory a Fiction?" the headline of the ad said, which both amused and intrigued him, as if memory were somehow a literary concept. He also remembered much more clearly, of course, since he'd been taking Memo, being late for the first meeting and taking a cab to get there, as he would again tonight. The organization's headquarters were on the third floor of a handsome brownstone on Beekman Place, near the East River. He couldn't help but be impressed by the spacious building the first time he saw it, but he was also disconcerted by the slightly disapproving stares of the initiates as he hunted for a seat.

"Excuse me, Sir," said Dr. Rossi, from the podium, a tall, extraordinarily pale-skinned man. "Are you Andrew Zorn?"

"Yes, I am. I'm sorry I'm late."

"Please sit down, Mr. Zorn. We're about to embark on a great adventure and there isn't a moment to lose." Dr. Rossi had waited a moment then extended his arms in his black suit like the wings of a giant black bird. "Welcome co-pioneers," he'd said, addressing the audience of about fifty. "Project Memo is indeed a great adventure as well as a unique one. It's an adventure that's grounded in firm science, but also promises to take us closer to the metaphysical center of things than man may ever have been before. In exchange for this adventure, this great gift, we ask only three things of you. The first is complete confidentiality, of course, which means not only absolutely no discussion about the project with anyone outside this room but also no recording or note taking. Once you fully experience Memo, taking notes will be a superfluous activity anyway. Second, we ask that you be punctual. We're always here on time, so you should be too. Punctuality is a golden rule of the organization. (Andrew remembered with great clarity nodding to reemphasize his regret for his tardiness.) Third, if you ever feel any anxiety or doubt about what happens here we ask that you come to us first to discuss it. In other words, trust us in all things regarding the organization. Remember, we're the only experts in this field, and we also have the assistance of first rate doctors and lawyers so we know how to help and protect you," he added with a slight smile.

Yes, thought Andrew, as a taxi finally pulled up to take him to tonight's meeting, he would never forget that introductory speech by Dr. Rossi—so forceful and reassuring. He got in the cab finally feeling relaxed enough that he decided he could take his last pill. At the meeting he'd get more, yet he always worried a bit that somehow he wouldn't. The e-mail said this was an emergency meeting of all senior members, and Andrew couldn't help but wonder if some serious new problem had arisen. But what could it be? He was almost afraid to speculate. Were there perhaps production problems with the supply that would cause the members to have to wait longer to get their next package of Memorosa? Or maybe a potentially deleterious side effect had been discovered? It was frightening to contemplate such undoubtedly farfetched scenarios, but he couldn't completely stop doing it. He knew his memory had increased since he'd been taking Memo but so, oddly enough, had his anxiety.

He was a few minutes early (as was his practice since the fateful first meeting) and walked directly into the auditorium, sitting just a few rows from the stage. The organization had done such a seamless job converting the apartment they owned into a functioning auditorium, complete with stage, podium, and curtain, that it really did look like it had always been one. He took a seat, felt the Memo begin to hit, and found himself recalling in incredibly vivid detail the sled rides he'd taken with his brother twenty-five years ago down the alleyway just in front of his back yard. Tears came to his eyes when he saw again the bright blue "magic mittens" he used to wear with the hole on top of the index finger. He shook his head from side to side to expel the memory. Such an important meeting required the increased concentration and later the power of recall that Memo alone could give him. That's why he'd taken it, after all, he said to himself in a chastising inner voice, not to once again indulge in his favorite sequence of memories when he was eight years old.

Turning his head, he suddenly realized that except for the guards, one posted at each door, there was no one else in the room. The stage was also empty. He felt another surge of memories threatening to inundate him, involving a day at the beach with his mother. This time he stared at the second hand of his watch to distract himself. Finally, at exactly 8 p.m., Dr. Rossi appeared at the podium dressed in his characteristic black suit.

"Good evening, Mr. Zorn," he said, in a voice that, if it had a British accent, would sound like Alfred Hitchcock.

"Good evening, Dr. Rossi," he said, quickly standing up.

"You've undoubtedly noticed that you're the only member present tonight. This was by design, for security reasons. I hope you don't feel in any way deceived."

"No, not at all, Dr. Rossi," he said, as earnestly as possible, although a part of him did feel slightly tricked. "I know you have your reasons," Andrew added.

Dr. Rossi said nothing to that. His silences were every bit as effective as his theatrical gestures and well-modulated voice.

"We have a special project to discuss with you tonight," Dr. Rossi continued. "Based on our research and general knowledge of you, we've selected you to help fulfill this project. Do you feel ready to begin?"

He could feel his heart beat, but also a sudden surge of pride that trumped his anxiety, at least for the moment.

"Yes, Dr. Rossi, I'm ready."

"Excellent. We thought we could count on you. You'll please follow the guards to the Special Projects room, where you'll meet with an officer of the organization. Oh, and one more thing that should go without saying. You are not to discuss this private meeting with any of the other members. They don't know about it, nor do we want them to. Is that clear, Andrew?"

"Yes, Dr. Rossi," Andrew said, feeling both surprised and pleased to be called by his first name. "Completely clear."

Moments later, burly, stone-faced guards were on either side of him indicating by nods of their heads that he should follow one of them while the other stood behind him, almost as if he, Andrew, were a prisoner they were guarding. They led him out of the auditorium, where the lights were now turned off, then down a well-lit hallway. Apparently the organization owned or rented much more of this apartment building than he'd thought.

"Where are we going?" he asked, in spite of himself.

For several seconds the guards said nothing as they escorted him down the floor. There were more rooms, mostly unlabeled, although he did see the word "laboratory" on one, "x-ray" on another.

"Here, please enter this room, sir," the lead guard said as he opened it.

"You can sit down," the trail guard said, just before they closed the door.

The Special Projects room was nondescript. A desk, three chairs, four full-sized filing cabinets, one rather old-fashioned schoolroom-type clock on the wall, with oversized roman numerals. No paintings or anything else on the off-white walls (except one discreetly placed photograph of Marcel Proust facing the clock), as if time itself was the only distraction recognized in the room. And yet time was passing so slowly.

How strange that this should be happening to him, he thought, a thirty-four-year-old librarian who worked for a branch of the New York Public Library, to whom such things were not supposed to happen. Not only was his career choice bland, but so was his slow rise to his current midlevel position—a rise based more on longevity of service than on anything brilliant or innovative he'd done during his career.

His mind was suddenly teeming with childhood memories he was struggling to resist because any moment his meeting could begin. Finally he let himself remember, in heartbreaking detail, the tricycle route he took when he was five from the lilac bushes through the rose trellis over the cracked sidewalk to the garage and back.

He really did feel that he'd been in the room a long time. Then he had an awful thought—could he be locked in? He stood up on his way to check the door just as an officer of the organization—who was also tall, at least as tall as Dr. Rossi—opened it and fixed his icy blue eyes on Andrew.

"Hello, Mr. Zorn. My name is Officer E."

"Good evening, Officer E," Andrew said.

E was tall, his height accentuated by his extraordinary thinness. Now that Andrew reflected on it, the overwhelming majority of members were thin, as if their immersion into their new powers of memory made eating irrelevant.

"Please sit down," Officer E said, permitting himself a trace of a smile. "You have been patient, Mr. Zorn, so I'll get right to the point. Perhaps you've seen the posters on the street or more likely read on the Internet about an organization that calls itself 'Oblivion'?"

Andrew shrugged to indicate that he hadn't or only in the most peripheral way.

"Frankly, there's every reason to believe that they've modeled themselves after us except, of course, their organizational goal, if one can speak of them as being an organization, is diametrically the opposite of ours. So then, Mr. Zorn, what exactly do you know about the philosophy and modus operandi of Oblivion?"

"Nothing really. Nothing more than what you've told me so far."

This wasn't completely true. It was Memo itself, he realized, that helped him to recall now the strange posters for Oblivion he'd seen on his walks around lower Manhattan, where he'd also noticed some pro-Oblivion graffiti.

"I'll give you a short briefing then. We also have some literature to give you about them as well, which you will read before you leave here, please. Did you take a Memo before this meeting?"

"Yes, sir."

"Good. Then you won't need to take any notes either." Officer E cleared his throat once, seemed almost embarrassed to have done so, and then continued. "Oblivion is the name of a group of emotionally or psychologically damaged people who claim to have developed a drug, which is also called Oblivion, that purports to obliterate only painful human memories. But what they don't tell you is that it's highly addictive and that taken enough, up to 90 percent of all memories can be destroyed, leaving one eventually with only the knowledge of one's name, address, and phone numbers and perhaps the ability to perform a minimal-competency-type job. This drug, by the way, which occurs in both pill and powder form, was not developed by bona fide scientists, nor has its safety, either short or long term, been monitored in any way. Our intelligence indicates that, unlike in our organization, no reputable scientists or doctors are affiliated with the group. . . . You might well wonder now, Mr. Zorn," Officer E said, his voice rising slightly but unmistakably, "why we concern ourselves at all with these morally derelict drug dealers who turn normal people into little more than zombies for a quick dollar. The answer is, our intelligence has recently learned that they have targeted us in ways we don't completely understand, but that they have targeted us is indisputable. Since enhanced memory, knowledge, and self-empowerment are anathema to them and they fear too many of their potential victims will be saved by Project Memo, it's perhaps not surprising. That's where we need you, Mr. Zorn."

He could feel himself grow rigid with attention.

"But first I need to ask you a few more questions. Questions that I want you to listen to very carefully to be 100 percent certain your answers are completely truthful."

It was odd to swear allegiance to a man he barely knew, a man so strange looking and noodle thin, with an occasional twitch in his left eye, but he heard himself say, "Yes, of course."

Officer E cleared his throat as if to signal that the process was about to begin.

"How would you describe the impact Memo has had on your life?"

"It's had a tremendous impact. It's changed everything."

"In what ways? Be as specific as you can."

He felt tears about to come to his eyes, as sometimes happened at the group meetings when he or others testified about their experiences, and he struggled against that feeling, not wanting Officer E to think him weak.

"It's like before Memo I was asleep. I didn't know it but I was. I was in a forgetting cycle, just like Dr. Rossi talks about, forgetting almost everything that happened to me and never learning from my past and so never being able to think clearly about my future. I mean, how much can you even care about your future when you know you're going to forget almost all of it right after you live it?"

Officer E looked profoundly sad. "You've articulated the tragic dilemma of pre-Memo consciousness very well, Andrew, very movingly. Now can you tell me concisely exactly how Memo has changed your life?"

"My general memory has increased tremendously, twentyfold, at least, which has had all kinds of practical benefits at my job and in my daily life, but all that pales before, if I may say so, the sheer beauty and joy of truly remembering my life. And as for those parts that are painful to remember, I now use them as great learning opportunities, as Dr. Rossi has been teaching us to. Also, I want to say that since I took the Special Focus Seminars with Dr. Rossi I've begun to develop my redirective abilities for the first time. Lately I've been focusing on my early childhood, five to eleven to be precise, and . . . well, let me just say that it's been the most incredible experience of my life."

"Again, very moving. Perhaps you should have been a teacher instead of a librarian."

"I wanted to . . . ," he said, then noticing a slight look of irritation in Officer E, let the rest of his answer go unsaid.

"I wish you could speak to some of those young gang members in Oblivion who still could be saved by Memo . . . and perhaps you will some day. How do you feel about Project Memo, then, Andrew? How do you feel about the organization that brought Memo into your life?"

"I feel very grateful, eternally grateful."

"Enough to do some important work for us that might even jeopardize your personal security?"

He felt his heart beat; it was what he feared from the moment Officer E began describing Oblivion, yet he heard himself once again say yes to Officer E and moreover felt a strong sense of pride doing so.

···

From the moment he agreed to go undercover and join Oblivion, everything changed, even the atmosphere around him. Though his training as a librarian perhaps made him prone to analyzing or "classifying" his feelings more than the average person, he couldn't find any way to describe this somewhat amorphous yet definite alteration in both his thoughts and surroundings. It was somewhat like a dream except that he was hypervigilant, as if always being watched or judged. It began after his meeting with Officer E, when he was finally out on the chilly November streets. He immediately felt he was being followed.

It was surprisingly late and he was hungry. The sky was already darkly purple as he started walking west toward Azure, his favorite cafeteria, where he often ate after the meetings. Before he'd walked a block he felt it—the same pattern of steps and silences by his pursuer, the same sense—confirmed the one time he turned to look behind himself—that he was being followed. Maybe it was someone from security at the organization, standard procedure that he shouldn't take personally. Yet it was hard not to feel concerned. They had just entrusted him with a tremendous responsibility. If they trusted him enough to do it why would they also distrust him enough to have him followed? Yet given the very quiet life he led, with so few friends or enemies, wouldn't his pursuer have to be connected to the organization? Who else knew him at this point?

He continued walking toward Azure, being careful not to increase or decrease his speed as his pursuer followed about fifty feet behind. Finally, just before entering the restaurant, he paused, as if looking at a newspaper at an outdoor stand, then turned to face him.

At first he saw nothing or just the late afternoon blur of New York. Then he finally recognized Wallace, a member of the organization as he recalled, although he hadn't seen him at the last meeting.

"Hey, Wallace," he said, waving at him and forcing a smile so it could all seem like a coincidence. "Over here."

Wallace, holding his hat, which covered his round, prematurely balding head, half ran across the street that separated them.

He forced himself to shake hands with Wallace, while keeping his smile intact, a difficult task that made him feel like a juggler. Meanwhile, he noticed an oddly embarrassed look on Wallace's face. Would the organization choose someone as ineffectual as Wallace to follow him and report on his activities?

"So what are you doing in this neck of the woods?" Wallace said, in what Andrew thought was a pitifully transparent attempt to sound spontaneous.

"I had some business near here and then I came here to eat."

"Oh, me too," Wallace said quickly, as if grateful that Andrew had provided him with his own cover story as well.

"Care to join me?"

"Sure," Wallace said, smiling more sincerely this time, which Andrew found convincing enough since Wallace had few friends and seemed to cling to anyone who showed a momentary interest in him.

"It's a self-service cafeteria. I hope that's all right."

"Oh sure. I ate here once before with you after a meeting. Didn't you take your Memo today?" Wallace said jokingly.

Andrew forced a laugh then entered the restaurant. He didn't attempt to talk to him again until they'd both gotten their food and were seated at a table on the upper level, where it was a little less noisy.

"So you never told me what *you* were doing around here today," Andrew said, before chewing a generous bite of chicken and couscous.

"Oh, business too, just like you."

"Really? Something to do with the organization?"

"It's a little embarrassing, but yes."

"Oh? What's embarrassing?"

"I thought there was a meeting today."

"Really?"

"Yes. I got confused so I went there for nothing as it turns out. And then I got hungry and went to this place just like you."

Andrew looked hard at him. Two preposterous coincidences delivered in a convictionless voice by a dubious man who was now almost chugging his beer. Andrew was concerned, but before he could think of what to say next, Wallace put down his empty beer bottle and spoke again.

"Can I ask you a personal question completely off the record while we're kind of on the subject?"

"Go ahead," Andrew said.

"Well don't be offended, but do you ever have any doubts about the organization?"

"Doubts? What kind of doubts?"

"Doubts in general about their modus operandi."

"What about it would give me any doubts?"

"Don't you think some of their methods are a trifle controlling, even militaristic?"

Andrew shrugged. Lately, he'd had similar thoughts himself, thoughts he'd generally try to kick out of his mind. For a second he wondered if Wallace had been given a different pill, which allowed him to read minds. "They're dealing with something that will have a profound effect on the world. They have to be very careful."

"Yes," said Wallace. "I considered all that. Still, the way they walk up and down the aisles like soldiers to make sure we're not taking any notes. And all the loyalty oaths they've made us sign, all the documented information we've had to turn over to them, whereas we don't even know any of their full names."

"What about Dr. Rossi?"

"I don't know his first name, do you? I mean, don't you find that just a little disturbing? Aren't they supposed to be doctors, so why are they acting like drug dealers?"

"You shouldn't talk about the organization that way."

Wallace shrugged—a mirror image of his own shrug a few minutes ago. Wallace Mirror, Andrew thought. That should be his nickname. "What about Memo?" Andrew blurted more angrily than he wanted to. "Do you have doubts about Memo, too?"

"Memo is a very powerful memory aid, no question. The question is, though, is it really ready for use by the general public? Is it really such a benefit to humanity or is it being rushed out before it's actually been tested, just so certain people can profit from it?"

"People *are* profiting from it *emotionally*, don't you see that? Don't you remember our last group testimony, how Elaine started crying while she described getting her memory back of the first rose she ever touched. What a moment of, of . . . priceless beauty for her. And there've been dozens of testimonies like that. You know that."

"That was very touching, true, but not everyone reacts so positively to Memo."

"I haven't heard of a single negative reaction in all the testimonies so far. I certainly haven't had any."

"Fair enough, but not everyone feels comfortable making that kind of confession in group. Many feel intimidated about confessing and frightened of the consequences if they really tell the truth. Some have even been actively discouraged from talking."

"How would you know this? Can you give me even one example?"

"Do you remember Jerome?"

"He stopped coming after the first two groups, didn't he?"

"Exactly."

"Is he even still a member?"

"Jerome had a very bad experience with Memo. It made him relive something extremely painful in his past—his father's suicide. He'd blocked it out before but Memo removed that block."

"Maybe he can start to work on it now."

"Jerome won't be working on anything anymore. He hung himself last week. The memories were torturing him, filling him with unbearable guilt. He left a note about it. My information is that the organization made a big effort to keep it off of the Internet and largely succeeded."

Andrew felt his heartbeat again. "That's a very serious allegation."

"It's not an allegation, it's a fact. As I said, there was a note."

"If you feel that way, how can you still be a member?"

"The truth is I'm not. I've resigned today in person and if you have any concern for your safety you will too. You look shocked, but are you really? I know they've probably got you on some special mission and maybe that's to follow me, maybe even to stop me from quitting. I realize that my telling you this may be a fatal mistake, but I had to."

"That's ridiculous. It was you who were following me and not the other way around."

"I'm just warning you my misguided friend," he said, getting up from the table suddenly. "Just urging you to get out while you still can," he added, before turning his back on Andrew.

"How can you talk that way about an organization that's given so much to you . . . and to the world?"

Wallace turned and looked at him.

"I did it to warn you, like I said. You won't see me again," he said, turning once more and walking quickly down the stairs.

• • •

Andrew had trouble sleeping that night. Of course he was thinking a lot about the charge he'd been given to join Oblivion, whose next meeting would be in two nights, but he also found it more difficult than he'd imagined to forget about his meeting with Wallace. Because he'd taken Memo he had an almost total recall of their conversation, which was both reassuring and disconcerting. After reviewing it he found a number of things that could undermine Wallace's credibility besides Wallace in general, who'd always struck him as a person who, for various reasons, was impossible to trust. Hadn't Wallace said, at first, that he'd gone to the organization because he thought there was a meeting, only to reverse himself a few minutes later and admit he'd already resigned? And was that even true? How could anyone give credence to such a duplicitous liar?

And yet Wallace had expressed, albeit in an exaggerated way, some of the secret doubts that he, Andrew, had about the organization, too. Moreover, the very fact that he kept thinking about what happened with Wallace reinforced some questions he'd had about Memo, mainly that it increased "obsessive thinking" at times, both in intensity and duration.

He turned on a light and tried to read a book. He'd called Wallace an underground man but look at his own lonely, little apartment, he thought, bereft of anything intriguing, or even comforting.

He shut off the light and closed his eyes yet again and this time saw Elaine's expression when she told the group about her rose memory, about touching each petal. Tears filled his eyes in the darkness and suddenly his crisis was resolved. Memo was bringing great beauty into the world and in that way was also changing the world. He knew again how important it really was and how important the work he had to do for it was too, work that lay just ahead.

...

He made his first contact with Oblivion by e-mail, Memo having provided him with the address. Then he waited, as instructed, until he received an e-mail an hour before their meeting telling him where to go and when. He was also told to wear a white shirt or sweater.

He was mildly surprised that they'd chosen Fanelli's in SoHo as the meeting place. It was a noisy bar/restaurant filled with artists talking shop and networking. The tables were all filled, but he found a seat at the bar, where, somewhat to the bartender's consternation, he ordered a ginger ale. (He'd already taken a Memo, which he knew shouldn't be mixed with alcohol.) After fifteen minutes he wondered if he was supposed to look for someone else wearing white, whether he'd gotten confused about that part although he'd been given more Memo than usual to use for the duration of the assignment.

Then he remembered a line from the literature he'd read at headquarters. "Oblivion members are notoriously late, perhaps because their goal is to forget the world instead of remembering it."

He was embarrassed but felt he had to order another ginger ale. Just after it arrived someone tapped him on his left shoulder. He turned and saw a strikingly attractive woman with dark eyes and long black hair.

"Are you here for the meeting?" she said.

"Yes. Is it going to happen here?"

"Tell me what meeting it is."

"The 'O meeting,'" he said, trying not to stare at her too intensely.

"You'll have to fill out some forms and provide us with some personal information, including your credit card number. Is that all right?"

"Yes, of course. My name's Andrew."

"We'll have to leave here now."

"Where to?"

"Follow me," she said, walking toward the nearest exit. He left a generous tip and watched as she walked ahead of him. She was wearing a black coat and big black boots that women wore back in the 1980s. He guessed her to be somewhere in the late-twenty to mid-thirty range. There was something vague in her expression that made it hard to tell, but she was certainly good looking, which was probably no accident. Perhaps her purpose was to stir up memories of lost loves, Andrew thought, to remind people of what they were missing in the present and so to make them want Oblivion even more than they already did.

She walked quickly, her boots making a strange kind of percussive music on the pavement. When he asked her name, she said, "I can't answer personal questions. My job is to escort new members to the meeting." When he tried another approach, commenting on the weather, he received only a one-word response.

After walking a few blocks she entered a loft on Wooster Street and pressed the button for an elevator. "Follow me," was all she said. He tried to keep his eyes off her and to stop his futile conversational forays as well. The one time he did look at her briefly she looked distinctly uncomfortable, as if the light of the elevator not only bothered her but was also somehow her enemy.

A smallish, sparsely furnished loft billowed out in front of him. They obviously don't have anything near the money Memo has, Andrew thought. They'll be pleased to hear that at headquarters.

"Can I ask your name?" Andrew said, now that she was out of the dreaded elevator and seemed composed again.

"Seven," she said tartly.

At the far end of the loft sat an undistinguished-looking man in his late thirties, early forties wearing a black T-shirt and black jeans. His sandy-colored hair was receding in an unflattering way but he had a charming smile.

"Wilhelm, this is Andrew," Seven said, then retreated to a chair at the other end of the loft.

Wilhelm shook his hand warmly. "Sit down," he said, pointing toward a straight-back chair with his thin, light-haired arm.

"Thanks," Andrew said.

"I prefer standing," Wilhelm said, with a slight German accent. "I hope you don't mind. There's a little speech I need to make and I feel more comfortable standing when I speak. OK with you?"

"Sure."

"I know you answered a lot of questions electronically when you signed up, but there are a few more Seven probably told you about that we'll need from you before you can really start our program. We're sorry but we have to be careful. Also, like I said, I want to give you a general idea about where we're at philosophically before we go any further. Is that all cool with you?"

"Absolutely," he said, mildly surprised by the informality of Wilhelm's language.

Wilhelm turned to face him directly. "OK then," he said. "Basically the world, as we see it, is divided between those who are trying to remember and those who are trying to forget. We don't have a problem with that. There are tortured veterans from, say, the Iraq war who, even though it ended five or six years ago, still can't sufficiently forget that part of their lives. but there are also aging people struggling to remember their own children because Alzheimer treatments still haven't been perfected. By the same token there are those who want to forget a lost lover and those who want to remember one. We accept that. We think there are more of us than them, but even if there weren't and we were in the minority, we understand that that's the way of the world, man, *capiche?*"

"Oh sure, of course," Andrew said, noticing for the first time a facial resemblance between Wilhelm and Seven. It was the shape of their eyes, he thought, or perhaps a vaguely vacant expression in them.

"Unfortunately there are people out there in organizations who don't accept our views and won't let us live our lives the way we want and deserve to. We know that increasing your memory can be valuable, even indispensable in some cases, but so is the ability to forget. Millions of people, who need to forget selectively and can't, suffer from anxiety, depression, paranoia, and sometimes end up committing suicide. But the so-called memory warriors in the name of the Great God Awareness want to force them to remember even more. They want to undermine Oblivion and make it disappear because we offer genuine relief to these sufferers in a way that contradicts their so-called research. So we're a threat to them, right, man? I think they're afraid we'll cut into their business, which, without meaning to, we already have. But that's free enterprise, right? You see the irony, don't you?"

"Yes, I do."

"So how do you feel about what I've been saying so far?"

"I completely agree with you. You've really expressed how I feel very convincingly."

"Good, I'm glad we're on the same page philosophically. But now I need to ask you why you want Oblivion in your life. I'm sorry if this puts you on the spot, but we have to know you really need it. Contrary to what you may hear on the street, there's not an unlimited supply of Oblivion and we have to constantly watch our reserves."

"Of course."

"We also know that Memo is trying to infiltrate Oblivion with a variety of spies and double agents. See, we're just too big a threat to them even though they're grabbing all the headlines. They're paranoid and very aggressive, man. I think they want world domination, I really do, so how can they let any alternative view stand in their way? They can't. They want to crush us like weeds, man, but we're tough weeds that won't go down. Ha ha! They didn't count on that, did they? Seven, come here and tell Andrew that's what Memo really wants to do."

Seven looked surprised to suddenly be addressed, flustered even, but she promptly got up and walked next to Wilhelm.

"He's telling you the truth," she said, and for the first time he realized her accent was German as well. Officer E had referred to Oblivion as "the Nazi drug" because a gang of Germans were said to be controlling the U.S. distribution, but Wilhelm and Seven seemed so kind and earnest—anything but the latest incarnation of neo-Nazis.

"What he's saying is one hundred percent truth about Memo and everything," she said, looking at him directly. He was startled to suddenly make contact with her ambiguous eyes, so full of promise and disappointment at the same time that he felt at once discovered and helpless.

"So you see we've been honest with you," Wilhelm said, "now it's time for you to be honest with us. Why do you want Oblivion?"

Of course he had a preplanned answer that the organization had given him, but he decided to tell them the truth about his life, which certainly contained things he wanted to forget anyway and which, he thought, would ultimately be more convincing. So he told them about his lonely apartment on the Upper West Side, where he often felt he was living in a cemetery. Instead of actual buried corpses he had memories all around him. Some of them from his childhood were beautiful but from his late teens on, many of them were often frustrating, in one way or another, or just plain painful.

What were they, Wilhelm asked? He felt himself hesitate, but then Seven asked him and he soon began telling them about his last two lovers, who each left him (they didn't seem surprised), and also that in his last relationship he felt deeply ashamed of how he'd behaved. He couldn't yet tell them what he'd done specifically, he said, but it was the darkest secret of his life, something he'd be ashamed of till the day he died.

"We can help you forget that," Seven said with great earnestness, and he looked at her and nodded, feeling touched.

He did go on to say that he tried to bury himself in his work, wanting desperately to do something constructive to escape his pain, which might have worked except he couldn't find any meaning in his job. He loved reading, but endlessly classifying and organizing books, attending meetings, dealing with library politics—yes, libraries had politics too—was killing that love. It was so soul killing, he went on to say, that he'd sometimes even had thoughts of ending his life. "Everyone needs the illusion of meaning," he said in conclusion, "but I no longer have any."

"Everyone needs to forget some things too, so they can have a fresh start," Wilhelm added with a knowing smile. "Your life is about to take a turn for the better this time, my friend," he said, suddenly producing a round, turquoise blue pill. "Are you ready for this? Are you ready for the peace and joy of Oblivion?"

He knew this moment would happen, Officer E had told him so. But he was also told that by taking Memo first, as he'd already done, the effects of Oblivion would be mitigated.

"I'm definitely ready."

Seven was pouring him a glass of water. He looked at the small blue pill—it seemed no more substantial than a drop of rain. He touched her fingers as she handed him the glass and a moment later he swallowed his first Oblivion.

They both applauded as Wilhelm's face exploded into a smile. "Congratulations, you're part of Oblivion. Here," he said, tossing him a black T-shirt Andrew hadn't noticed before. "Take off that pasty white shirt and put on the black one. That's what we wear at Oblivion. That's it, just leave the other one behind you. Now, how would you like to go to a party with us to celebrate, Oblivion style?"

"Sure," he said, and for some reason he knew he meant it, though he wasn't sure at all that the organization would approve of him going to any Oblivion event high. And what kind of party would it be anyway? His hosts kept that a mystery, saying that they didn't want to ruin the surprise.

The next thing he knew he was out on the street laughing with them as they walked toward the party. They kept telling him it was a short distance but it felt like a long one. Still, he laughed because he didn't care how long it took. And when they told him they'd only been walking three minutes at most, he laughed even harder.

At Prince Street, Wilhelm pressed a buzzer and they were let into a loft. "Your sense of time is changing, man, and it will change again, where time will pass more quickly before it regularizes."

"I don't understand a word you're saying," Andrew said, laughing hysterically as he hadn't laughed since he was eleven.

Inside the loft some kind of loud "computer rock" was playing. He saw a sea of mostly young people dancing, dressed in black T-shirts or sweaters and black jeans. So it *was* an Oblivion party, but there was nothing sinister about that, was there? He wondered if he'd even bother including it in his report or if he'd even bother writing one. That made him laugh, too.

Meanwhile, a number of people were hugging Wilhelm and Seven before Wilhelm introduced him. He had all he could do to control his laughter and a minute later couldn't remember their names. He walked away and began circling the loft, feeling the strong high surging through him while watching the dancers. He must have circled the loft three or four times before he suddenly stopped. He wanted to be with Seven more than he remembered ever wanting to be with anyone, but she was at the other end of the loft still socializing with the guests. Then someone tapped him on the shoulder. He turned and saw Wallace.

"Hello there," Wallace said. "Having a good time?"

"What are you doing here?"

"I guess you've found me out. I'm a member of Oblivion now. The real question is what are you doing here? I didn't know it was a party for double agents," Wallace said with a mischievous smile. How Wallace loved these situations, making people who intimidated him suddenly squirm themselves.

"I'm not a double agent."

"Anyway, whatever you are, you should know there's been another Memo suicide, did you know that, so I really hope what you tell me is true. If it is then congratulations, you've made it to the other side. . . . Well, sayonara for now," said Wallace, who turned and suddenly disappeared into the crowd of dancers.

Andrew never thought of calling after him. It wouldn't do any good if Wallace had heard him and returned. What could he say? It was all over now. By not admitting to anything, he'd blown his cover—and to Wallace, which was like telling the world, or at least the world of Memo and Oblivion. He had to get out of here. Wallace was probably on his cell phone right now calling Officer E or Dr. Rossi to report him. There might even be Memo security on the way to the loft already, where they'd be waiting to work him over, or worse, once he set foot outside the loft. They certainly wouldn't let it pass without some response. They'd interrogated and researched him. He'd sworn allegiance and now he was at an enemy's party, having taken Oblivion itself while being flooded with desire for Seven. Yes, nothing like sleeping with the enemy, or wanting to, on your first night on the job. Yet he had to admit he'd also never had fun like this before, certainly not as an adult.

He continued to pace around the periphery of the dancers, who were gyrating with more frenzy than ever as the music also became increasingly frenetic and atonal. Finally he realized there were two hopes to which he could still cling. Perhaps the organization would believe that he'd made the decision to take Oblivion and go to the party to gain extra information. That he'd made a strategic blunder (any decision that Memo didn't prescribe would be viewed by them as a mistake) but that his motives were pure. He'd actually had fleeting thoughts like that at one point, though he knew it wasn't his real reason for going to the party. How easily swayed he was, how weak! Still, he might be able to pass the organization's inevitable interrogation, which he'd heard involved a new kind of truth pill. The other possibility, which he couldn't entirely dismiss out of hand either, was that Wallace really was a member of Oblivion and not a double agent at all (with a little research he could possibly find that out one way or another). If Wallace had joined Oblivion, and there was a plausible case that he had, then it became imperative to convince him that he, Andrew, was now a member as well. And that could be done maybe more easily than he imagined.

He suddenly felt lighter, happier, could feel the high coursing through him again as if he'd suddenly learned his life had been unexpectedly saved. Then he began to search for Seven. He wouldn't be so diffident this time but would compel her to talk with him. Finally, he found her walking off the dance floor, looking both sad and angry. She was walking toward him without realizing it and away from Wilhelm, whose back was turned to her in any case.

"Seven," he called out twice before she stopped and looked at him. She'd clearly been crying and also, for the moment at least, appeared not to recognize him.

"Seven, it's me, Andrew."

She half nodded, making no effort to smile. He was going to ask her how she was enjoying the party but that seemed ridiculous now and, moreover, false. He'd been working on this project for Memo for three days and he was already sick of dissembling.

"You look upset. Are you all right?" he blurted.

"Was that what you wanted to tell me?"

"No, I wanted to talk with you."

"You're right, I am upset, too upset to talk."

She looked at Wilhelm, who was now dancing with a tall blonde, and he thought she seemed to be coming to some sort of decision. Then she turned toward him in her characteristically dramatic way.

"I'm leaving now. You want to come with me?"

"Yes," he said, although he felt by doing so he'd now completely betrayed both Memo and, in a way, Oblivion too.

She barely talked to him on the street—just one- or two-word answers to his questions. What would happen if this continued? Finally he asked if she wanted to go someplace and have a drink.

"A bar?" she said, almost contemptuously. "I met you in a bar. Don't you have anything at your place?"

He tried to form a mental picture of his tiny, amorphous kitchen. There was only some cooking wine; he was not a drinker.

"Maybe not what you want."

"Doesn't matter. I've gone old school and got some pot. Remember when it was a big thing, before everyone started wanting all these memory drugs? Anyway, I've got some and it mixes well with O. We can smoke it at your place, can't we?"

"Sure," he said, his long neglected penis suddenly stirring again.

In the cab she said, "You're kind of ambivalent about O but you definitely want me, right?"

"Is it that obvious?"

"I still have insight into people. I used to have really good insight but it tortured me. O took away a lot of that but there's still some left. Don't look so sad. It was my choice, after all."

At the door of his building he said, "My place is small and there's not much to it."

"Don't worry, I'm never gonna remember it."

The remark both set him at ease and hurt his feelings. Did it mean she'd never see him again—that this was only a one-night stand? He asked her about that while she was rolling a joint on the desk in his bedroom.

"My goal is to get rid of my memories, not increase them, I thought you understood all that. So why would I remember your place? If we have fun I might remember you," she said, with a smile that revived his temporarily lost erection.

He should have kissed her then, he realized later, or else right after they smoked, but instead he asked her about Wilhelm. He saw her face constrict as if he were aiming an intense flashlight on it.

"I don't want to talk about Wilhelm."

"What did he do to you?"

"Hey, Mr. Andrew, you want to spend time with me, don't talk about him, OK?"

"Fair enough," he said, deciding that this time he really would shut up before he ruined everything. Besides, it was all he could do to inhale the marijuana right without making a coughing fool out of himself. The reward, however, was an immediate, blissful high. He looked at Seven, who seemed to be feeling the same thing. He remembered thinking it was human nature to let your enthusiasm for something—be it Memo or Oblivion—drive you to extreme positions. In that sense there was really no difference between the two. Then he started kissing Seven and soon after that they took off their clothes.

He didn't see it until afterward—noticed something for a second, like a shape in a dream, but didn't really see it till she got up to use his bathroom. Then he knew he would see it forever. It was written in black, the color of Oblivion, underneath an image of a pair of eyes—the single word "Wilhelm" just above her bottom. He felt a burning throughout his body as if he'd been set on fire. He thought, I'll give her my life savings if she'll just get it removed.

She returned from his bathroom wearing only her panties and looked at him.

"So you saw it. Did it ruin your good time?"

"I knew you two were lovers anyway."

She began dressing herself slowly but methodically.

"People do things they regret but they deserve to forget them," she said. "Isn't that why you joined Oblivion? Anyway, Wilhelm's not my lover. Our relationship is just the business now."

"It's hard to believe that. I saw how angry you were when he was dancing with that blonde."

"It's not what you think. We made a pact not to date any members, but he continues to violate it and then flaunt it in my face."

"If your relationship is over, why do you still care?"

"My relationship with him will never be over."

"So, you're still lovers then?"

"Stop giving me the third degree. Stop it! I won't stand for it."

"Sorry. It's been done a lot lately to me too."

But he couldn't stop himself. It was as if the part of him that was asking questions over and over was operating on its own, like an independent entity. As far as he knew, he was still terrified of losing her, yet the question still wouldn't stop, though her face had gone first red with rage, then white with shock. Finally she screamed at him, "OK, OK. God damn you, he's my brother. Are you satisfied now?"

"Jesus Christ."

"Yes, Jesus almighty Christ. You still remember him. I'm impressed."

"How could that happen?"

For a moment he saw a sad smile on her face, before she looked away from him. She was talking now—a flood of words like a waterfall—but he couldn't make sense of it other than she blamed her father, who had done unspeakable things to both of them.

"Wilhelm got us away from him. He saved my life, so how can I hate him?" she said, crying a little. "Do you expect him to be a normal man after what my father did to us? We both want to forget, that's all. What else can we do?"

"I don't know," he said, trying in vain to make eye contact with her, and then looking away himself.

"Of course you don't know. You screw me but you don't know. You only know I'm a permanently ruined woman, right? That's why I plan to forget you."

He looked up and saw that incredibly she was already dressed.

"I'll tell you what else I know," she said, looking sharply at him. "You're a weak and terribly confused man, yourself. You're playing some kind of dangerous game. I know that much and Wilhelm knows it too. Maybe it's with Memo, maybe not, but it's a dangerous game that could have a very bad ending."

"Did you tell Wilhelm that?"

"I don't have to. We think the same thoughts. Things are going to be closing in on you very fast, Andrew. My advice to you is to get out of here right away. Get out of all your lonely-hearts clubs and leave New York right now. You're from someplace else, right?"

"Yes, a town in Mass . . ."

"Don't tell me, it will be one more thing I'll have to forget. Just go back to it."

"But can't you give me a chance to talk with you first?"

"Just forget it," she said, letting herself out his door and slamming it behind her. All she had left (he noticed a moment later), whether by accident or design, was two more Oblivion pills. He stared at them as if they were a pair of eyes to which he was drawn, wondering how much they could help kill his pain. But there was no time for such self-indulgence because his fear was even stronger. She'd warned him, but what exactly had she said? He took a Memo to remember it more clearly. Almost instantly her words came back, as did his meeting with Wallace at the party. Which one, if either, could he trust?

He began frantically packing his suitcase, thinking that both Memo and Oblivion knew his phone number, e-mail password, credit card number, and address. Had he left any incriminating e-mails? He didn't think so, but there was no time to check. Had they tapped out his credit card by now? He'd better take as much cash as he could, especially since he couldn't fly directly to his parents' home—he'd have to go to Boston first.

He continued to think the key was Wallace. If Wallace was a double agent, then Memo would be coming for him soon. But if Wallace was working for Oblivion, he could be equally as dangerous. He felt the same uncertainty about Wilhelm and Seven. For all he knew they could be double agents working for Memo too. He felt a pain again as he thought of Seven. If her warning was sincere, maybe she'd felt something for him after all.

How could he have gotten himself into such a mess so quickly?

He'd simply wanted to remember his childhood better, to improve his memory, and somehow he'd gotten into a situation where his very life was in danger. There must be some flaw in him that caused this to happen. But why had Memo chosen him? Was it his very blandness and reliability that influenced their decision? One thing he knew, he wasn't suited to work undercover for anyone.

The phone rang and he stood frozen in his spot before answering on the fifth ring. Whoever was on the other end listened to him say hello and then hung up. Instinctively, he looked out his window on West End Avenue and thought he saw someone move behind a dumpster. Reaching in his pocket, where he'd put both kinds of pills, he swallowed an Oblivion. He decided then to leave from the basement exit, which he didn't think either organization knew about.

If I think about my home, things will get better, he said to himself, already forming an image of his aging mother's welcoming arms, as he got in the elevator and began his descent.

"Do You Like This Room?"

"Do you like this room?"

"Yes, it's very nice."

"You don't say that with much conviction," he said, leaning forward in his chair, which faced her on the sofa.

"It's a fine room, really. It looks like it's your entertainment center."

"Why do you say that?"

She pulled back some of the hair that had fallen over her eyes, hair that she now realized was the same color brown as his. "Because there're so many things here that are entertaining . . . like your giant TV and your stereo."

"Do you think the TV is too big?"

"No, it's a wonderful size. It must be great to watch movies on."

He seemed to relax a bit but was still looking at her intently, as if checking her face against an identification card.

"Did you like the restaurant we went to tonight?"

"Yes, very much."

"The food, the service . . . did it live up to your expectations?"

"It exceeded them."

"And was your crème brûlée all right? I remember you hesitated before choosing it. Was it too sweet or too bitter?"

"It was too good. I hadn't meant to eat all of it. I meant to share some of it with you, but I guess it turned me into a little pig," she said, laughing for a few seconds.

He nodded and watched her drink her gin and tonic.

"So did the restaurant seem the kind of place you thought we should go to? I mean on a second date. Did it meet those expectations?"

"Yes, of course. I mean I didn't have any expectations . . . I"

"Why not?"

"Anything would have been fine but what you chose was excellent, just right. Why are you asking me all these questions? It's starting to make me a little nervous."

"Do you really want to know?"

"Yes, I do," she said, finishing her drink and setting it down on the glass table in front of them. He watched her cross her legs—her skirt just above her knees—before answering her.

"It's because of the last woman I was with."

"Oh."

"There are probably other factors involved, but for the most part I lay this at her feet."

She made a supportive sound that stopped just short of being a word.

"You look mystified," he said. "See, just before she left me she said I never asked if she was happy, so now I've learned to ask."

"OK, I understand," she said, nodding.

He also nodded, as if imitating her, and finished his drink. "You may be wondering why I didn't ask you any of these questions during our first date. It's because I figured I'd get my answer when I asked you out again. That if you said yes it meant you liked the first date."

"I did like the first date. I liked it quite a bit."

"I guess you think I'm being silly saying all this since you're here in my condominium, right?"

"It's not silly," she said, straightening her skirt so that it was at knee level now or perhaps just below.

"Hey," the man said, his green eyes suddenly becoming animated, "are you in the mood to play a game?"

"What kind of game?" she said, smiling and wondering if he was finally going to make a move.

"A surprising game. A game you would never think of playing."

She looked at him—it was as if a whole new side of his personality was suddenly opening like a door revealing a garden. It gave her more hope about him since he'd seemed a trifle bland until now, although also very nice.

"Everyone likes surprises if they're fun," she said.

"Would you like to play one of the games I invented?"

"I'm not sure I understand. You mean a board game or . . .?"

"No, this isn't the kind of game you could buy in a store. We play it with our minds."

"Well, maybe you could tell me about it first."

"I invented it a few minutes ago while you were asking me why I asked you so many questions. Here's how it works. One of us plays the role of God, I mean the typical Christian all-knowing God, and the other plays a person, or is just ourselves. Don't worry, we can switch roles. Anyway, God asks the person questions about how he likes the world, and the person asks God if He approves of his behavior as a person."

She told him she wasn't sure she understood, while trying to camouflage her disappointment. He assured her she would understand and said he'd start off by playing God.

"Did you like the sunset I created today?" he said. "Go ahead, answer."

She looked a little flustered. "Yes, it was beautiful," she said, managing to smile.

"Now ask about something specific you did and whether God approves of it. Go on."

"I don't know. I can't think."

"OK, OK," the man said, holding up his hands. "You play God and I'll ask you the human questions."

"All right," she said.

"Did you hear my prayer last night? It was windy where I lived, almost a storm, and I didn't know if you heard it."

"Yes, I heard it. I hear everything, my son," she added, smiling.

"Go on. It's your turn now."

"OK, OK. Did you enjoy the stars I made last night? Did you notice the patterns they formed over your head?"

"When I remembered to look up I did, though it was just for a few seconds because I live so far away from them and I don't know exactly what they're for and why you made so many of them in the first place. You never tell."

"Good line," the woman said, hoping her compliment might lighten his mood, which had turned serious again just when she was feeling encouraged.

"Sometimes I wonder if my prayers bounce off them on their way to you—if your stars just bat them back and forth so they never get to you."

He looked at her and noticed a sour expression on her face. "Are you upset by my implicit criticism of you . . . my *God*," he added, to be sure she understood.

"No, no, my Phil, I understand and forgive everyone."

"Since I can't do either, that puts me at a great disadvantage. Go on, it's your turn again."

She looked at him uncertainly. "Did you enjoy the flowers I created that were in Tower Grove Park near the restaurant where you ate last night?"

"I did enjoy the flowers," he said, "as well as the stars, though they require two opposite motions of my head to see. You've made so many things but you've placed them too far apart and in so many directions I'd have to have a very flexible head, like an owl, to appreciate them all, or even a hundredth of them."

"One billionth of them would be more like it."

"Yes, my head would be very sore even noticing one *trillionth* of them. My head would be sore and useless and probably fall off."

"I wouldn't let that happen to you, my son," she said, adjusting her skirt again so it revealed more of her leg.

"But you do let many people's heads fall off all over the world. I watch this on my giant television and am puzzled."

He looked at her quickly and noticed her sour expression was back. Her name was Courtney, he suddenly remembered. He didn't know why he kept forgetting it tonight—didn't think he had on their first date. He could see she was a little high, too, which had originally been one of his goals, but now it didn't matter. He was thinking of Melanie, the woman who left him. Courtney asked her question and he heard himself say, "I don't think my game is a big hit with you."

"No, no, Phil, it's really interesting. I'm just not very good at playing God or talking to Him either."

"Even though you're a therapist?" he said.

She forced a laugh then excused herself to use his bathroom, leaving him alone with his thoughts. When she returned he said, "I'm sorry for what I said about you being a therapist. It was just a little joke."

She made a disparaging little gesture with her left hand. "I know, it was a joke. It was funny, really."

"I respect you a lot for being a therapist. It's very important work."

"Thank you," she said, smile intact.

"You know, I prayed about our date last night."

"Really?"

"Yes, I prayed that you'd like it and would want to see me again."

"Well, I did like it, but now it's getting kind of late so I'm afraid I . . ."

"Why didn't you tell me before?" he screamed. She thought he might have pounded the table with his fists, too. It had all happened so fast—like a lightning flash—that she couldn't be sure.

"I'm sorry," she mumbled.

"Excuse me, do you suppose we could have a little sincerity here? Wasn't that one of the points of the game we just played, the game that bored you so much?"

"It didn't bore me and I have been sincere," she said, raising her own voice, although it trailed off by the end of her answer.

"What I'm asking is, once you wanted to go home, why didn't you say so? Why did you only bring it up after playing the game much longer than you wanted to? This, after all the questions I asked you before to try to find out what you liked or didn't, trying to tell exactly what pleased you just so I could avoid this kind of humiliation."

"No, no," she said, gesturing vaguely with her right hand.

"No, no what?" he said. "You've got to explain better than

that. You're a therapist, for Christ's sake. It's your job to explain things, isn't it?"

"I enjoyed playing the game. I enjoyed all the other things we did tonight, too, so much that I didn't realize about the time and then as soon as I did, I merely said I needed to go home to get some sleep, 'cause I have clients in the morning."

"And whose home are you in now?"

She said nothing. She thought she'd made a diplomatic answer but it didn't seem to have made any difference.

"You're in my home now, aren't you, which I guess makes you *my* client."

"Yes, of course."

"And a man's home is his castle, am I right? I didn't pluck that saying out of the air, did I?"

"No, you didn't pluck it out of the air," she said softly, feeling that her lips were starting to quiver and wondering if he noticed because he was looking at her in a kind of inhuman way, like a camera recording everything.

"I can stay a few more minutes," she said.

"I'll say how long you can stay."

"I don't understand what's happening."

"Seems clear enough to me," he said, staring directly at her.

"I don't understand why you're talking this way to me—it's scaring me."

"It's a pity," he said.

"What? What is?"

"That understanding so often lags behind activity, or to put it another way, a therapist understands but a God acts."

"OK. That's interesting. All your ideas are, but now I really do have to go." She said this in what she considered a fairly even tone of voice, though she felt she was shaking a little when she stood up and that he noticed it, of course, looking at her the way he was, like some kind of x-ray machine.

She took a definitive step or two before he sprang up from his chair tiger-like and, grabbing her arms just below the shoulders, forced her down on the sofa. She let out a little half scream just before his hands fastened on her neck.

"Be quiet. Don't ever scream again in here or things will get a lot worse for you."

She said nothing. She was breathing heavily, felt for a moment that she might pass out. His hands were holding her firmly—not quite causing pain, but more like a relentless pressure.

She looked at him closely. The physique that he'd bragged about on the Internet, that had attracted and surprised her on the first date by being almost exactly what he'd described, was now her enemy. He was a little older than her, but still in his thirties, and he was taller and of course much stronger, too.

He released his hands and walked a little away from her.

"I'm sorry. I don't know what I did to make you so mad but I'm sorry," she said.

"You tried to leave after all the reassurances and tawdry little compliments you threw my way."

She nodded, as if acknowledging a crime.

"Even after I told you how I prayed about this date, how I bothered God Himself about it. *That's* why I'm keeping you like this. Do you think you understand now?"

"I understand," she said.

"You should understand. You're a psychotherapist, aren't you? Isn't that what you told me?"

"Yes."

"Doesn't your training cover people like me? People who are really in pain."

She said nothing, and bowed her head. She suddenly felt exhausted and wondered if he'd somehow drugged her. She heard him walking across the room, but still kept her head down. Maybe he'll just go into his room and let me leave, she thought. But his steps were getting closer now instead of further away.

"I asked you a question," he screamed, and her head jerked up and stared at him in disbelief. He was standing five to ten feet away from her, pointing a gun directly at her with one hand while gripping some kind of bag with the other.

"Jesus," she said.

"No, it's Phil. Jesus isn't here now, Dr. Courtney, but I am."

"What? What are you doing?"

"I'm commanding your attention. You were starting to fall asleep and I think therapists who fall asleep should lose their licenses, don't you? At the very least they need to be woken up."

She gazed at him. He seemed much taller now—as if holding the gun had suddenly turned him into a giant.

"Please put the gun away, please, so we can talk."

He shook his head no, so rapidly it was like a twitch. "I'll tell you what I *will* do," he said. "I'll even things up a little."

"Please," she said. She wasn't aware that she was crying, and the tears falling down her face felt like another shock.

"Let's play a different game," he said. "This one might interest you more than the last one."

He was withdrawing something from the bag, then in one fluid motion it came flying at her like a bat, landing beside her on the sofa. She let out a gasp and saw the light come back into his eyes.

"Yes it's real, you can touch it if you want. It's a real gun and it's all yours to use as you wish as long as we play the game."

"Please don't . . ."

"Please don't what? Play the game? Why don't you hear what

the game is before you reject it? The rules are simple enough. One of these guns has bullets in it, the other has blanks. If you have the gun with bullets you can leave now simply by shooting me. You look surprised, but don't be. And don't assume I know which gun is which. They're twin guns, have you noticed? They're linked forever, just like you and me."

"I know that woman hurt you. I know you're feeling a lot of pain."

"*Do* you know what I'm feeling? Haven't you already generalized me away into some psychological category—the better not to really know me."

"There's some truth in what you say. I know there are psychologists who are too analytical and not always empathetic enough. I've had them myself."

"Then you've had problems, too? Problems you apparently couldn't manage."

"I've had issues I needed to have some help . . . dealing with. It's very frustrating when you feel a doctor doesn't understand the uniqueness of your pain, no question. Now could you please put . . ."

"And what side of the fence are you on as a therapist: analytical or emotional?"

"Can you put the gun away first?"

"No. Answer me."

She could feel herself trembling slightly while she spoke. "I like to think I'm both, but if I had to be on one side I'd say I'm more on the feeling side."

"Do we really get to choose which side we're on?" he said, taking one step closer. She looked at his gun, couldn't help it, then at hers a couple feet away from her on its side against the sofa pillow.

"I could talk about this a lot better if you'd put the guns away."

"We've talked about that already. That's not an option for you."

"OK, would you like to talk some more with me about this?" she said, feeling it was crucial to keep a dialogue going.

"I'm all ears," he said tonelessly. "No, literally, I'm sometimes entirely made up of ears. I paid a doctor to sculpt some of my ears so they'd fool you by looking like other body parts. But that's just an illusion. Look at my mouth more closely. If you do, you'll see that it's really an ear."

"Did your ex used to talk too much? Did you feel you weren't listened to?"

He laughed ironically.

"Your mother, too, perhaps?"

"When you're composed entirely of ears it's kind of hard to compete as a talker, wouldn't you say?"

She tried to force a smile to show she appreciated his humor. She had to still try to believe that empathy could have some impact on him, although he appeared to have none for her whatsoever.

"What's the matter? You're not saying anything. I thought therapists had mouths as well as ears."

"I know that being disappointed by someone you love is the worst pain in the world," she finally said.

"You're a fool if you only become disappointed *after* they leave you."

"What do you mean?" She couldn't tell if he'd said something insightful or not. She kept looking at the gun that was still pointed at her, although its angle was less direct now.

"Disappointment begins way before a person leaves you. Even ear people know that. The question is: is there enough there to counteract the disappointment? That's what love really is, it's just tolerated disappointment. You're lying if you define it any other way."

"I don't know," she said, thinking of the man who'd recently broken up with her (a professor of architecture at her university). "Maybe you're right."

"Seems like I'm right about people more than you are. Of course, I don't have a license, so what good does it do me?"

"Insight is always valuable, what else do we have?"

"I have insight into what's wrong with a lot of things, but what good does it do if you can't ever fix any of them?"

"You can use your insight on yourself, can't you?" She was leaning forward, as she often did with her clients when she was excited about making a point.

"Sit back," he said sternly. "Don't get too close to my gun. I already gave you your own, didn't I?"

. . .

It got darker outside. It was a cold night in early spring and there were lots of clouds out. She could see through the Venetian blinds that were still open until he finally noticed and closed them. What was she thinking by going back to his place in the suburbs? They could have gone to an after-hours bar in University City. She could have stayed in the city with him until she knew him better. Why hadn't she? Her rule of thumb was to go to a man's place only if she was prepared to sleep with him. She didn't think she was thinking that with Phil (although lately she'd been feeling so lonely), so why had she broken her own rule? It was because his behavior was so impeccable on the first two dates—considerate, generous, animated but not aggressive. Also, he seemed to be doing well at his business, which she couldn't quite remember but had something to do with computers. So there were no warnings, at least none that she caught until they were already at his place.

It had gotten hot in his condominium but she was hesitant to mention it. Maybe she'd just take off the pink cardigan sweater she was wearing—the one she had picked because it looked so good with her black skirt.

"What are you doing?" he said. He was a little further away, but his gun was still pointed at her.

"I'm just feeling a little warm. Is that OK?"

He didn't say anything. She felt it was all right to take it off (she was wearing a white blouse underneath) because so far, thank God, he'd shown no sexual interest in her. Meanwhile, he lit two candles on the glass table in front of them. (It was ironic, she thought, about the candles. On her Match.com profile, which was how they met, she'd listed candlelight as one of her turn-ons.) She placed the sweater carefully beside the gun.

"Hey, what are you doing?" he said again.

"What? I just put my sweater down."

"I thought you might be reaching for your gun, which is OK, of course, I completely encourage that."

"I don't believe in guns. I wish you'd throw them away."

"Why's that?"

"Because they're dangerous—they can kill people and I don't want to be part of that."

"But you are part of that now, aren't you? From an objective point of view, I'd say you should keep your gun. You can never tell when you might need it, when it might be all you can reach for in this world."

"What do you want from me? I don't understand," she said, starting to cry again.

"I'll answer that question when I feel like it, Herr Doktor, or maybe you'll just figure it out in time . . . speaking of which, time passes slowly in here, doesn't it. It's not at all like a therapist's hour."

She stopped crying and tried to laugh at his joke.

"It's funny how things happen," he said, stroking his chin for a moment with his free hand. "For many years I was very unlike other people and then after my ex, I began to do online dating, which is how I met you, and I became more like other people then, but now, I'm not acting like other people at all, am I? I've come back full circle to my original oddness."

She snuck a look at her watch and was shocked to see it wasn't even 1 a.m. He'd said he was keeping her here all night—did he mean that literally? Although he often spoke in riddles or metaphors, he was also at times literal to a childish degree. In that case, her night might have just begun, and who knew what it would eventually include? So far, he hadn't been violent since he pushed her down on the sofa, but she could still remember the pressure of his hands on her neck. He hadn't made any sexual demands yet either, but who knew when that might happen or what the meaning of his long looks at her was? One time she knew she'd caught him staring at her legs.

. . .

It was stupefying, how slowly time passed. Sometimes he talked in manic little fits and starts about his ex, whose name was Melanie, a name he never said again, as if saying her name would make her even more intolerably alive. Other times, there was unadorned silence, which made her listen for the little noises that every home makes, yet his didn't, as if it were as silent as a vault in a museum.

118

Always she tried to keep eye contact with him and always he kept his gun pointed at her, until she thought she might lose her mind.

Then she needed to urinate but was afraid to ask him—afraid he would go with her to the bathroom and who knew what would happen then? Maybe she should take her gun with her, but that might provoke him somehow. Probably it was better to somehow hold it in and if worse came to worse, do it in her underpants. But what if some of it trickled onto his sofa? Who knew how he'd react to that? In his cosmology his sofa might be sacred and that might be all it would take to make him shoot her.

"You seem restless," he said, without a trace of irony.

"I'm OK."

"Are you worrying about what's going to happen to you?"

"Yes . . . to a degree."

"Are you afraid I'm going to attack you in some way?"

"No, I don't think you'd do that."

"How do you know what I'm going to do? Why do you say that?"

"I don't think you really want to hurt me."

"What am I going to do then? Tell me what I'm going to do."

"I think you want me to stay so you won't be alone . . . with your feelings. I think maybe you'd like me to help you. Maybe that's why you answered my ad and wanted to ask me out in the first place?"

"Because you're a therapist?"

She smiled and shrugged.

"What else do I want from you? . . . assuming that you're right about any of this."

"Maybe you want to see if you can trust me or any person, after what happened to you."

"Trust you to do what?"

"Stay here with you tonight. Listen to you, if you feel like talking."

He turned his face away, staring into space.

"Do you think I should trust you?" he finally said.

"Yes."

"Because you're a therapist?"

"That's only part of it. I haven't given you any reason not to trust me, have I?"

"Women are trained to lie. To act and flatter and deceive and lie. It's what we call their personality."

"I don't believe that," she said, although there was some truth in what he said, she thought. But that was only because women had always been oppressed, didn't he know that? Didn't he understand about social conditioning and sexism?

"You're the exception to the rule, I suppose," he said.

"I don't believe there is a rule."

"But as a 'good' woman, and certainly as a psychotherapist, you would never break a trust, would you? You would always keep your promise and never manipulate me, right?"

"Yes. You can definitely trust me. I'll stay here with you tonight."

"Along with your gun."

"I told you I don't want it."

He smiled and nodded ironically.

"I prayed for something else about you tonight," he said.

"What was that?"

"I prayed I wouldn't hurt you."

"That prayer has been answered."

"You think so?"

"Yes, I do," she said, trying not to let her voice shake. Have you done it before, she wanted to ask, rape or worse? He'd seemed so affable and solicitous (albeit slightly nervous) on both dates—he hadn't even tried to kiss her good night. But she saw now that he was just waiting for the chance to terrorize her, that that alone made him feel alive.

"A man is always alone," he said calmly but definitively, as if commenting on the weather. "In the end, he's deserted by everyone, his parents, his women, and of course by God, the original deserter, and he's left only with regret, his infinite regret and his anguish."

"I haven't left you. I'll listen to anything you want to tell me. Maybe if you tell me the story about your ex you'll feel better."

"There are no stories—at least that's the way it is for ear people like me. For us, stories go in one ear and out the other. Anyway, I'm going to make a leap of faith and trust you, simply because I have to use the bathroom. But I'm leaving the door open a little so I can hear you very easily and I'll only be fifteen or twenty feet away with my gun in hand and all my ears wide open, and then I'll be back in less than a half minute."

She nodded to reassure him as she watched him cross the room, go into the bathroom, and close the door but not completely shut it. The moment she heard him urinate she took her shoes off, grabbed her pocketbook and gun and bolted for the door, leaving it open so perhaps he wouldn't hear her from the bathroom. She ran down his steps, worrying that she'd fall, then past two or three houses until she went into a neighbor's backyard. That way if he chased her she could scream and someone might hear her.

It was extremely dark out—a cloudy sky covered a hint of a

moon. She nearly bumped into an enormous tree, then put her hand on the tree trunk to steady herself. She was not one who ran regularly, or even exercised, and was out of breath—panting heavily—which made a strange kind of music in the night as she put her shoes on.

She had a horrible thought then, but it disappeared as soon as she reached in her pocketbook and found her cell phone. Why hadn't she taken her car on this date? Why? Finally she felt herself get her breath back, then realized how cold she was and that she'd left her sweater—her favorite one—back at his place. She opened her phone to get a little light and call 911, when she realized she didn't know what street she was on and wasn't even sure of the town—was it Ballwin, Wildwood? Perhaps at 911 they could tell where she was, she wasn't sure. But what could she tell the police? There'd been no rape—no sex at all—and as far as violence was concerned, just the time he threw her down on the sofa and pressed his hands on her neck. But there'd be no sign of that either. Nor would there be any sign of the threat he constantly posed to her with his gun—which he would have hidden by now or perhaps even had a license for and wouldn't need to hide. She opened her pocketbook and felt the gun he gave her, cold and heavy like a snake. What would she say about it? She didn't know. (She wished she'd taken her sweater instead.) She only knew that she'd throw the gun away as soon as she got home.

He'd been clever, diabolically clever, she saw that now, in his self-restraint—turning her night of torture into a long mock therapy session of a kind, more than anything else.

"Bastard," she muttered, and started running again to get further away from him. But after a couple of blocks she began thinking differently. He was, after all, ill. She couldn't lose or compromise her humanity because of him. She thought instead

she'd eventually try to show some mercy toward him, only tes-
tifying against him if he would be sent to some mental health
facility where he could get help, instead of jail. That would be a
good thing for her, might even help her self-esteem, since she'd
been feeling so blue lately. She would look at him as a person
grappling with some of the painful riddles of the world and try
to respect that, but meanwhile keep running till she found some
light and could read a street address to call a taxi from because
every town had a yellow cab, didn't it?

• • •

It took fifteen seconds, twenty at most before he realized he was
alone. How could he not hear her leave? It must have been the
fan that went on when he turned on the light. Then, when he
realized what happened he was stunned, as if he'd turned into
a giant frozen ear, which gave her five or more seconds to get
away before he raced to the door, gun in hand, and looked out
but couldn't see her. Then he bowed his head and turned back.
Fifteen or twenty seconds—that's all it took to become a ghost,
at least in this room, he thought. He stared at the empty sofa,
just as he did a month ago when Melanie had been sitting there,
and noticed Courtney had taken the gun with her. It was like a
little cavity was now on the sofa. He walked to the hall closet,
unloaded the blanks from his gun, replaced them with the same
bullets he'd put in her gun, turned around and walked back to
his original spot. This time he noticed her sweater, even saw
that it was pink before he started seeing it as flesh colored and
then finally saw Courtney herself in it as if she grew out of the
sweater.

"How could you?" he said. "What's your point? Aren't you
supposed to help people, not run away from them?"

He kept staring at the sweater, asking it questions intermittently, until some time later he saw that it was really Melanie leaning against the sofa, and not the therapist at all. He said "Melanie" or whispered it as he moved toward the sofa to embrace her. Yet when he reached it, she'd disappeared. He blinked rapidly several times, then gasped. It was a hollow, futile sound, like a muffled wind in a shed. He felt his face, then realized he could see it as if he were looking in a mirror. He gasped again, louder this time. His face was completely covered by ears squirming and multiplying like little fish. Immediately he put the gun to it and shot into the school of earfish before falling forward onto the sweater, the red of his blood merging with the sweater's pink, as if the two colors were always destined to coalesce.

Mission Beach

It begins in the ocean with wave following wave, breaking over his head and sometimes over yours. You're on vacation again with your twelve-year-old son, Andy, on crowded Mission Beach in San Diego and he's jumping up and down in the water, laughing and squealing. You love the waves too, especially bodysurfing with them. It's a passion the two of you share (although his version of bodysurfing isn't really bodysurfing at all, something you never point out to him, of course). Andy's in the black wetsuit that you bought for him in the sporting goods store in Philadelphia, and seems oblivious to the chilly seventy-degree air. When he temporarily disappears under a wave and then emerges from it he looks like a slender little seal. In contrast, you are wearing the thickest, and one of the ugliest, T-shirts you own. The sky is a tug-of-war between sun and clouds. It gives relief one moment and removes it the next. You're shivering and want to leave but you stay because Andy wants to. Although he's improved his swimming a lot in the last year, he only weighs seventy-seven pounds, and with the strong undertow and waves you have to be extra vigilant and keep your eye on him virtually every second. Yet he also badly wants you to bodysurf (as do you), so you develop a technique of turning around the moment your ride ends and zeroing in on him. Meanwhile, the faraway lifeguard sits in an elevated tower of sorts like a cliff atop a distant island.

There are other temptations besides the waves. There are a lot of women in bikinis or less in the water, many of whom appear to be playing a game to see whether they're revealing more of their breasts or more of their bottoms. There's a very well built brunette near you in whom the competition appears to be a tie. Since Anna left, you haven't made love with a woman, though God knows you've wanted to, which makes the mermaids of San Diego that much more difficult to disregard. Just before a new, mountainous wave arrives you do look at the brunette before telling Andy that you're taking the wave. He's rapt with attention. He makes fun of you a lot in playful ways (calls you "Face Wad," for example), something you tolerate and actually encourage because you don't want him to be in unapproachable awe of you, as you sometimes were of your father. But in the ocean you're his water hero. You taught him how to swim and float and dive and never take foolish chances.

You hit the wave well and have a long, exquisite ride. Just before it comes, you think the brunette is looking at you and moreover realize she's the same person you've been exchanging looks with in your hotel. When your ride ends you look for her for a second but don't see her. Then you look for Andy and for a few horrifying moments don't see him either. Finally his little head pops up, and after relief suffuses you, you feel a stinging self-contempt that never completely leaves you no matter how you intermittently try to rationalize it for the rest of the day, though you do manage to keep it hidden from your highly perceptive son.

Because of your lapse in judgment in the water you stay in much longer than you intended, which greatly pleases Andy.

Eventually you stop bodysurfing, and when Andy complains about that you take his hand and invent a wave-jumping game that the two of you play. You also look away from that woman or any other that swims or boogie boards across your path.

Meanwhile your shivering is increasing. To help deal with that, you think of your father, already over sixty at the time, going out in a pouring rain and with a pretty bad cold to buy you some boxing gloves when you were seven or eight because that was your passion at the moment, and when you're that young a moment is all of time. Then you think of your mother, who sat with you while you cried because you were sick and were going to miss the first game of the seventh grade basketball season when you were set to be a starting guard. At one point, as if it were contagious, she even started crying herself. You continue to shiver but these memories help.

Finally Andy's bluish lips start to quiver and he admits that he's getting cold, so the two of you start to leave the water. Because of the fierce undertow, he lets you hold his hand until you reach the sand. Your soaked through T-shirt seems to be making you even colder. It's like wearing a bar of ice and you take it off as soon as you find your beach bag. Meanwhile, Andy claims the hotel towel—the only one you brought because it's the only clean one left.

The sky is completely gray now and the wind is strong. Still, Andy doesn't want to leave the beach. For a moment you look out at the ocean, where the woman from the hotel, who you now remember sat at the table next to you at the hotel restaurant, is just now coming in from the water. Then you focus on the expression in Andy's eyes. You think of those awful moments when you couldn't see him in the water, and when he asks you again you tell him you'll go back in the water after you both eat lunch.

...

Mission Beach is full of questionable-looking characters; the street that leads away from it to your hotel, even more so. You'd wanted to return today to the much more upscale and safe beach at LaJolla Shores, where even the waves are more genteel, but Andy lobbied vigorously for the more thrilling Mission Beach you could get to much faster, and you ultimately gave in. Walking back to your hotel you're almost as vigilant as you were in the ocean. The street is filled with liquor stores, head shops, and tattoo parlors. A number of shirtless, heavily tattooed men with grimly vacant expressions are smoking a variety of things while staring at the passersby. You have a fair amount of cash and your credit card in the pockets of the shorts you're carrying in one hand while holding Andy's hand with your other. You have to navigate three blocks like this. It's a lot like navigating the waves. You realize that you can't eliminate everything potentially threatening in Andy's environment, but you can't help trying. You also can't seem to stop the fantasies you have of someone hurting him physically and then your rage-filled, violent response. You do this when you walk him back from school, too, where you often imagine some bully suddenly picking on him before you come to the rescue.

You know that you are a bit overprotective of Andy but there are reasons. He's short at this point (his bone age lagging two years behind his chronological age). The doctors have assured you that eventually he'll be average height, but you can't explain all that to kids. You've been at schools your whole life and know what kids are like. Andy's also very shy with children his age. He's been raised his whole life by two single parents, as you and his mother divorced before he was born. Despite some definite bumps in the road, his mother and you now have a good collegial relationship concerning Andy, though you realize it hasn't always been easy for him transitioning between his two homes in Philadelphia.

But to be objective about it, Andy also has a lot of things going for him. He has a strikingly beautiful, blue-eyed face, like one of the children Renoir loved to paint. He's also extremely smart, funny, very imaginative, and has an exceptional memory. It's too bad, you often think, that computers to a large degree have made memory an increasingly insignificant talent, but he will still probably be able to put it to some good use down the line. He's also loved a lot by both his parents and, because you inherited some money, is already quite well traveled and will be well provided for after you die.

You are thinking all this while waiting for your food at the Japanese restaurant, the first restaurant you saw away from the menace of Mission Street. It's funny how Andy often requests going to different restaurants when he ends up eating the same thing at all of them—French fries or plain white rice. This lunch today is obviously a white-rice occasion. Shortly after it arrives, he begins telling "the story," his favorite thing to talk about by far. Over the years the characters and their situations have changed, but it is all part of the ongoing story—an imagined world that you two act out together.

It started when he was four or five with animal stories centered around Baby Claw, a winsome if somewhat rebellious crustacean; Tail, a rodent, who was Baby Claw's best friend; Tiny Duck, a frustrated comedian; Tony Frog, the ultimate rock star; and the psychologically challenged Happy Hedgehog. That story lasted over three years. Not only did he act out the story for at least two hours a day with you, but he also drew their daily adventures, made meticulous maps of the town and the school they attended, and tape recorded with you fourteen school "Talent Shows," mostly improvised songs with some stand-up comedy by Happy Hedgehog and Tiny Duck. During those years there was almost no conversation between you about what was happening in your "real lives." (Because you had your share of career and love-life disappointments, this was sometimes a relief for you.) When you'd ask him how school was he'd say "horrible," grow visibly distressed, and change the subject. Yet he was doing well in school academically and making some progress socially. Still, when his classmates talked to him he'd invariably look down at the ground and either say nothing or mumble an almost inaudible "hi."

Sometimes, during breaks from the school where you taught, you'd visit him during recess to give him some Skittles (the only candy he'd eat). A few times you couldn't resist spying on him for a moment. The other kids were talking, laughing, and running with one another, but Andy was running in straight lines back and forth by himself, as if in an isolated training for some kind of grand, imaginary track meet.

Then the animal story suddenly stopped. He refused to say why. But you were encouraged that the next story was about people—albeit highly eccentric ones who lived in the mythical town of Kingsville, Ohio. One of the most memorable of these characters was Burl Lee, the town's chief thug, who ran Kingsville's nefarious amusement park, Burlyworld. Burl Lee was a sadist and Burlyworld was in his image. The only soft spots in his heart, besides Burlyworld, were for his pet lion, Burlio, and his pet bird, Vulcan Vulture, who could speak a form of English. These two Burl Lee loved unconditionally, and, accordingly, trained them to be superlative thugs in their own right.

Burl Lee & Co. lasted about two years. Again there was no explanation, but the next and current metamorphosis of the story soon followed. This time it involved an entire continent named Crasia and the characters from two rivalrous bordering countries —his homeland, Rodnesia, and yours, Rudolpha. Once more there were incredibly detailed maps not only of Rodnesia and Rudolpha but also of all the countries in the continent, from the melancholic Blubberland, whose people perpetually mourned their lost empire, to Rationalia, where reason reigned supreme.

That day while you were eating lunch in the Japanese restaurant, you two were discussing the new wave of dog shows that were getting so popular on Rodnesian TV. Often Andy's desire to tell the story or to make maps or lists about it is so strong that he ends up staying indoors regardless of your appeals about how beautiful it is outside. At such times he always had a ready argument to stay inside.

"Why do you want to go out all the time? The outdoors is so twentieth century," he'll say. Since your body aches from the waves, you're hoping that this will be one of those times and that the two of you can go back to your warm room and lie down while you talk about the new dog shows *Fi Do Do* (pronounced "dough, dough"), *the Wonder Dog* or *Dog Thugs* and where your greatest challenge will be simply to stay awake. So after telling the story in the restaurant you ask if he'd like to go back to the hotel and continue it there and he looks stricken. "Why do you want to leave the beach?"

"I'm tired."

"How can you be tired so quickly?"

"I'm a lot older than you."

"But, Face Wad, you're the most outdoors person I know, and you promised."

"OK, don't get upset. We'll go back to the beach in a few minutes."

"Is that a promise, you wad?"

"Yes," you say quickly, and that settles that.

· · ·

Back at the beach you force yourself to bodysurf for as long as you can—about twenty minutes—until you begin shivering again. Then you tell Andy that you just can't do it anymore, because you're too cold.

"You should have gotten a wetsuit like me, you have to admit that."

"You're right. I definitely should have. I just couldn't believe it wouldn't be warmer than this in San Diego in July."

You then promise to stay in the water and watch him jump waves for as long as he wants.

"Aren't you going to jump them with me, Face Wad?" he says, his blue eyes opening up wide behind his goggles.

"Maybe in a little while," you say, and then assume your standing position, and block out the skimpily clad, frolicking women while fixing your eyes exclusively on Andy, who looks back at you for your invariable thumbs up after each wave he jumps or dives under.

But you can't control what happens in your mind as easily. You start thinking of Anna, who you used to take to the beach a lot, too. Odd that with a twelve-year-old son who, despite his prodigious intellect, is in certain ways socially much younger, you should have hooked up with a middle-aged German woman who didn't speak English very well and who was emotionally around twelve. Though, if you are really honest with yourself, you know you've done this before, that it's your own needs that make you pursue childlike people, especially women, perhaps because you are childish yourself.

You remember the first time Andy and Anna met in your apartment in Philadelphia. He was deeply into making train set-ups then, with his Thomas the Tank Engine toys. You advised Anna to compliment his setup and, in general, to let him take the lead. Instead she started giving him unasked-for advice and then building a setup of her own, as if in direct competition with him. It set the tone for a lot of what followed for the next five years.

You remember trying to explain to her about Andy's shyness with other kids and the skeptical way she received the news, as if you were somehow trying to pull the wool over her eyes. She always felt you were too sympathetic and protective of him and not enough toward her. Meanwhile, when you talked to Andy about her, he said, "the only thing I don't like about Anna is you pay too much attention to her instead of me."

You were caught in the middle but, of course, you put him first, which in turn ate away at Anna. She had her own daughter who she lived with and was very close to (though her daughter was a fully grown woman), but she still couldn't accept your feelings toward Andy and, like a couple of your other former girl-friends, resented the amount of money you gave to his mother and your friendly, albeit strictly platonic, relations with her.

For years Anna would bring up marriage with you, but she was spending less and less time with Andy. She always seemed to have a reason not to see him, though you made it clear you couldn't live with someone until they got along well enough with Andy to make him feel relaxed with them. You didn't expect her to love him, you said, but you did expect her to be his friend.

In spite of this, your feelings toward Anna somehow continued to grow. Since you thought that if Anna really wanted to get married she'd start spending more time with Andy (and you didn't really care about marriage, yourself), you decided to accept the status quo and just let things ride. But Anna had other ideas and one day, while you were in bed, in her typically blunt style she told you that she'd met another man she was attracted to. A month later she told you that she'd slept with him. "You did not make me yours," she said by way of explanation. "Instead, you do everything for your son." And that ended that.

"Andy, Andy," you yell into the wind as yet one more dinosaur-sized wave crashes over him, seems to swallow him, and then a few vertiginous seconds later releases him to the world again.

"Are you OK?"

"Face Wad, did you see me bodysurf that wave?"

You give him a thumbs up. You are shivering even more now but a half hour passes before you leave the beach.

● ● ●

"Pretty big waves today, huh?"

It's the woman from the hotel, the same one you were looking at in the water when you should have been watching Andy. You are both getting food at the dinner buffet table. She's wearing fairly tight black pants and a low-cut turquoise blouse.

"Bigger than I knew what to do with," you say, turning to face her.

"I don't know about that. You looked like you really knew how to ride them. You seemed pretty fearless to me."

You can't think of anything to say (it somehow doesn't seem appropriate to say thank you) and you actually feel yourself blushing. She compliments you again and you feel like you're regressing to adolescence at a rapid rate. You check her face and see that she's smiling in what appears to be a genuine way, and also notice that despite her fairly extensive makeup she's a little older than you thought, which only makes her more obtainable and so more appealing to you.

"Was that your son I saw you with today?"

"Yes," you say, looking at your empty table. "He's using the bathroom right now," you add by way of explanation for his absence, which you realize is apt to be ten or even twenty minutes because whenever he has to go he takes a long time, "to make sure I get every little part of it out."

"He's really adorable," she says.

"He keeps me laughing."

"I'll bet."

You two continue moving along in the line, chatting a little more easily now as you tell her a bit about Andy. You each take salad, chicken, and fruit. She passes on the rolls and dessert; you don't. You can't help thinking of Anna, who was always trying to get you to eat healthy foods and to work out, neither of which you ever really did.

You wonder if you should make some kind of parting remark and then remember that she's sitting at the table next to you. You both arrive at your tables at about the same time, look up at each other and smile again. The two of you are only five feet apart.

"How long are you here for?" she says. She has a slender but attractive face framed by dark brown hair that falls to her shoulders. You realize she's being pretty aggressive but she's doing it in what you consider an understated way.

"Just three more days. What about yourself?"

"I'm kind of playing it by ear."

"Oh?"

"Yah, my plans sort of got disrupted."

"How so?"

"The gal I was traveling with met a guy here and sayonara— she just took off with him."

"Really?"

"Yah, really. She said she was sorry but she knew that it was the real thing this time and had to do it. Love at first sight and all that. So I had to try to understand, you know? The thing is, she's already been divorced three times."

The two of you share a short laugh while you check the hallway where the bathroom is, but there's no sign of Andy.

"That's really a shame, for you."

"Hey," she said, finishing her glass of wine. "All I can do is wish her the best, right? And just try to be philosophical about it."

Immediately, a waitress springs up next to her to ask if she wants another drink. You're not surprised when she says she does. If you weren't with Andy this would be the ideal time to buy her and yourself a drink. Instead you look, again, at the hallway near the bathroom, waiting to see him, and turn down the waitress because you don't like to drink in front of Andy. It was something else Anna disapproved of because she loved getting high.

"My name's Janice," she says, extending her hand.

"I'm Eric," you say, shaking it slowly. You get the feeling that both of you are instinctively checking out the other's hands for wedding rings. At any rate, you don't see any on her.

"Is Andy your only child?"

"He's my one and only."

"Is his mother here with you two?"

"No, his mother and I are divorced."

"Oh, I'm sorry."

"Don't be. It was long ago, before he was even born," you say, wondering why you've revealed this hard-for-others-to-understand detail.

"So you've been a single parent his whole life?"

"Yes, I guess I have, and his mother has too. We split our time with him so he's always very well taken care of and very well loved."

"I'm sure," she says.

A strange look passes over her, more regretful than anything else.

"You're an unusual man," she finally says. "I mean that in a good way."

Her compliment gets to you (you always were a compliment junkie) and you feel yourself start to get excited. This would definitely be the moment when (if you were alone) you'd not only finish your own drink but also touch her some place that wasn't too tasteless, considering you're in public, but that definitely showed intent. Maybe briefly on her shoulder and possibly for a few seconds on her knee. Instead, you say thank you. You want to ask her if she has any children but think it too invasive a question. Besides, something tells you that she has an even sadder story to tell than the one she already has.

"I had a chance to have a child once," she eventually says, "but my ex was a selfish man. He wanted all the attention for himself, so . . ."

"It never happened?"

"No, it never did."

You two become quiet, she looks to be uncomfortably close to tears, and you think that once again, though you sensed it coming, you didn't act quickly enough to prevent a woman you desire from becoming unhappy and instead uttered an ill-considered remark. It happened less often with Anna, who in some ways was pretty thick-skinned and laughed as a first reaction to almost everything, but it happened quite a bit with her predecessors. Typically you now can think of nothing to say to make things better. Instead, Janice changes the subject by asking if you've used the hotel pool yet.

"I saw it, yes. I love all the trees and flowers around it, but I didn't swim in it yet."

"Oh, you have to! Of course it doesn't have any waves," she says. "It might not be exciting enough for you."

"Oh, no, Andy and I both love pools."

"It's heated, too."

"Sounds really nice."

"It stays open till eleven at night, and it's lit up with these colored lights that really make it look kind of magical."

"So obviously you've been swimming there?"

"Yeah, it's a nice way to end the day—gets rid of my stress, for a while."

"I'll bet," you say, turning toward her, and remembering how she looked in her bathing suit again.

"I was planning to go there tonight around nine thirty or ten. If you want to come, I'll be there."

"Very tempting. If I can, I will," you say, gesturing toward the bathroom as if to explain that because of Andy you're on a very short leash.

. . .

It's odd to pursue someone as you were pursuing Janice, in your mind at least, and then to retreat from them, as you did to a degree in the restaurant. You suppose that's a typical experience of single parents of a certain age (and you are definitely of a "certain age"), but then it's odd to discover that you are typical in as many ways as you are. A number of years ago, after your divorce, when you were on four different online dating clubs and dating one woman after another and getting high and feeling sorry for yourself every night, you finally began to realize that there are people who can only love their family in a relatively selfless way, and then still others who can only love their children. These people "fall in love" all the time and go through all kinds of contortions to get it and keep it and all kinds of self-flagellation when it ends, but it's usually more lust and self-delusion than love. What was even more surprising was to learn that you are probably one of them. Though you don't want to be, your past record certainly seems to indicate it.

You are telling the story with Andy and he's running across the room or jumping up and down every minute or so from excitement. As fate would have it, the picture window in your room overlooks the pool, and after nine you get up from bed and sit in the chair, where you can see the swimmers because the pool lights are on, as Janice promised, and there is still light from the sun-streaked sky. Also, as promised, she appears in the same skimpy white suit she wore on Mission Beach. You even get to see her dive neatly into the pool, as if she's demonstrating how dexterous her body is. Once again you have trouble not watching her and begin to wonder if it would really be so wrong to leave Andy in the room for a half hour or so after you read to him and he falls asleep.

The problem is he's highly ritualistic about sleep, and the earliest you could expect him to sleep would be an hour from now. Could you be an hour late for a woman like Janice and still expect her to be there? Maybe Andy could let you go for ten minutes, during which you would explain to her that you'd be free later, when you'd either meet her in the pool or else buy her a drink at one of the hotel bars? Still another possibility would be to bring Andy with you, ignore the look of disappointment on Janice's face, a look you'd seen before from Anna and some of her predecessors, and tell her at the first opportunity that you'll be back alone later after he goes to sleep. Of course that would involve talking Andy into going to the pool when he'd be ecstatically in the middle of one of his stories.

"Which do you think will be a more successful spin-off from *Fi Do Do, the Wonder Dog*?" Andy suddenly asks with great earnestness, "*Aqua-Dog* or *London Mutt*?"

"*Aqua-Dog* is aimed more at the six-to-eleven demographic," you say, "*London Mutt* at a slightly older audience, with the hope that it can jump from the Saturday morning super-dog shows to an early prime time show."

"But which will be more successful within its demographic, Face Wad?"

You smile. He wants his answers precise. "*London Mutt*," you answer.

"Yuh, I think so too," he says, before beginning another series of runs up and down the room.

You know now that there will be many more questions before he'll let the story go for the night and ask you to read to him. Still, in spite of all this, you can't help looking out the window at the pool every thirty seconds or so, where Janice is still swimming.

"What are you looking at, Dad?" Andy says during one of your viewings, which you try to sneak in whenever he starts jumping or running.

"The pool. It's still open and people are swimming in it. It looks really cool. Wanna see?"

"Sure," he says, standing in front of you now to get a better view. "Cool" is his one-word verdict.

"Hey, you wanna go swimming there now?" you say enthusiastically. "It might be really fun."

"No, I'm OK."

"Oh, OK," you say, trying not to show your disappointment and finally getting up from your window seat and sitting on his bed. You know your fate is sealed now. You know that he will ask you one question after another until his reading time, and for a while he does. But then something you didn't foresee happens. A half-hour before his normal reading time, he "hits the wall," as it were, and lies down on his bed. Then, within five minutes of reading to him, he's deeply asleep. Miraculously it's only 10:30. You tiptoe to the window and see that Janice is still in the pool, sitting in the Jacuzzi. You could leave Andy a note (for months he's been begging you to leave him alone more anyway, and you'd be within his view the whole time) and join Janice in the hot tub. You look at her once more and get the feeling that she's perfectly built for you and you start to get erect again. Your bathing suit is on top of a chair about five feet from you and you can't help imagining swimming with her. First, laughing with her in the water, then buying her a drink at the poolside bar and sipping it after you dry off at one of the candlelit tables by the pool. She tells you more of her story then. You listen to it effortlessly and give her sympathy and support. It was terrible how her friend abandoned her, you say, terrible also how her husband treated her. You feel her loneliness as you feel your own. She sees that, and doesn't want to be apart from you now. She takes your forty-five-year-old high school English teacher's face in her hands and kisses it for a long time.

Back in the present, you get up and take your bathing suit from the chair. It's a little damp but it will do. Andy will never know any of this, and you can leave notes all over the room for him if he wakes up. You can even lay his bathing suit and goggles out for him so he could join you. It's now merely a question of finding a shirt that you won't be too cold in and start to shiver while you have your drink with her but also one that won't make you too warm, either. You certainly don't want to start perspiring at a table while you sit at the pool bar waiting to make your move.

Suddenly you remember a night when you were six or seven years old and you couldn't get to sleep because you were either too hot with the blankets pulled up to the base of your neck, or too cold when you took them off. You must have told your father about your trouble sleeping after he said goodnight to you, or else he came in to check on you on his own. "Let's try this," he said, as he first lowered the blankets and then raised them up to your shoulders, stopping to rest for a few seconds at each place where the blankets landed before resuming the process, back and forth, back and forth, like the rhythm of a gentle ocean, until you finally fell asleep.

You look at Andy and wonder again how the jumble of adult and childish things inside him will turn out. You hope he will find friends, you hope for many things. Yet his face looks so composed it almost hypnotizes you. Then you drop your bathing suit on the floor (where you know it will stay) and move closer to his bed to see him more clearly.

What a private and paradoxical thing sleep is. So private that everyone does it in their own way, yet while you do it alone you also want company or at least some potential company nearby because you don't know what your dreams will bring or whether you'll be cold or too hot later on, you think with a smile. You feel a great clearing in your head then while you watch him.

It's strange how you learn things so slowly, but you love it anyway.

The Dolphin

It was really just a smile he saw for a split second, but it made Parker stop walking and go back to her. She was a young black woman in a cheap but pretty purple dress. When he stood in front of her, she smiled again.

It didn't take much after that. In less than a minute they were walking together—money hadn't even been discussed. Then he looked at her more closely and noticed that one of her front teeth was chipped, but she was still beautiful, he thought. They walked another block together, talking easily while he kept looking for a cab because he wanted to get out of this part of Boston called the Combat Zone as soon as possible. He couldn't wait to get her to his apartment, couldn't remember ever feeling this eager in a situation like this, and his eagerness made him talk more than usual.

Then halfway down the next block he suddenly knew. He turned to look at her once more and said, "Wait a minute, are you really a man?"

Her smile had a tinge of sadness now.

"Only in one place," she said.

"I didn't know. I'm sorry. I'm not interested then."

He walked away quickly, afraid to look back. He was stunned. How could he not tell a man from a woman after all these years? Why did it take him so long to find out this time? To think that because of his illusion he'd come so close to taking her home and yet, at the last minute it was as if he'd known all along.

• • •

Parker was sitting in a bar where they sometimes had music and strippers. It was called The Dolphin, but he couldn't see even one image of a dolphin anywhere. He realized he was still upset and ordered a whiskey sour, which he drank moments after it arrived, then ordered another. At such times he often fell into a state of repetitious thinking—what he called a "thought loop"—which was very difficult to stop. He hoped he could head this one off by drinking but it was too late, he was already in another loop.

He was thinking how often he'd been deceived in his life (sometimes, of course, contributing to it himself). Even as a child he was confused, far longer than he should have been, about the sun and moon. He used to think the moon was just how the sun looked at night—that they were two words for the same thing. For a long time he'd also never really believed that the earth was orbiting in space. He knew it "intellectually" but never felt it to be true. The world tricks us, Parker thought. Maybe that's why people trick each other so much.

A moment later a thirtyish man (around his age) sat next to him. He was wearing a black leather jacket, dark sunglasses, and was slightly unshaven, which accentuated his overall menacing appearance. Dear God, Parker said to himself, don't let there be a conversation.

At first there was a minute or so of silence, then the man asked him if the dancer had performed yet.

"No," Parker said. "I've only been here ten or fifteen minutes but no dancer yet."

He'd answered clearly while avoiding eye contact—the best of both worlds under the circumstances, he thought, though if the man really wanted to talk the window of opportunity was still there.

"Came here to see a dancer," the man said. "Her name's Trudy. You know her?"

"No, I don't know any of the dancers. I've never been here before, or maybe just once years ago."

Parker looked at the man, noticed he seemed somewhat reassured, at any rate down a notch of intensity. The next thing he knew, the man was extending his hand.

"My name's Nick," he said, as they shook. It was a strong, overbearing handshake, clearly meant to send a message about his masculinity and strength, Parker thought.

"Why you happen to come here?" Nick said.

"No reason. I was just walking, not feeling too great, saw this place and thought I'd try to feel better."

"You probably could have made a better choice, but, hell, you're here now so drink up."

"I have been."

"Not enough, I can tell. Bartender, bring this man another on me."

Parker's heart sank—there would be a price to pay for this, he knew. He would have to talk more and on a night when he was feeling both desperate and ineffectual, without a clue of what to do about it.

"So you sure you don't know Trudy?"

"Yah, I'm sure."

"Maybe you know her under a different name. She uses as

many names as the number of men she's screwed." Parker laughed a little. "Seriously, I think everyone who did her knows her by a different name so I'll tell you what she looks like. Long brown hair that she wears in a lot of different styles so she can look like different people if she wants to. She thinks that makes her more interesting. But when she combs it out right after a shower it goes down to her belly button. She has brown eyes too, the same color as her hair. Nice eyes, really nice, but she thinks they should be bigger. You know how all these bitches in the movies make their tits and lips bigger? Trudy has a device that makes her eyes look bigger. Didn't even know about it or suspect a thing till she told me herself. Still don't understand how they work. You ever know one who did that to her eyes?"

"No, I don't think so."

"Yah, she's one of a kind. Anyway, you'll see her body soon enough. It's good, real good—not a pound of fat on her. She works out and diets all the time, like an athlete or something. She's very ambitious that way. She wants to be the top stripper in Boston, then go to New York and get discovered. Thinks she can wind up in the movies that way. 'Look at Anna Nicole,' she'll say. 'Look at Tracy Lords.' I'd say, 'They were whores, Trudy,' and she'll say, 'Oh,' kind of tonelessly, as if to say 'and the problem with that is?' or else she'll just say nothing.

"Yah, she wants to be the city's number one stripper, works on her dance moves all the time. Has to have the best moves too. She'll fuck anyone—man, woman, in between—just cause they could show her something new to do with her pole, you know? Or help her get a better gig somewhere. Yah, she's real ambitious in a twisted way, I'll give her that. So you probably wonder why she's dancing in a dump like this?"

Parker shrugged. He'd been wondering why Nick was wearing his sunglasses in a dark place like The Dolphin, but it was slowly beginning to make sense, for some reason, the more he talked.

"She'd say it's 'cause her tits need to be bigger and she needs another operation. I say it's 'cause she takes too many drugs and the wrong ones too, like crack. These club owners aren't dummies. They don't want to hire a crack addict who's apt to cross the line with the customers or with an undercover cop. I tried to tell her all of this. I tried, but guess who won the argument, and guess who ended up paying for her new tits, which are plenty big enough now, believe me."

Parker made what he hoped was an empathetic sound. He wanted to say, "That's harsh" or "That's cold man" but was afraid it might sound too flip and only aggravate Nick. He could tell Nick had a short fuse.

"Hell of a world, ain't it, where you can't tell if the eyes you're looking at are real or not."

"I know what you mean," Parker said, thinking about the black hooker he'd picked up, then how he'd spent the first twenty years of his life trying to figure out if he loved his parents or hated them and later whether he loved or hated his girlfriends, until ultimately he'd walked away from them all and, in effect, from his parents, too, without ever really talking about it or reaching a conclusion.

"And if the lips aren't real, what chance is there that you can believe the words that come out of them?"

"Not much. None," Parker said. He was feeling nervous now because Nick was nearly yelling. Even the seen-it-all bartender was giving them a funny look.

"Let's move to a table, OK?" Nick said in a voice that was more of a command than a question.

"Sure. I can do that."

"I'm not getting a good vibe here. This bartender doesn't like me. He's sick of me. I think he wants Trudy for himself. We'll be better off at one of the tables. We can see the dancers better too."

"Sure," Parker said uncertainly. He was surprised that Nick chose a table directly behind a pole that half obscured the small, slightly elevated, spotlit stage.

"Don't worry, some whore will be waiting on us in a second. Drinks are on me."

"No, I'll get the next one."

Nick ignored him, wanting to make an additional point.

"That's what they do to the old strippers—demote them to waitresses—long as their legs still work."

Parker finished his drink and thought he could see Nick's eyes darting around behind his sunglasses but wasn't sure.

"Yah, lucky for her I paid for her chest before I found out what she was doing behind my back. Kind of like collecting her life insurance all at once, she must have thought."

Parker didn't know what to say and merely nodded, not sure if Nick detected it in the half dark of the bar.

A waitress in a black miniskirt and fishnet stockings approached the table, and Nick ordered two more whiskey sours.

"I told you they'd pounce on us right away, just like alley cats."

"Yah it was just like you said."

Nick took a long swallow then placed his drink down on the small circular table with emphasis. "Don't you think there ought to be a line, something you can see clearly, in your head at least, that once it's crossed you have to do something about it?"

"Sure."

"I mean *really* do something. Like if the line is clear and the other person knows where that line is, can see it as clear as you, then you have to take a stand, right?"

"Sure."

"You wouldn't be a man otherwise, would you? If you knew the line got crossed and you just pretended you didn't see it 'cause you were hallucinating or something or had some kind of instant amnesia and you forgot the line, forgot the thing you'd based your life on, then you'd just be another pussy yourself, am I right?"

"Right," Parker said softly, and then nodded as if to further indicate his support.

"You can't go through life in blindness—that's not what we're here for. Look, look at my eyes," Nick said, taking off his sunglasses.

Parker looked but it was hard to see them right, maybe because he was staring too hard at them.

"I don't know you very well but I'm gonna tell you anyway 'cause I'm not a pussy, OK? You know what I got in my jacket?"

Parker shook his head.

"The answer to her crossing the line, that's what. I'm talking about moody Trudy, OK? You want to feel it so you know I'm not lying?"

"What, what are you saying?"

"I'm *saying* I'm gonna blow that bitch's brains out the second she steps on stage—which is any minute now, right? Any second."

"Are you serious?"

"God damn it, man!" Nick said, pounding his fist on the table. "Don't I sound like I'm serious? Why don't you feel my fucking gun? I already said you could."

"I believe you. I believe you," Parker said, holding his hands up as if Nick were pointing the gun at him. "I just think you ought to consider all the consequences if . . ."

"I've been 'considering' all my life. You have any idea how much time I put into her? How many times I fed her, and took her to the hospital, and cleaned up her puke? You know how much money I spent on that bitch? Have you 'considered' that?"

"I just meant to think about what will happen to you, if you, you know, do what you said."

"You think I give a fuck about myself anymore? You think I'm a regular flesh-and-blood person like you are? Or maybe you think I'm a vampire 'cause I'm dressed in black. I don't want her whore's blood if that's what you think. I don't need anyone's blood to live. I'm wearing black 'cause I figure I'm already dead. Yah man, you confused me with the living but I'm actually dead. Death is really different. Only thing is, they don't tell you that you get lonely when you die. Yah, that's why I'm gonna take her with me. It'll solve my loneliness problem real fast."

Parker pulled his chair back, rehearsing various exit lines in his mind.

"You getting ready to run out on me?" Nick said. "I'm getting a little too freaky for you, maybe? Hey, it's too late to leave now man. You gotta stay and watch the show. I'm serious, man. Hey, your face has gone all white. Maybe you're dead too and you're really a ghost."

"I do feel like I'm dead . . . sometimes," Parker blurted, surprised that he'd said something so personal at a moment like this. "Dead in the sense of feeling hopeless."

"Dead in the sense of feeling hopeless," Nick said. "I like that. If you look at it that way then half of Boston is dead," Nick said, laughing. Parker thought Nick's laughter might be a good sign and forced out a laugh himself.

"My problem is I'm dead in the sense of dead," Nick said, "but I like your line 'dead in the sense of feeling hopeless.' You must have gone to college to come up with that. You a college man?"

"Yah. That's where you start to meet the hopeless *and* the dead," Parker said, hoping his little joke would keep things lighter.

"No, I didn't go to college. Couldn't afford to—spent all my money on a certain whore I told you about. Just think, any minute you'll get to see her. Maybe I won't do her right away so you can get to see her naked first? You like that idea? That's a dumb ass, non-college idea. Yah, I wanted to go to school but I was too busy becoming dead in the sense of being dead."

"Well, I may not be as dead as you but I'm still dead, so we could still do something together."

"Do something?" Nick said, fingering his gun, which was now partially visible. "What're you talking about?"

"Like go outside and take a little walk. You know, dead men walking."

"You hear a thing I've been saying? Maybe you're deaf instead of dead?"

"I just think it would be a good idea to go outside now and talk there."

"A good idea?" Nick said, mockingly. "Tell me, college man, what makes something a good idea? Is something 'good' if it's what you want? Does that make it good?"

"Sometimes ideas can be good for both people," he said, looking directly at Nick's eyes for the first time. It must have upset him in some way, Parker thought, because Nick put his sunglasses back on, though they'd only been off for a few seconds.

"How would it be good for me? Can you tell me that? Why at this exact moment would it be a good idea for me to go outside? You trying to keep me from doing her? I thought we agreed that she crossed the line?"

"We did. I just don't think you should do, you know, what you planned. You're too young to throw away everything like that."

"You never killed anyone, did you?"

"No," Parker said softly.

"So how could you know whether it's a good idea or not?"

"It's because you're both too young for this to happen."

"Hey, brother, if sins counted as years, that lying bitch would be a thousand years old."

"You never lied to her?"

"I hand-washed her blood-stained underpants. I wiped the vomit off her clothes. I kept her from OD'ing three or four times. Yah, I lied to her but it didn't matter. So, it's not the same thing."

"What do you mean?"

"My lies didn't hurt her. She didn't care who I screwed as long as she had money or crack. I could do it right in front of her and she wouldn't care."

"Come on," Parker said, "I'm gonna go outside now, why don't you come with me, huh?"

. . .

From the moment they were outside Nick began to look different. He seemed thinner and somewhat shorter, too. His face looked almost gaunt, his seemingly flawless leather jacket was faded in spots and had two tears in it, and his body, which leaned forward aggressively in the bar, was now slightly stooped.

I have no reason to be scared of him any more, Parker

thought. Then he remembered the gun, but it still didn't seem to be enough of a reason. He didn't know if it was even a real gun with real bullets.

Nick looked at him as he took his sunglasses off. "You want to shine the light of truth on me? Is that why you brought me out here?"

"I brought you out here 'cause I don't want you to do what you'd planned."

"Don't think I'm evil enough to do it?" Nick said sarcastically.

"No, I don't think you're evil. I think you're good. Here," he said, withdrawing a pill from the breast pocket of his shirt and handing it to Nick. "Take this. It will calm you down, help you sleep."

Nick swallowed the pill without looking at it. Meanwhile Parker was thinking that before *he* could sleep he'd have to speak to the bartender or someone else about Nick and also speak to Trudy too, and that he'd have to do it as soon as Nick left.

"So you think I'm good, huh?"

"Yes, I do," Parker said. He could hear the music from The Dolphin, the music that Trudy would dance to, and he knew that Nick heard it too.

"So if you're right, I owe you a lot."

Parker shrugged. "Just forget about it. You don't owe me anything." He turned so he was facing the street and could hail a taxi.

"Maybe they teach you how to be kind in college. Is that it? Course, if you're wrong and you've misjudged me I could come back the next night and blow her away, couldn't I, and you'd never know if you were right about me or not."

Parker looked away from him at the streets. They were filled with bars, sex shops, sex movie theaters, and a few shabby hotels.

The hookers were already out in force. It was a warm spring night, ideal for business. He wished suddenly he were in the Boston Commons or any kind of park. When he was young he loved it when his father took him on the swan boats in the Commons. Of course he loved his parents, he thought, they were not who they said they were, but who was?

"You're being really quiet, bro. Maybe you're wishing you were with one of those ladies of the evening instead of old Nick?"

"I was with a hooker earlier tonight just before I met you."

"Oh yah? She any good?"

"She was nice and very good-looking but a couple of minutes after I met her I realized she was a man, so that ended that."

"A man, huh? You should have blown him away on the spot. I would have done it in a second. Hey, maybe I should take out one of these whores you're looking at now? You know, it could be like doing one of them instead of Trudy. They could be the substitute or the symbol, right? Is that how they put it in college? It would be symbolic. So's that what you're wanting me to do?"

"I was just wishing we were in the Commons, or any park. Some place with grass and trees and no sign of the Combat Zone."

Nick turned away for a moment, then readjusted his sunglasses before he spoke.

"One time Trudy took a lot of sleeping pills, so many I had to help her hurl and walk the floor with her till my legs ached—till she could puke out enough pills. She slept a long time, while I watched her, almost the whole next day. When she woke up she wanted to die all over again. So I took her for a walk at this playground in Brookline, of all places, where I was living. We were making pretty good bucks then, which is how we could live there. I was pretty much her agent then and was getting her good gigs, and I had a couple of other businesses going too. Anyway, we were walking slowly 'cause she was still weak. I'd driven her to this park, although it was nearby, just because she was so weak. But I really thought she should get some fresh air. Yah, at that time I could even afford to lease a car. It was nice out too, about this same time of year maybe two or three springs ago. Even though it was warm, and still in the afternoon, she was bundled up in a trench coat and scarf and dark sunglasses. She looked like a mummy, man. Except for her nose, there was barely an inch of her face exposed. She was also being as quiet as a mummy. This is a woman who could talk as fast as a roller coaster and nonstop too. Just twenty-four hours before she was ranting about all the club owners who'd cheated her and all the dancers who'd stabbed her in the back and then the men who'd beaten her and then back to her childhood (which really was a horror show), about her alcoholic mother and her father, who abused her, but now she was suddenly completely silent. At first I thought it was the drugs she took, her system still reacting to them, her brain still exhausted, but then I realized that she was shy, without her pills or crack or a drink, she was shy, you know? I missed the old Trudy with her wild energy but I also wanted to show her that it was OK with me if she didn't want to talk, if she suddenly felt shy, you know what I mean?"

"Yah, I think I do," Parker said, who was just then hailing a cab. "Maybe you should always remember the way you felt then, no matter what."

"What do you mean?"

"Just to remember who she really is and what you really felt."

Nick turned his head away, for a moment, once more fiddling with his glasses.

"But I did remember, didn't I? My problem is I remember too

much, not too little. What I'd really like to do is kill my memories, man."

"Yah, I hear you. That's something I'd like to kill too—some of them anyway."

"Yah, it would be nice if we could get to choose."

"Here," Parker said, handing Nick a twenty. "You got the drinks. I've got a taxi for you, see it coming up? Just go home and lie down, OK?" Parker said, starting to give Nick a goodbye hug. Nick backed away immediately.

"Don't be doing that bro. You want the driver to think we're a couple of queers?"

Parker laughed and they shook hands.

"Seriously, thanks man. I really appreciate what you did," Nick said.

Parker opened the door and Nick climbed in with his stooped posture and Parker said, "Take it easy," and Nick said, "Yah, take it easy bro." Parker waited till the cab turned the corner, wondering if Nick would look back and couldn't remember the last time someone had thanked him like that. Still, he would talk to the first person in authority he saw at the club about Nick and make sure Trudy found out, too, but he wouldn't look at her while she danced. That wouldn't be right. Even if she approached him afterward he wouldn't do anything with her. It wouldn't be fair to Nick.

It had gotten dark now, but the Combat Zone suddenly seemed softly lit, like a strange kind of Christmas tree. Just before Parker opened the door to The Dolphin, he looked up and saw a half moon in the purplish sky.

At least I know it's a moon now, he thought.

The Justice Society

It began when the air in his apartment changed. It grew heavier, becoming almost filmy, and had a faint but definite acrid smell. When he started to feel hotter and woke up in the night perspiring, he looked in his bathroom mirror. His hazel eyes looked watery and his hair seemed grayer—his whole face looked as if the pale gray of his hair had spread over, it covering his normal color. Was it the flu? His doctor ruled that out. Of course, his doctor knew about his somewhat hypochondriacal nature, also knew he'd been a painter once. He all but said it was due to his easily stimulated imagination or to staying inside too much where he now worked with his computer. But whatever it was persisted—his apartment still felt occupied—and tonight when he felt something move (not on the floor exactly, but over it) and the air smell worse than ever, he finally became convinced that hell had invaded it and he ran out of his place to find a bar.

Would his drink never come? He'd taken a wrong turn and missed his usual place and was now at one that seemed to be run by the lazy and will-less. When it finally came he took two deep swallows and closed his eyes, trying to imagine he was at a beach or else in a grove filled with pine needles that led to a clear lake.

"Hey, bud," someone said, forcing him to open his eyes. Sure enough, a surprisingly well-dressed man was sitting next to him, and Mason immediately tried to recall whether the man had actually said, "Hey, bud" or "Hey, bro." "Bro" would be more ridiculous, although a warmer attempt at communication, whereas "bud" was more appropriate for the occasion but also, somehow, more anachronistic.

He moved his head a few degrees toward the man and nodded, then returned to his drink. Already he'd made up his mind to leave probably after his first drink and definitely after his second. He wouldn't go home, of course, not after what happened. Instead, he'd go to the bar he meant to go to in the first place, where people left you alone.

What was this now? The man had turned toward him again and cleared his throat. He was either going to gargle in front of him or else assault him with more words.

"Hell of a wind out there tonight," the man said. His blue eyes darted around uneasily as if a wind was moving them.

"You got that right," he said, to say something, but worried that now he'd encouraged the man too much. Then a silence followed while the man drank. Perhaps it would be over now. Once more he altered the angle of his head to his left, but the man began talking again anyway.

"You come to this place much?"

"No, this is my first time. Took a wrong turn somewhere and wound up here. What about you?"

"I've come here once or twice, when other places were too crowded."

"Yuh, there's not much here, is there?"

"It's pretty minimal," the man said.

"Sort of how I picture hell," he said, then regretted his words, shivered even as he thought of his apartment, but the man laughed.

"I hear you," he said.

Hear what? Know what? Just what do you think you could know about me, he thought, thinking of his home with a shudder, and how could you know it, Mason wanted to say, but of course had to keep what had happened to his home a secret.

"There've been many nights when I felt the same way, when it was like being in a part of hell. Fortunately, that doesn't happen anymore, but it used to."

He turned toward the man again.

"So, what's the secret? Why doesn't it happen anymore?"

The man sighed a little. It was barely audible but Mason heard it almost as if the man felt *he* was the one being put upon.

"You really want to know? OK, first I had to absolutely come clean with myself." The man paused as if to let the impact of his fatuous revelation sink in. He cleared his throat portentously again before resuming. "Then I heard about an organization that could help people like me, people being eaten up by their sense of injustice, and fortunately I gave them a chance and went to their meetings, and that's really what turned me around."

Mason nodded rapidly a few times. It was odd not to know if he were interested or not. "What's the name of this organization, or is that a secret I shouldn't be asking about?"

"It's called the Global Justice Society, GJS for short, and I'm actually heading over there for a meeting in a few minutes."

It had been a long time since he'd thought about that word—"justice." It sounded both vengeful and satisfying and so ultimately unreal.

"What does the society do exactly? Sounds like it has a pretty ambitious agenda."

"It does have an ambitious agenda and now that you mention it, it has a pretty intimidating title, I suppose. But the society really works with just one person at a time."

"How so?"

"It interviews you to determine the source of injustice in your life and, more importantly, what you can do about it, and then it puts you into the right division that will help you get what you deserve."

"That sounds more like heaven than any society I know of."

The man laughed. "You have a good sense of humor, and I don't blame you for being skeptical," he finally said. "When I first heard about Global Justice I was, too. I mean 'Global Justice,' that sounded way too grandiose for me. But the thing about the society is, it doesn't try to change the world, just help one person at a time in the way they need to be helped. That's really it."

The man talked a little more about it and then invited him to go to their meeting, adding that they served hors d'oeuvres and free drinks.

. . .

Incredible that he was walking with the strange man from the bar in South Philly en route to a justice society meeting, no less. Just before they began their walk the man told him his name was Archie—which didn't help. He hadn't known an Archie since the character in the comic strip he used to read as a kid, and yet he went with him anyway. They walked down Broad Street past the University of the Arts. While they walked Archie talked more about the society (although he hadn't asked him to), as if he were a tour guide obliged to point things out. Mason didn't listen to much of it. It was a January night and quite cold out and they were walking further away from his apartment with each step.

Maybe I dread going back there even more than I realize, he thought. Maybe I can never return. He did manage to hear Archie say that tonight there was an awards ceremony at the society, held by the literature division but open to the general public. When he asked what kind of award, Archie said, "The National Book Awards—the Justice Society National Book Awards, that is. You look confused, but really you don't think that any of the other world's literary awards are fair, do you? That there's one scintilla of justice in their selection? They're as corrupt as can be, just like the Academy Awards or any other of their awards. It's all deals and politics. That's one of the things we correct at Global Justice."

He mumbled something, letting the wind eat most of his words while they kept walking. At the outskirts of Center City Archie took a left on Walnut Street, explaining that the meeting was being held at a private residence. Soon, in fact, Archie was ringing the buzzer in what appeared to be some kind of code until the door opened and they went inside. About thirty people, quite dressed up for the occasion, were seated in the large living room of a three-story townhouse. He had to sign some obligatory papers asking for his name and address.

"It's a good thing we're fast walkers," Archie said, "looks like the ceremony's about to start any minute."

Mason nodded then watched Archie waving and shaking hands with a few people near him and saying, almost proudly, as he pointed to him, "I've brought a guest," after which he felt obliged to smile and shake hands himself.

...

He couldn't pay much attention to the ceremony because he kept visualizing his apartment and wondering if hell really had taken it over, and if so, how he could ever go back there to get his things.

From what he could tell it was an absurdly bloated ceremony, as most ceremonies were, filled with meaningless thank yous and transparently ridiculous attempts at self-modesty. He didn't even hear the names of the first few awards. Instead, he was remembering taking a bath as a child and wondering how many years his father, then in his late fifties, had left to live. His father had been dead for a long time now, and lately he'd been wondering during the baths he still took how many more years he had left himself.

Finally, a hush fell upon the room and he heard the master of ceremonies say, "And the winner of the National Book Award for Fiction is Geoffrey Crumple."

Instantly the room burst into applause, and a bearded man in horn-rimmed glasses and a suit that was too small for him rose to accept the award. He'd never heard of Geoffrey Crumple. He was not the best-read man in Philadelphia but he still read, fairly avidly in fact, until a few years ago, and yet he'd never heard of him. Even more absurd was why this modest, local ceremony was called the National Book Awards. Clearly it was not the real National Book Awards, so why steal its title?

As the Justice Society cleared the chairs for the reception, which he thought he would attend just long enough to get some free snacks and drinks, he asked Archie about this.

"Geoffrey Crumple is a brilliant novelist and deserves the National Book Award far more than the person who supposedly won it."

"Where can I buy his books?"

"Geoffrey's too uncompromising a writer to be published

commercially. You can read him for free on the Internet. Just go to his website, www.crumple.com."

"Are the other winners published exclusively on the Internet too?"

"Yes, all of them are. Just pick up a program before you leave and you'll find their websites."

He nodded and mumbled, "Will do."

"So, Mason, what do you think? Pretty impressive ceremony, wasn't it? You'll have to come next week. We'll be awarding the Nobel Peace Prize—it's maybe our biggest event of the year."

This time he nodded silently then turned toward the table at the far end of the room where a bar was set up and excused himself. Now he only needed to stick to his program—have his drink or two with some of the hors d'oeuvres on the table and make his exit, stopping to say a brief thank you to Archie, but absolutely not giving him his address or any other contact information. The last people he wanted to hear from, especially given his state of mind recently, were Justice Society members. Though they seemed like benign enough lunatics, they were lunatics nonetheless, with their National Book Award and Nobel Peace Prize. At least, in their total devotion to healing their own egos, they didn't appear to be harming anyone else's, although it could be argued that their delusional ceremonies were increasingly separating them from reality. Not that he couldn't understand their kind of separation firsthand—he had merely to think of his apartment—but that was really all the more reason to keep these people at bay who were now joking and laughing and drinking as if a real event of consequences had just taken place that they were all privileged to attend.

He put down his mostly emptied drink, thinking he would

get some food from the hors d'oeuvres table. These lunatics were well financed, he thought, as he put some olives onto the chef salad he was constructing. Just then he noticed a quite pretty redhead in a purple dress a few feet away from him in the fruit section. He looked at her and thought he hadn't felt attraction, much less love, for anyone for a long time. There was injustice for you. I wonder if the Justice Society ever deals with people like me, he thought, as he unconsciously moved into her section.

"You look like you're building quite the culinary masterpiece," the redhead said, indicating his salad, which was embarrassingly large. He immediately decided he wouldn't add any fruit to it.

"Once again, my eyes want what I can't or shouldn't have," he said.

"I know the feeling."

Apparently everyone knows everyone else's feeling, he thought, and yet people were so alone.

"I haven't seen you here before. Are you in the arts division?"

"I'm here for the first time, actually, so I guess I'm not in any division at all."

"Well, welcome to the Justice Society. My name's Julia."

He told her his name and they shook hands. He hadn't held a woman's hand in some time and wasn't eager to let it go.

"So what do you think of the society so far?"

He finally released her hand and looked slightly past her, where Archie was talking to someone but also apparently looking at him.

"It's all very new to me. I'm not sure I completely understand."

"I know I was confused at first," she said. "I was like 'who are these people and what do they think they're doing?' Is that how you feel?"

"Something like that."

"Hey, you want to talk about it for a little while? There's a table over there where we could sit, unless you're with somebody?"

"No, no, I'd love to talk with you about it," he said, as he followed behind her. Now, don't sound angry, he said to himself as they were sitting down, and control your sarcasm. Then he resumed looking at her face, which was even more pleasing in this setting.

"So how can I unconfuse you?" she said, just before taking a bite of her fruit salad. He couldn't seem to concentrate on an answer and ended by releasing perhaps the most ineffectual gesture in his repertoire, a shrug. This, in turn, provoked a brief look of frustration in her. Then he could see her concentrate again as she rephrased the question.

"I guess I don't understand what you don't understand," she said, smiling pleasantly at him again. "Go on, fire away. Like I say, I've been there, I won't take offense."

"For one thing, I don't understand why the society calls them the National Book Awards. There already are National Book Awards."

She looked directly at him with a serious look on her face. "These are *our* National Book Awards."

"So you think the winners all deserve them?"

"Of course. We support each other totally in the society, and you can't support someone if you don't believe in them, can you?"

"Even though all the winners self-publish on the Internet?"

"We've learned not to confuse 'success' with merit. Certainly not success in the other world."

"What do you mean by 'other world'?"

"The unjust world. The world outside the Justice Society."

"So you don't find it strange that the best books of the last year were all written by members of your society?"

"Kind of a miracle, isn't it?" she said, smiling broadly, without a trace of irony.

He looked at her closely and thought he wouldn't hate being in his apartment so much if she were in it with him, even though she was a little crazy. Besides, he thought, what she believed was no more delusional than what a lot of religious people believed, what with their talking snakes and virgin births and resurrected people. But now he had to keep the conversation going. She had that concerned look on her face again.

"So, are you up for any awards, too?"

It must have been a good question because she smiled again. "I'm in a different division, nothing to do with writing or any awards."

"So, what determines which division you're in?"

"That's what the interview process is for before you become a member."

"You can't choose yourself?"

"Of course you help choose, but you need guidance, too, to make such an important decision. The guidance counselors at GJS are super. They help you find where you really need justice in your life the most and that's the division you enter."

He continued to look at her closely.

"Can I ask what division you're in?"

"Sure, we have no secrets from each other. I'm in the marriage division. I've had a very unjust love life, so far. I married a couple of cheaters from the other world so now I'm waiting for my reward."

"How is that going to happen, exactly?"

"The society will find me a husband. I have faith in them and so I can be at peace with myself until they do."

"I wouldn't think you'd need any help with something like that."

"Why thank you, Mason."

She was smiling so fully and spontaneously he decided to say more. "You're so pretty I'd think every man you'd meet would want to marry you."

"My goodness," she said, putting her hand over her heart, "such a wonderful compliment. At the society we call them 'sweet justices.' So thank you for the sweet justice, Mason."

He smiled and felt himself blush, though he tried to stop it. He decided he should ask some "serious questions" then, so she'd think he really wanted to be a member (otherwise how would he ever see her again), and asked her how and when the society started. She told him it started just three years ago and that next month there'd be a big anniversary celebration. When he asked her who started the society, she quickly said in a reverential tone, again completely bereft of irony, "Our founder, Mr. Justice."

"Is it just a coincidence that his name is 'Justice'?" Mason said.

"We don't know or care what his name was in the other world. Most of the members think of their former names as being slave names. I mean, if there's no justice in your life you really are a slave, don't you think? Julia Seeker is my new name, my real one. Except for the IRS I never use my other one."

He cleared his throat, reminding himself again not to sound sarcastic (which he thought had cost him a number of women in the past). "So is Mr. Justice here tonight?"

"Wouldn't it be wonderful if he were? But no, he's in L.A. de-

veloping our West Coast branch. I did get to meet him once—
he's an amazing man."

"You mean you're not just a local group?" he blurted.

"Oh no, our mission is much bigger than that. We started
right here in Philadelphia but then branches followed pretty
quickly in New York and Boston and in D.C., too. And now
we're in the West Coast, in Santa Cruz and L.A., and soon we'll
be in London and Madrid."

"They certainly could use some justice in D.C.," he said with
a smile.

"Gotcha. But really everyone needs justice everywhere, so I'm
not surprised by our success."

He asked her then how they grew so fast and whether they
advertised a lot. Again she had an immediate answer, as if she
knew his question in advance, saying they weren't about being a
big, slick organization that advertises a lot. "We don't really have
to advertise," she said, "'cause you know what our best form of
advertising is?"

He made a gesture to show he was completely mystified.

"Word of mouth. When you have a great idea that the world
really needs, people tell each other. It's like Founder Justice says,
'the need creates the demand.' How did *you* find out about us,
for example?"

He looked across the room at Archie, who still appeared to be
staring at him. "I just started talking with a guy named Archie in
a bar and he told me about it."

"Oh, yes," she said with an uneasy expression. "Well, the important thing is you're here now."

"So anyone can just come in to your meetings?"

"Of course, we're not secretive. We have no hidden agendas or
secret rituals and we ask for very little money beyond our dues,

too. Any full-fledged member can swear you in. If you'd like, I could make you a member tonight."

He raised his eyebrows, as if to slow up his response. "That sounds quite possible."

"I'll have to ask you a couple of fairly personal questions," she said, pushing back a few strands of auburn hair from her eyes.

"That's OK, but do you think we could go someplace a little quieter, maybe get a cup of coffee and do it there?"

The uneasy look flitted across her face again. "I'd love to, but unfortunately there's a senior members' meeting after the ceremony and sometimes they go on for a pretty long time."

"Of course," he said, noticing that Archie had just gotten out of his seat and was walking toward him in a straight line.

"Could you possibly give me a number where I could call you to set up my membership meeting with you?"

She looked a little hesitant. "Sure, if you like, but anyone here could do it."

"But I'd feel more comfortable doing it with you since you've taken the time to answer all my questions."

"Gee, thanks again for the sweet justice." She began writing in earnest on a scrap of paper. "My cell is probably the better number to try me on," she said.

Just as she handed it to him, Mason looked up and saw Archie standing two feet in front of him.

"Hello, Julia," he said.

"Hi, Archie."

"Hello, stranger," Archie said to him, in a voice that made him immediately uncomfortable.

"Do you think I could borrow Mason for a minute?" Archie said, not looking at Julia as he asked the question while also continuing to stare at him in a way that suggested he'd just learned some incredible secret about him. But he couldn't know anything about what was happening at his home or, more importantly, what Mason now believed caused it. He hadn't let anything slip about it when they talked in the bar, had he? At any rate, Mason soon found himself standing up from the table.

"Of course you can. I think Mason's gonna be another terrific new member," she said. Then she looked at him and quickly mouthed the words "call me" before they both said good night.

With Mason in tow, Archie walked about ten feet from the table and spoke to him in a low, commanding voice. "You seem to be completely charmed by Julia."

"She's very nice."

"I hope you think you've talked enough with her and might be ready to leave with me now."

"Leave, where?" he said, trembling a little, in spite of himself.

Archie looked closely at him—his eyes had stopped darting. "Am I misunderstanding something here?"

"Could be," he said.

"I thought you were with me tonight?"

"I walked over here with you. I don't remember discussing any other plans."

"Then obviously I've misread the situation."

"I didn't know there was anything to read into."

"I guess I owe you an apology, as well," he said, but his voice was still icy.

"There's nothing to be sorry for. It's just one of those things."

Archie continued to look hard at him. "I don't agree. I think someone should be sorry because it's a very awkward, unjust situation for me and it didn't happen by chance. I, myself, have never misread a situation like this before, have you?"

"Maybe once or twice."

"Once or twice," Archie said softly, but with unmistakable sarcasm, "and tonight makes thrice. So what's the deal—do you go both ways?"

For a moment he was stunned. It had been a long time since anyone asked him anything about his sex life.

"These days I'm not going *any* ways but when I did, it was only with women."

"I see. I see very clearly, but I still think you misled me. At any rate, I'd strongly advise you not to mislead Julia or to try to take advantage of her in any way. In case you don't know, she's a candidate for a justice society marriage, and I'm on the committee that will help select her spouse. You'll find that I'm on a lot of committees, that I'm quite a prominent member of the Philadelphia branch, so stay clear of her, and for that matter I wish you'd stay clear of the society in general."

Mason nodded and turned away from him. He's crazy, he thought. They all are. He had to admit he wasn't unsympathetic to the idea of a replacement world that finally made its inhabitants feel proud of themselves, just not one in which someone like Archie played an important part. He thought of Julia then and felt his heart beat. She had gone to the other side of the room, but they exchanged a look before he left the building.

· · ·

As soon as he shut the door of his apartment he knew for sure what had happened. Again he didn't see anything specific move on the floor but felt it all around him instead, like the invasion of a new atmosphere. Even in the dark he knew it was different by its persistent, now strongly acrid smell. Then he turned on the living room light and saw it in the filmy look of the air, as if he were living underwater.

It was all much stronger now—there was no longer any doubt. He didn't know it would be like this, never thought that hell could be portable and travel to him. It was like the instant recognition of a cruel foreign language—learning its modus operandi. So this is how it looks and smells and feels after it invades you. It waits like a thief till you leave your home and then surrounds you as soon as you open the door. Doesn't say a word to you but lets you know it's there. That was how the real hell worked, he thought, not with devils or fires, although he was perspiring and there was a strange feeling of heat in his place—heat, that is, with a kind of cold filling in the middle.

Will I scream? Should I scream? He thought. Would it even be right to ask for someone to help him, which might mean placing that person in hell, too? His life was not that precious to him. He was just a man alone, worrying about money like everyone else, worrying about death like he used to worry about his father's death as a child in the bathtub. A man who had sinned many times, he knew, but not spectacular sins, he didn't think, no more than most people, and yet he had been selected, targeted, and finally captured and all without knowing why, of course, which was the way of the world.

He wondered if he could trust his thoughts. Did hell already control them? Would he be able to tell?

He reached in his pocket and withdrew the piece of paper where Julia had written her phone number. Stared at it in the sickeningly watery light of the room as if he expected her number would have been burned off the page or just gone missing. He said it aloud three or four times until he memorized it, then walked toward his phone. It didn't feel safe to even walk, as if the air was full of a kind of invisible quicksand.

Then he stopped. He couldn't call her while this was going

on, not at night anyway, when hell made its fullest appearance. A minute later he left his apartment heading for a hotel in Center City, where he spent a largely sleepless night.

. . .

He called her the next morning from his hotel room. It was her office, where she was a secretary.

He apologized for disturbing her at work, mumbled something about wanting to become a member, and invited her either to lunch or an after-work drink. She chose the latter option, which was perhaps encouraging, he supposed. She worked in Center City, so he chose the most expensive place he knew that was near her office, figuring if things worked out he could take her to Le Bec Fin or some other chichi restaurant for dinner.

He got off the phone with a smile on his face that quickly disappeared once he realized (how could he not always realize?) that he couldn't do his job because his computer was back in his apartment. He wondered how many of the clothes he'd packed had that acrid smell. It was there in most of them, but he found one uninfected outfit that he quickly put on his bed to wear. He was so relieved by this discovery that he fell asleep on the bed with his clothes on.

When he got up there were still three or four hours to kill, so he went to a branch of the public library near Rittenhouse Park and read about hell on the Internet, looking for an account similar to his. He found a couple of ambiguously similar reports but nothing exactly like what had happened to him. Perhaps part of hell's "genius" was to never repeat itself in its dealings with people.

He left the library earlier than he needed. On the way out he noticed its bulletin board was plastered with notices about the Justice Society's National Book Award Winners. He felt his heart beat. They may be delusional but they were definitely hell-bent on replacing, piece by piece, the world that had excluded them, until they occupied it much the way hell occupied his home. He shook his head as if to expel the thought, then began walking through the park toward the restaurant to meet Julia.

...

She was wearing a white dress and he was in black. We look like pieces in a chess game, he thought, a game he was never good at. Yet he couldn't stop looking at her dress, which seemed to sparkle in the dark restaurant where they sat, and when he told her she looked beautiful he meant it.

"It has a symbolic significance," she said.

"What does?"

"My dress. The society officially annulled my other marriages for being grossly unjust, and now that they've expunged them I can wear white again."

"So you're able to date again, too?" he asked.

"Sure, as long as they're approved by my marriage committee. My whole marriage is in their hands."

"Is Archie on that committee?"

"Yes, actually, he is. How did you know?"

"He mentioned it to me."

"Oh. He must think highly of you. Usually you have to be a member to know something like that."

She was trying to compliment him but he felt his face fall. So Archie had told him the truth about that and also that he'd never let her go out with him. Of course Julia didn't think of this as a date anyway, merely a chance to "do a justice" as she called it, by signing up a new member.

He swallowed his drink quickly. "Am I allowed to buy you a drink?"

"I shouldn't really, but I guess one won't hurt my judgment. I'm going to have to ask you some pretty serious questions before I can pledge you, though."

He turned just in time to order drinks from the waitress, who seemed to understand his intent and brought them right away.

A few minutes later Julia began questioning him in earnest. "You're going to have to tell me about your injustice. I know it's very painful, but you have to tell us so we can place you in the right division and help you better."

He finished his drink and said, "I don't think of my life as being particularly unjust."

"Nobody likes to."

"My personal disasters have happened to a lot of people. I got older, I wound up alone, my career fell far short of what I wanted, and like everyone else I recently lost a lot of money, but I've got enough to get by."

"Their world is an unjust world. We're going to replace it . . . and sooner rather than later."

He looked at her, letting her words vibrate in the atmosphere. He was convinced she meant them. "There is one very unusual thing, I think, that has happened to me recently," he said, figuring he had lost her anyway. "Should I tell you?"

"Of course, that's what I'm here for, that's why the Justice Society exists."

"It's going to sound extremely weird and scary, too."

"Just tell me. You can be sure I've heard a lot of things."

"I don't doubt that. OK. But first can you tell me what hell means to you?"

"Hell, the concept?"

"Hell, the place."

"Hell is a 'place' the unjust created to punish their victims. It's just a concept the powerful use against the weak. That's what hell means to me."

"That's what it used to mean to me, too."

"What do you mean?"

"I mean I used to believe like you did that it was just a concept invented by people in power, that it wasn't real. But something changed."

"What was that?"

"This isn't easy to tell you."

"Go ahead. You can tell me anything. I have a just heart now," she said, staring into his eyes.

"OK. Recently I found out that hell *is* real and that it travels—it's portable."

Predictably, she looked confused.

"It came to my home and took it over. It's living there now, OK?" He looked hard at her, waiting for her to talk. "So now you're probably plotting how to get away from me as soon as possible."

"Not at all. I'm not like that. I won't leave . . . until the membership process is finished. You're safe with me, really, and with the society, too. You have a new home with them. Believe me, the justice society is strong enough to take on hell," she said, forcing a laugh, which he decided to do as well.

Then she turned as the waitress passed by and ordered another drink.

"So you want to tell me how this all began?" she said. He told her about the distinct sense of something moving over his floor, about the change in air, the smell, his night sweats. She listened to him closely, looking very serious, not trying to dismiss it all at any point. Why did it take him so long to meet a woman like this? Why did he only meet her now, when it was too late?

When he was done talking he was afraid to look at her. "I notice you aren't saying anything, now that I've finished my story. So, I'm sure you think I'm just crazy."

"Not at all. I was wondering if you're a religious person?"

"No, no way."

"Were you raised as one?"

"No, my father considered the question of God beyond the comprehension of man, which is the truth of course. So I guess he'd be labeled an agnostic."

"Forget the labels. The other world likes to label you to death. What about your mother?"

"She was a far more conventional person. She made me go to Sunday school for a while when I was a kid before she gave up. But she wasn't as big an influence on me as my father was, anyway."

"Still, she probably made you aware of sin and of hell, too."

The new drinks came and she swallowed hers quickly.

"So this must be a new one for you to listen to?" he said. "Kind of hard to know what to say, isn't it, hearing something like this."

She looked down at the table when she spoke, for the first time not making eye contact with him. "Actually, something like this happened to a friend of mine not too long ago. A woman who had suffered a lot . . ."

"What? Here in Philadelphia?"

"Yes."

"What happened? Could you help her?"

"I did help her. The society helped her."

"What about me? Can you help me?"

"You have to become a member first. You have to believe in it before it can help you."

"Lack of belief is one of my sins, but sure, OK."

"Here," she said, withdrawing some papers from her pocketbook and unfolding them while she spoke. "Sign these," she said, handing him a pen. "And then you'll also need to pay your membership dues for the first year, which is only two hundred dollars, though you'll probably end up wanting to donate a whole lot more than that—everyone does."

He signed the documents then wrote a check in the half dark of the restaurant. She had a big smile when he gave them to her.

"Congratulations, you've just left the other world."

"I've always wanted to, so now I finally have," he said, with a little laugh.

"But seriously, to help you, you need to tell the society about the injustice in your life. You need to tell me now."

"You don't think having hell take over my apartment is unjust enough?"

"Tell me what happened *before* that."

"You think my behavior caused it to happen?"

"Of course not. That's what the other world wants you to think. You've left that world now and you're taking your first steps in the new one, but you still need to face what happened to you before. For instance, in your work, did you do want you wanted to?"

"Does anyone?"

"Did you achieve what you deserved?"

"I was a painter once. I had some talent, I thought, but I didn't know the politics, didn't know how to succeed."

"The art division can help you there. What about in your love life?"

"I didn't know how to treat women."

"Nobody in the other world does."

"I ruined every chance I had."

"Your life isn't over there either. The marriage division will find you a partner, I know that firsthand."

He looked at her longingly.

"Do you have any children?" she said.

"No. I was the child I tried to take care of," he said, remembering himself as a seven-year-old then, alone in his bathtub.

"It isn't too late for children either. The Founder will soon have some exciting news about getting children into our lives, or into the lives of those people who want them."

"OK. All of that sounds great, but none of it's gonna happen as long as I'm literally living in hell, right?" he said, more angrily than he wanted. He felt the veins might even be sticking out near his forehead, veins his hair was no longer there to cover.

"You're not in hell anymore," she said, looking at him calmly.

"How can you know that? Is that what happened to the other woman you helped?"

She nodded. "She was given justice, and hell can't survive in a just environment."

"So can you really help me?"

"What would you like me to do?"

"No, it wouldn't be right. It could . . ."

"Do you want me to go to your apartment and face down your hell? Is that it? I'm not afraid to. Is that what you want?" she said.

. . .

It was almost preternaturally easy to get a taxi, as if the two of them were never really in the restaurant at all.

Mason sat with a kind of rigid attention, as if he were a soldier assigned to guard himself, while Julia kept assuring him about their trip to his apartment. But when they got out of the cab he started muttering, "I shouldn't be doing this. It's a sin, don't you see? It's a sin."

"The only sin was your enduring the injustice in your life and now you've finally done something about that."

"No, no, I've sinned against others, always putting myself first and now I'm doing it again."

"Hush, Mason," she said, putting her hand to her mouth as they approached the door to his building. "I've done this before even though I shouldn't be doing it now. I mean I'm breaking the rules a bit 'cause it's work outside my division, but I think they'll understand. Is this your building?"

"Yes, I'm on the ground floor." Then he told her to turn back even as she was turning the key in the lock. "I was often disappointed to find out the world was real," he said, "that things stayed in their place after we left them."

"Why? What does that mean?"

"Because that made my failures real, too."

"Don't talk that way. Is this your door?"

"Yes," he whispered.

"Don't worry. I have my cell phone with me if anything's wrong."

Your phone won't work here, he thought.

"Give me your key. I'll open it."

He handed the keys to her thinking he'd just given her the key to hell.

And then they entered his apartment as easily as if entering a smooth pool of water. Immediately he could feel the heat and smell the bitterness in the air, which seemed to have grown still stronger. She turned on the kitchen light and gasped, then tried to muffle it, hand to her mouth. They each took a step forward and stopped. The air was coiling like water stirred by wind, and though it was invisible, there was an unmistakable sense of movement around them.

"Oh my god," she whispered. She looked like she'd been electrocuted, eyes rolled back in their sockets for a second like Little Orphan Annie's. Then they both looked at the door behind them, which was shut.

"I'm sorry," he said, but she wasn't listening, had instead begun talking out loud more to herself than to him.

"This is worse than what I saw before, this is worse. I shouldn't have come here, I wasn't supposed to and now I've ruined myself at the society, now I'll never get married."

"Why? What?"

"I broke my pledge, don't you see? I'll have to confess it."

"What should I do?" he said. "What can I do?"

"Go to a hotel. Don't come back here, it's too late."

He decided not to tell her about the Holiday Inn where he was already staying.

Then she started dialing her cell phone. "Archie, is that you?" she said. "Can you come here right away? I'm in trouble. I have an injustice to confess. I'm so ashamed and scared. Please come here as soon as you can. I'm with member Mason."

A moment later she asked him for his exact address, so she could give it to Archie.

"He's coming. Archie's coming to save us. I wouldn't touch anything if I were you—it's probably all infected."

"No, I won't," he said.

"Archie said to inhale as little as possible and not to move until he knocks."

He nodded, wondering if he would throw up from the air and everything else that was making him sick. Then they waited without moving, like statues.

"When is he coming?" he finally asked, feeling like a child, and wondering if he'd just spoken in a child's voice.

"He's just a few minutes away. Be strong," she said, but he could hear her crying softly, like a muted violin, then wondered with a shudder if it was really hell that created that image in his mind.

...

The knocking came in triplicate, reverberating like drumbeats. The two of them came unfrozen and ran to the door, which opened quite easily despite his fears that it wouldn't.

In the hallway she fell into Archie's arms, sobbing. He held her while staring bullets at him.

"I've committed an injustice, please forgive me. I only meant to help him."

"We'll discuss it," Archie said tersely.

"Please don't tell the Founder, please."

"You know I'll have to."

"But he'll expel me, he'll . . ."

"We'll discuss it later," he said firmly, separating himself from her so he could look her in the face. Then he turned his gaze on Mason.

"You," he said, pointing a finger at him. "In the name of the Founder, I hereby expel you from the Global Justice Society forever."

Then, grabbing her hand, they walked briskly, almost running to the front door, which roared like thunder as it shut behind them.

He stood still, staring at the outside door after it shut behind them. Or rather, he stood in place but was shaking as if the hell winds of his apartment were still blowing through him. He realized he was stunned by the suddenness of their disappearance even more than by hell's sudden invasion of his home. It's as if the door murdered Julia, just as a different door brought her into my life, he thought. Was hell just a variation or subset of time? Then he began shaking more, and his teeth also started chattering, as if determined to play their part in the sickening symphony his body was playing in spite of his efforts to stop it.

"This is the end of reality," he thought, as he ran toward the door. Yet it opened as if only too eager to let him escape into the streets. "Taxi," he started yelling, "taxi," already yearning for his hotel.

• • •

He was sitting in the bathtub with only the hotel's bed-table light on. It was like dusk. He felt he'd been in the tub a long time but really he didn't know how much time had passed. Tomorrow he would look for a new apartment and buy a new computer, too. Some new clothes also, he supposed. Certainly he wouldn't miss his old place. Without a woman in it all that time it had already been like hell long before hell took it over.

He shut his eyes. He didn't want to think but it was hard to stop. He saw an image of Julia's face, which quickly disappeared, then an image of his father, which stayed. It was just a picture of his father's face smiling at him when he was a child. Hell hadn't destroyed that, at least. Yes, that was a kind of justice, he thought. That and this good hotel bath water.

The Interview

The jeans were a disaster—a failure on every level. Not sexy enough, not classy enough, too preppy, like something from a different era. What was she thinking to even consider them for the interview? Her mind had been off lately, she knew that, as if it were taking delight in sabotaging her with one trap after another. Even this morning, just after Eric left, she found herself thinking about the farm in Chester Springs, jumping from the tractor that she used to climb every day as a little girl and landing in the hay below, then laughing after she landed when she looked around her—suddenly surrounded by a yellow world.

And then, no sooner remembered, than the guilt for remembering it. It was a Pennsylvania memory, and Eric didn't want her to remember Pennsylvania. He'd bristled when she'd first told him about it—pretended he didn't but really did—which was so often his way. She was supposed to be from the South just like him, the self-styled "cowboy director," was supposed to be from Arizona though he really grew up in New Jersey. It would hurt both of them if that came out, not just her, but both of them, he'd said, staring hard at her when he first told her, as if he were her father catching his little girl in a lie. It was like acting, Eric said. Once you accepted the part you had to live it completely. If you started remembering things that didn't match up with the part, the next thing you knew you'd be talking about them and then you'd betray the character and lose the role. She had nodded and agreed. Who was she to disagree with Eric West, the great director, when he talked about acting? But what she wondered was, if you weren't allowed to remember yourself, who were you? Maybe that was why she wanted a baby so much, to have something she could remember that would be real.

She was doing it again—giving in to the bad thoughts that these days were always just a second away. She opened her closet in search of the right jeans and felt like she was entering a forest. It was obscene to have a closet this big, the way people were living all around the world. But even the most socially activist stars lived like royalty, every single one of them from Angelina on down. Who was she, to think that if she ever became one and had her own money that she'd live any differently? It was just another self-sabotaging fantasy, she supposed.

She began thinking about her conversation with Jaime two nights ago at Lillian's party. He was obviously an intelligent guy, kind of attractive, too, in a non-Hollywood way. Of course she assumed it was Eric he wanted to interview. Why wouldn't she assume that? When they met people, journalists or otherwise, they stared at her breasts for a few seconds, then turned toward Eric and quickly told him how much they loved his movies and proceeded to ignore her for the rest of the night, treating her more like a poster than a person.

Ah, these were better, she thought, taking a new pair of jeans with her as she emerged from her closet, then throwing them on the bed next to her prospective shirt. Sky blue jeans and a pink shirt. Was it too cute a look? Too "Barbie?" She caught a glimpse of herself in the wall-length mirror and held her stomach in. She ate too much last night when Woody was over. She was nervous around him (she thought even Eric was a little wired), and when she was nervous she ate too much, drank too much, too. Who wouldn't be nervous around Woody Allen? She'd kill to be in one of his movies. And now, as if it were a punishment for the dinner, she could see the results in her stomach. Stomachs were like cancer, when you thought about it. They only got worse with time. Almost everyone had one when they died, too, no matter how hard they'd tried to get rid of it. If that was your fate in life, your stomach fate, why not get one from having a baby? Even Eric had laughed when she tried that line on him. "You gotta do comedy, babe, you gotta. You're a really funny broad," he'd said, tapping her on the bottom, while avoiding what she wanted to talk about once again. Still, maybe she really was funny. Eric told her a funny woman with a hot body was "a million-dollar combination." "Look at Pamela Anderson," he'd said. "Think how much she's made. You look hotter than her, and you're younger too. You could be the next Pam, if you let me market you that way."

She loved Eric when he talked like that, as if he really believed in her. It didn't happen often but when it did it was sweet. Jaime thought she was funny too. She remembered how hard he'd laughed at one of her jokes at Lillian's. She was telling him how she hooked up with Eric and Jaime was encouraging her, as if it fascinated him. A lot of those journalists, especially the younger ones, were still in awe of movie stars, even a very minor one like her.

"I was just a bit player in one of his movies," she'd said to Jaime. "I think I said ten words in the picture, but one day during rehearsal our eyes met in a special way and he invited me to dinner that night and then boom, we just clicked."

"It was that way with me and my fiancée too," Jaime had said.

"So, yuh," she'd continued, cutting him off, "I was crazy about him right from the start, but I also had a lot of hang-ups about dating a man who was so famous and, you know, older—a man who knew so much more about the world than I did."

"But your hang-ups all went away, obviously."

"Not completely," she'd said, laughing as she finished her drink. "I mean, you see the nice tits," she said, pointing to them for a second, "but behind them beats the heart of a hick."

Jaime had laughed then. It was a real laugh, too—he even spilled part of his drink, and she'd laughed as well, holding his wrist for a few seconds as if to steady him. So maybe there was something to this Pam Anderson idea, after all. Maybe there really was.

...

There was less than an hour left and she still hadn't done anything with her hair or makeup. He'd be right on time. A young guy like that with his own new magazine interviewing Eric West's wife would definitely be on time. But she knew now that she needed a more classic look with her jeans and top if she wanted Jaime to take her seriously as an actress—which was the whole point of the interview, wasn't it? He'd even agreed on using that angle on the phone, and flattered the hell out of her in the process. So maybe not show off her new breasts (Eric's best present yet!), maybe not show any cleavage at all and that way make a statement. Of course, that's what she should do, how could she not have realized it?

She picked three new pairs of jeans from her closet (she was still ruling out a dress) and two new tops—one beige, one black, and began trying them on in front of her mirror. Sometimes everything in her life seemed like an audition. Even the first time she made love with Eric (the first few months actually) she felt she was auditioning to be his girlfriend and constantly worried if she was pleasing him enough. Of course, she did everything he wanted and acted as if she loved it all. What choice did she have? There were a million girls in Hollywood who would trade places with her, who would pay her a lot to trade places. It was a fluke, a one in a million chance for a hick like her from a little farm town in Pennsylvania to even get to be mentioned in a gossip column with Eric West, much less marry him. So all the things she did (even though some of them really hurt) were well worth it. His cheating was harder to take, of course, but it was still all worth it, she'd be a meaningless speck without him. And, besides, she'd gotten him back for his cheating more than once, and though she worried about it, it made her feel like she wasn't such a dupe after all, and that was a good kind of feeling.

She had to start her make up. The make up and hair issues had to be addressed now. After all, Jaime already knew what she looked like dressed up. Her yellow dress had been a hit at Lillian's, and he must have liked the way she looked to want to interview her that quickly and to promise her a cover too. She wondered how much money he had, then, and whether the magazine had its own money or was largely his.

· · ·

It always happened when she was about to meet someone important. She'd suddenly have to go to the bathroom, which was where she was now. Was Jaime important? Her body obviously thought so even though his magazine hadn't even come out yet. She should have asked him what kind of distribution deal he had. If it wasn't at least a million copies it wasn't worth it, that's what Eric always said.

Maybe she should have told Eric about the interview. A man was coming to his home to interview his wife. He probably should have been told. Besides, she could have used his advice in general and about her clothes in particular. But he said he had meetings all day long and a lot of things on his mind, and she also wanted the satisfaction of handling something as essentially simple as this, by herself.

She got up from the toilet. The cramps were stronger now so she swallowed more Mylanta. Then she sat down again, and in the intervals between her intermittent pain began reviewing Jaime's phone call this morning. It started with his asking very modestly if she remembered him from Lillian's the other night.

"Of course I remember youuu . . ." she's said, extending the "u" to a comical degree and then letting him hear her trademark giggle. "We sat next to each other at Lillian's and had that fascinating talk about babies and then about art and immortality. 'Art is the last illusion,' you said, right?"

"Right," he said, laughing a little himself.

"See how well I remember? I'm not as dumb as they make me look in the movies."

"Of course not, I'm very impressed."

"You're the publisher of a magazine, too, that's just about to debut, a film magazine."

"You've got a fantastic memory," he said. "That's actually one of the reasons I called you, though I didn't really expect to get you on the phone."

"Why wouldn't you get me? I gave you my number, darling, who else would answer my phone?"

"I thought your secretary or someone like that."

"Eric and me always travel alone when we come to New York. We like to keep it simple. That's why we never have any help staying with us in our New York apartment. That's a no-no. Otherwise they end up selling stories to the tabloids."

"I see your point. Well, I certainly won't do that."

"Oh no, of course not. You're going to write a novel, I remember that too. I know what a great *intellectual* you are."

He seemed stunned by her compliment for a moment but managed to say thank you. She had a habit of overcomplimenting people, even by Hollywood standards, and Eric had told her to work on it, so why did she keep doing it?

"I was hoping, though I know it's a long shot, to try to schedule an interview," he said.

"I'm sure that'd be cool," she said, cutting him off. "But Eric's in meetings all day today, and tomorrow we're off to L.A."

"No, no, I was calling about interviewing you."

"Me? Really?" She really was surprised, shocked even.

"Yes, I thought I told you that at Lillian's. Of course I'd be deeply honored to interview Eric West at some point, who wouldn't, but I wanted to interview you as an example of a terrific young actress and rising star. I think your story would fascinate our readers."

"Wow, I'm really flattered. I don't know that I have that much to say. My career's been pretty much just showing off my body so far. You could blink and miss the *acting* I've done."

"I'm sure you have lots to say," he'd said, polite as ever.

"Well, I do have a few free hours early this afternoon. What would we do about pictures?"

"I can send a photographer the next time you're in the City or fly one out to L.A. at your convenience."

"OK, I'm starting to like this, Jaime."

Then he'd suggested a number of restaurants for the interview, but she'd said she didn't want to risk dealing with the paparazzi.

"Eric pretends not to care, but it really pisses him off when these lies about us come out in the sleaze rags."

"Of course," he'd said. "Who wouldn't be angry?"

"And let's face it, because he's so famous and also, well, an older man, although he's the youngest man I know in energy and spirit, they pounce on me every time I'm spotted with someone around your age and write these awful stories about my cheating on Eric, which just about tears my heart in two."

"That's awful."

"So if it's OK with you I'd rather do it right here in my apartment, so long as you promise not to take any pictures of me I don't approve."

"Of course not. I won't take any pictures at all during the interview. What about a tape recorder? Would you like me to tape it or not?"

"Yah, I think I'd rather you tape it. I'm not exactly the world's best speaker and sometimes I blurt out things I wish I hadn't and then Eric gets upset. So if you tape it and type it up and promise to send me a copy, I can read what I said and get a chance to edit out the stupid parts, which will probably be about half of it," she'd said, laughing, and he laughed too.

• • •

He arrived on time, as she knew he would, only a few minutes after she was finished in the bathroom. She left the apartment door open and told him from her bedroom to come in and make himself at home, then decided to let him cool his heels while she did her final primping. Let him feel the lush, thick carpet, see the big, velvet chairs and then, of course, the paintings—

the only real tip-off that this was a multimillionaire's apartment were the paintings judiciously placed on the walls. Originals by Chagall, Modigliani, and Diego Rivera. There was even a small etching by Picasso, and one by Giacometti, too. He'd probably never seen a living room like that. Let him realize who she was for a minute or two before they began.

Five minutes later she walked into the living room wearing her skintight blue jeans and a low-cut yellow blouse that revealed a generous view of her newly revamped breasts.

"Hey, Jaime, thanks for coming," she said, extending her hand then leaning in for a hug and peck on the cheek. He could smell her perfume; expensive and delicious.

"Thank *you*," he said, feeling, no doubt, her artificially enhanced breasts brush against his chest.

He was wearing an expensive blue Yves St. Laurent sport jacket with matching tie. At least he knows how to look like he might have some money, she thought.

"Your apartment is beautiful."

"Thank you."

"And your art is amazing."

"Most of it's back in L.A., but we left a few good ones here."

"I'll say."

"Eric's been collecting a long time. It's all his taste. I don't know much about art but he's trying to teach me. Do you need to set up or . . .?"

"Oh, for the interview? No, my tape recorder is very discreet, very diminutive—you'll barely notice it, see?" he said, taking it out of his jacket pocket and holding it up.

"It *is* small. Do you want to just sit on the sofa then and put the recorder on that glass table in front of it?"

"That should work fine."

"Fabulous. Now I just have one more question for you: would you like a drink now and some really super hors d'oeuvres left over from a little dinner we had last night? I've already had a drink or two so I'm way ahead of you."

"A drink sounds good. I'm trying to diet so I'll pass on the hors d'oeuvres, but thank you."

"Are you sure? Woody couldn't stop eating them last night."

"Woody Allen?"

"Yes, he and Soon-Yi were over last night."

"Well, that does make me curious," he said, with a smile that soon became an appealing kind of blush.

"Be right back," she said, getting up to bring the hors d'oeuvres and knowing that he was checking out her body as she walked a slightly modified version of her model walk into the kitchen.

• • •

There was no more postponing it—the interview had begun. She was surprised how nervous she felt. It was like taking a test in school.

"When did you know you wanted to become an actress?" he said, turning to face her (she was only a few feet to his right on the pale green sofa), "and how did you know it?"

"Wow, what a question," she said, smiling even more broadly at him. "That's pretty deep. I think I always knew, I mean, I think I was seven or eight and had a part, OK, the lead, I admit it, in my school play and it just gave me a feeling I never got in any other way."

"What was that feeling?"

"Oh, just the fun of pretending I was someone else and making it all seem real. And then of course the applause was nice. The first time you hear it, there's nothing like it on earth," she said with a smile that revealed her straight, gleaming teeth—her main, model smile.

"Did you ever study formally?" he quickly asked, "and if so, at what point in your career?"

"Oh, no, I can't claim to have studied with anyone formally," she said, realizing she was using her Marilyn Monroe voice, which was definitely the wrong one for the interview, so she transitioned partway through to more of a Meryl Streep. "Of course, I learned a lot from a lot of different actors and actresses and then when I met Eric, especially from him. I mean—who wouldn't? He's one of the world's great directors."

"Of course."

"I remember a talk we once had early in our relationship. I don't think he'd mind my telling you this," she said, swallowing the rest of her drink. "I'd asked him if he thought I should study—join an actor's studio or whatever, and you know what he said?"

"What?"

"He said, 'You don't need to study, babe. You're a natural. If you studied, they'd just fuck you up.' Wasn't that sweet of him? I think it's the greatest compliment I ever got—especially since it came from such a genius."

Jaime nodded and said something supportive, reminding himself to keep well hidden the contempt he felt for West's movies. One day, sooner rather than later, when his novel was published, his work would bury that fake cowboy's.

"Who are some of the actresses who've influenced you? I mean your approach, to acting." It was such a typical question that for a moment it embarrassed him.

"Oh, there're so many. Meryl Streep is great, Eric loved working with her, and he loves Julia Roberts, too. And you know who else Eric and I always loved is Angelina. She can do it all, don't you think? And then, of course, we both loved Marilyn. She was the greatest, right?"

"Definitely," he said, though he barely understood what she was saying. He felt he was in a movie himself, not acting in it, but photographing it and not as the photographer exactly, but more like a magical camera floating invisibly in space. An invisible camera with a little tape recorder inside it that kept asking questions. Already he couldn't wait to tell Sarah. She'd say, "I'm marrying a publishing genius," or some other absurdly excessive compliment that he had to admit he loved. God, he was so lucky lately, getting this high-profile interview, which would put his debut issue on the map, and then, of course, marrying Sarah in less than a month—a woman who had finally shown him that he really was straight, once and for all, and who was also largely bankrolling his, admittedly, modestly financed online magazine. Good, steadfast Sarah, something to count on in this world of illusion.

"And what about actors?" he said. "Have they influenced your work as much as actresses have?"

"That's a really interesting question, Jaime. Let me think . . . I think we've all been influenced by Jack and Marlon and by Bobby De Niro. Of course all those guys are geniuses and I'm, well, I really feel that I'm just starting out. So far I've just been kind of a tit queen, but I aspire to be much more. I guess that's why being interviewed like this is making me kind of nervous."

"You're nervous?"

"A little."

"That's hard to believe," he blurted. "You're such a talked-about young star. I thought you were wonderful in Eric's last movie," he added.

"*Rainbow Café?*"

"Yes," he said, hoping he sounded sincere, since he hadn't seen it.

"I love being in Eric's movies 'cause they have so much substance and, and . . . meaning, don't you think?"

"Of course."

"He gives me a chance to really act because he really believes in me. At least, I think he does."

There was a silence until he said, "Have you ever thought of doing any independent films?"

"Yah, sure, I think about them all the time. I was even going to be in one by . . . well I shouldn't mention the director's name."

"Why not?"

"Cause . . . some bad stuff happened."

Jaime raised his eyebrows to show he was interested. "You're being very mysterious," he said, then regretted it. He didn't want to possibly offend her by acting like a sleaze-rag journalist, himself. His magazine was going to be different, classy—revealing the real complexities of people in the film world.

"Well, this director thought he was in love with me. Least that's what he said, but it was more like he was in lust for me. He started writing me these crazy letters and making lots of phone calls and naturally Eric noticed and got upset, so I had to withdraw, and there went my independent movie," she said, with what looked to be a real tear in her eye.

"I'm sorry it didn't work out."

"Don't be," she said, although her eyes were now clearly tearing up. "I'm so lucky. I mean look at this," she said, gesturing with her arms to indicate her apartment. "And I have a beautiful home in Beverly Hills and a house in the south of France."

"Really?"

"Yah. Eric doesn't talk about that one so let's keep it off the record, OK?"

"Of course."

"And then we have an apartment in Paris, too, even though we only go there one or two times a year. I guess I always make a fool of myself in Paris 'cause I can't speak any French. It irritates Eric no end."

He decided he wasn't going to get into that and instead said, "You have an amazing life, don't you?"

"Believe me, I pinch myself all the time. I know how lucky I am. You think I think I deserve this? What have I done? Just married the right guy I guess," she said, laughing, as she put her empty glass on the table.

"Now all I really need to be happy is a baby, and we're working on it . . . or I am. If I could only convince him to have one more. Eric already has a lot of kids you know . . . well, he's had a lot of wives."

Once more they laughed in unison.

"I guess that's what keeps him so young."

Sure, thought Jaime, that and his daily thermos of Cialis.

"I remember your talking about wanting to have a child at Lillian's," Jaime said.

"That sounds like me, always blurting out private stuff to people I've just met. Eric hates that about me, he's warned me many times to stop it, but I can't seem to help it—especially when I'm a little tipsy, like I am now, screwing up this interview."

"No way, you're doing great."

"See, my only problem is I worry about him 'cause so many women want to have affairs with him and a lot of them are more beautiful and smarter and more talented than me and wouldn't bug him about having a baby, either. Do you see what I mean?"

He stared at her in silence while she finished another drink.

"Did I say the wrong thing? Am I talking too much again?"

"No, not at all."

"It's just that you've gotten so quiet," she said.

"I'm just listening to you, that's all."

"That's a wonderful quality, Jaime. Women really like that, 'cause they don't meet many men who ever really listen to them. Eric doesn't really listen to me much. Sometimes I think he'd like it better if I never talked at all. Anyway, all I'm trying to say is sometimes I get nervous being married to such a great and desirable man. You know, people are saying he's the new Orson Welles. Did you know that? They used to compare him to Robert Altman but now they compare him to Welles, you see what I'm talking about, and I'm just a Hollywood body that's never even had one of his kids—like three other women have. Can you understand what I'm feeling . . . Jaime?"

"Of course, but I don't really think you have anything to worry about."

"Thanks, but I do worry. Most nights I have to take pills just to get to sleep."

"Really?"

"'Fraid so. Well, now I'm definitely talking too much."

"Don't worry, I won't print that."

"Oh thank you, darlin'. You're a true prince. Please don't print any stupid stuff I say, OK? 'Cause, you know, half the time I really don't know what I'm saying." She was slurping the rest of her drink, or maybe starting a new one while she continued talking.

"You really are a prince," she said, "you're a really special prince to look out for me this way."

"Thank you," he said softly.

"I think you really do understand what I'm feeling, don't you? You know what I'm going through. Even today, he's been gone all day and I don't really know what's he's doing."

She looked down at the carpet. She was aware that she'd been talking in an excited burst of words that had nothing to do with his questions, but she couldn't help it. It was as if the waterfall of her words was too strong not to overflow. "Can I talk to you off the record for a second," she said, suddenly forcing eye contact between them.

"Of course."

"Are you sure?"

"Absolutely."

"When he leaves me alone at night, or even sometimes in the afternoon like he did today, it's like I die a thousand deaths imagining him being with some woman, maybe even a hooker. I mean, everyone wants him, so he could do anything with anyone. I'll feel it then like it's gripping me by the throat and then a rage will go through me. . . . You look surprised but it's true, I'm ashamed to say it's all true. I'll feel rage even though I don't have any proof that it's anything more than my mind working overtime, being overstimulated and turning on itself. . . . Well, OK, a few times I really did have proof, I mean I figured out the code in his appointment book, I'd smell the woman's perfume on him (I have a very sensitive nose, maybe 'cause it's the only part of me they didn't reconstruct, much). Once I even kind of had him followed . . . and I'll think 'Jesus, I didn't ask for any of this, I didn't ask for this,' you know."

He heard the glass go on the table then heard her crying and once again didn't know what to say.

"Give me a hug, will you, Jaime? OK? I really need one."

They moved closer to each other, then she was in his arms, breasts against his chest, his arms covering her like a tent.

"It feels good in here," she said, "really good."

The next thing he knew her tongue was in his mouth, then he didn't think anymore, just felt her tongue. He wanted to close his eyes but kept them open, unable to resist the sight of Louise Leloch, bona fide Hollywood sex symbol, kissing him. He only wished he'd brought his camera so he could photograph her. Meanwhile, her tongue was making a series of complicated loops and probes all very skillfully executed, and he had to concentrate to be able to respond properly. He could hear her breathing, could feel her hands—finally he closed his eyes. But the moment he did, he saw an image of Sarah's face with that eternally hopeful, believing expression in her face when he proposed. Who was he kidding? He wouldn't be able to do this under these circumstances. Sarah was the only woman he'd been able to have sex with in almost five years.

He waited till one of her deep probes ended and then pulled away from her.

"What's the matter?" she said.

"I'm sorry, I can't."

"What?" she said. "Are you kidding?"

"No, I can't. There's someone I love, so I can't. It's my fiancée."

"Sweetie, I love someone, too. What do you think I've been talking about all afternoon?"

He shrugged, in spite of himself. Looking down, he was surprised to discover that one of his buttons was missing from his shirt. She must have torn it while she was massaging his chest.

"You know how much I love Eric, right?"

"Yes," he said, "of course I know."

"I can barely say two sentences without talking about him. I mean, this was supposed to be my interview, but it ended up being all about him just like all my other interviews."

He looked up from his shirt and saw that she was watching him closely.

"Well," she said, straightening her own clothes, "this is a first. I thought you were going to say you were gay or had some kind of injury or something."

"No, it's just that . . ."

"Don't say any more, OK?" she said, holding up one of her hands. "I heard you the first time. It was just a mistake I made— it's no big deal."

"OK. Well, would you like me to finish the interview?"

"I'd like you to go now, Jaime, that's what I'd like."

"All right then, if that's what you want."

"And I don't want you to print that interview, all right?"

He looked at her. Something in her tone of voice frightened him, reminded him of her deep pockets and powerful connections.

"OK then."

"I'd feel much better if you'd give me the tape right now. Then I think we could be friends and there'd be no more issues between us."

He felt another jolt of pain at the thought of handing over the tape and closed his eyes again for a second. "Here," he said. "Here's the tape."

· · ·

She couldn't help seeing the symbolism as she flushed the toilet. It was like flushing away another botched interview. Yes, another potential boost to her career floating away along with another bit of her self respect. Her record was intact—always a before the interview trip to the bathroom and always one after, where she had to deal with her weakness and ineptitude and now her fear that Jaime would try to find some way to sell what he heard and what happened between them. Another thing she'd have to try to explain to Eric, who'd be home before she knew it.

· · ·

He was late—which she expected—but she wouldn't say anything about it. She was watching TV in bed when she heard the key turn in the door. Then she shut it off and jumped up to greet him, feeling like an oversized poodle—but she knew he liked her to be at the door the moment he arrived. Amazing how trained her ears had become that she could always hear the sound of the key immediately through the TV or music she was listening to— through anything. She was wearing a short black silk bathrobe the size of a miniskirt and a pink thong, both of which she'd bought at Frederick's of Hollywood. That was the way he liked her to dress around the house, like a Playboy playmate. He'd even said to her before they married, "if you're not wearing any underwear when I come home, that means you want me badly; if you're wearing a thong, that means you're persuadable; if you're wearing that fifties kind of underwear you used to wear when I met you, that means you have cramps, or something worse, and if I do you, you can consider it rape."

She was standing in front of him in her "playmate pose" awaiting his next move, but all he did was kiss her half-heartedly. Not even his usual "playful" spanking. He suspects something, she thought, turning to get him a drink.

"You want the usual?" she said.

"Make it a double."

She saw Jaime's face again while she fixed his Scotch, and shuddered. She waited till it ended before she handed Eric his drink because she could never be sure he couldn't "see through" whatever expression she'd put on her face and know what she was really thinking—as easily as he'd read the headlines in *Variety*.

"Tough day?" she said, forcing herself to make eye contact, lest he wonder why she wasn't.

"Don't even ask," he said, turning away from her. He looked tired. It would be another night when he wouldn't want her, and even though everything indicated it was her best day to get pregnant, she wouldn't say anything more about wanting a baby tonight, that was for sure.

• • •

She told him she needed to clean up some things. After all, they were going to L.A. tomorrow—and he bought it, or was too tired to care. She puttered around the living room and kitchen and in less than ten minutes heard him snoring. She knew she was supposed to go to bed herself then but drifted toward the picture window instead. She looked down at the soft, lemony-looking cars, as quiet as plants, as they moved along Park Avenue. She couldn't believe Jaime had rejected her. She felt she could have gotten pregnant for sure with him and with Eric's ego, he'd never question it.

She looked at the cars again. It would be quite a disruption if she jumped and landed among them. It would probably make her immortal—Eric always said death was the ultimate publicity stunt for anyone under thirty (which she still was, or at least looked like).

She closed her eyes to picture her jump of death, but when she did, she saw herself jumping again, as a little girl, from the tractor into the hay below—a happy prisoner once more of her yellow world.

Single-Occupant House

I would have stayed in the other place longer but the false teeth in the bathroom upset me. It was like walking along a beach looking for shells and suddenly seeing a dead lobster. A bad sign, a bad omen, so I knew I had to quit the house and go to the other I'd been considering on Silver Place. I couldn't even remember now why I hadn't gone there before and wondered what that said about me.

The outdoors was full of scares. Tried to keep my eyes closed as much as possible and find my way to Silver Place like a bat. It had taken weeks to learn about the house—its locks and security system—(I used to be a locksmith years ago). I even posed as a sewer worker, which was a risk since I lived nearby, but it worked! Found out it was a single-occupant house, the best kind for me, and that the lady of the house was planning an out-of-state trip to visit her daughter. Managed to find that out by chatting her up a bit. I also saw how I could get in from the cellar. Then one day I noticed her car was gone—twenty-four hours and counting—making her garage look like an enormous, empty mouth. It was time. I was on the main floor and it was as if I'd climbed to the main floor of my memory, too. I saw the cab again, heard the conversation.

"Why are you driving so fast?" he said from the back seat. I could hear and see him again so clearly it was more like watching a movie, than a memory. I didn't answer him at first but he repeated himself.

"I'm thinking," I said.

"Excuse me?"

"I need to think."

"Could you just slow down a little? I don't want your 'thoughts' to kill me, OK?"

"That's what I'm thinking about," I said.

I shudder now, as I should have then. It's odd—most bad memories are about the start of something or the end of something but this one was both. It was the end of my driving for Sun Cab Company and the start of my visit to this house and it was all decided that day. Because I certainly couldn't stay in my apartment after what happened with the passenger, who I knew would call about me. I thought that after I stopped answering the phone they would come to my home and so decided I had to go to others, which I'd been doing more and more often anyway.

I walked through the first-floor rooms quickly. It was like moving under water, with small life forms floating around me. Went into the family room and saw a blue reclining chair, a La-Z-Boy. I stared at it as if it might dissolve at any moment into a shattered reef of blue dots. Eventually I sat on it, turned on TV, watched it too until I saw an ad for Plavix. "Plavix saves lives," the ad said. "If you save lives, why aren't you free?" I said to the TV. Then I shut it off.

...

When I'm in people's houses I don't steal or eat their food and rarely use their bathrooms, much less ever hurt anyone. I thought this and then I said it to myself on my La-Z-Boy, or her La-Z-Boy, to be more precise. Of course it'd give her an awful scare if she came home suddenly and saw me, but I'm very careful about that. That's never happened either. I've developed a sixth sense about when I should leave a house, almost as if the house warns me in advance. I'm really not a person who dreams of doing harm to anyone. Yet I've been told otherwise.

"OK, just stop and let me out now," he said.

I heard him again in my mind movie.

"We're on a highway," I reminded him.

"Just slow down right now, OK? Slow down or I'll call the police. I mean it," he said, brandishing his cell phone like a little spear.

I lightened my pressure on the pedal, reducing the speed. But that only seemed to make him angrier.

"What's the matter with you?"

"It's my thoughts . . . what I'm thinking."

"Your thoughts? What about your goddamn thoughts?"

"They upset me. I told you."

"What thoughts? You didn't tell me your thoughts. Why should you?"

"I told you about my apartment. How it's turned on me."

"No you didn't."

"I told you in great detail."

"Whether you did or not is beside the point. Whether you did or not doesn't give you the right to drive so fast you could kill me."

I heard him, but said nothing. Soon he was yelling at me again.

• • •

I've left the La-Z-Boy and am walking through the first floor more slowly this time. When you're in someone's house it's like being in their mind. A house can hide its secrets, for a while anyway, but it can't hide its mind. Not that its mind is everywhere, but you'll find it in one of its rooms. When you find it, it's strangely satisfying—you're no longer alone then.

I think the mind of this house is in the living room. There's a row of knick-knacks on a wooden panel above the fireplace there. I look at them and see a blue glass horse with one leg raised, a three-inch bronze head and some of its upper body, a wooden hand, a carved statue of an oriental woman, and a small white marble elephant. I'm not an art expert, but these are magical things. So much time in them, so much hope. They were meant to save memories, and what could be more magical than that? Without our memory we'd be like a giant flock of crazed bats. We wouldn't be human, I don't think. In my apartment I have nothing like those mementos. In my home I can't feel myself. That's why I spend so much time in other people's.

• • •

I don't envy other people's houses, even though they're always nicer than mine. Just the opposite, I feel grateful to them (although they don't know it) for the time I spend there. I've seen many lovely things but have never taken any. (Besides, once you stay in someone else's home, even if it's only for an hour, it becomes like one of your homes, and to take something from it would be like stealing from yourself.) Not that I haven't been tempted. Once I saw a photograph on the refrigerator of a lovely little girl with yellow, sun-like hair. She was in her bathing suit and had been digging in the sand, in her sandbox looking up, on cue, just in time for the picture to be taken. There's a little bit of surprise in her eyes that's heartbreaking. I'd rather own it than the most precious jewels, and I've seen quite a collection of those too, in jewelry boxes during my house visits. Still, I'd rather have that little girl's picture and some others that I've seen. But I never took anything, like I said, jewels or photographs alike. I touched both but I never took either.

• • •

Don't touch me, I heard myself say to myself. Don't touch me or I'll crash the cab.

"You're still going almost as fast as you were before. Don't you realize you're gonna die too if we crash?"

"I haven't decided if that's what I want."

"You decide? What about me? I've got a wife and kid to come home to."

I saw him again in the cab mirror. If he were an animal he'd be part wolf, part fox. So I started to think of him as wolf/fox.

The veins were out in his forehead; his eyes extended too, like bug eyes. I noticed that his eyes were silver blue, his hair streaked with silver too.

"Look, I'm sorry that I yelled at you, OK? I'm sorry if I wasn't listening as well as I should have. Why don't you slow down a bit and I promise I'll listen this time."

I was silent. There were conflicting thoughts in my head so I said nothing, but I slowed down. We were still on the highway.

"I remember you had an interesting theory about the secret purpose of the Internet. Had something to do with aliens. You could tell me now, couldn't you? You could even pull over to the soft shoulder and tell me there, where it would be quieter."

He had misrepresented me and I told him that.

"What I said was the Internet makes us more connected and so more tolerant of other people around the world. I said that maybe that was God's plan to prepare us, through the Internet, to tolerate the aliens we're going to meet when we start exploring other planets. That's what I said."

"That's a really interesting idea," he said. "You should write an article about it."

"But I don't believe that anymore. I told you that. Now, I don't think God has any interest in developing us."

"Why do you say that?"

"He's stayed away too long or was never there at all."

...

I hear a noise and the next thing I know the blue horse explodes in my hands. A few of the pieces fall on the floor, like chips of blue ice. The rest is in my hand. The noise goes away but it was enough to make me squeeze the horse that I hadn't realized had even been in my hand. It's the first time I've ever broken anything during one of my house visits. Now they'll know someone was there, I thought.

I was upset after I broke the horse and thought about going down to the cellar to isolate myself for a while, but instead I went back to the La-Z-Boy to think.

When I was a kid I went to the cellar in my house almost everyday. It was cool and dark even in summer and it was a good place to hide. In that cellar is also where I became a man. It's where I pleasured myself until it erupted and my fluid fell all over the floor. I nearly fainted from the pleasure. Then the next thing, I imagined how furious my father would be if he knew.

My mother would be shocked too, but my father would be furious. It seemed to take forever to clean it all up.

I stopped going to the cellar after that except when I was told to bring up the laundry from the clothesline. And I've never lived in a place where I had a cellar again. Also, in all my house visits I've only gone to the cellar once. Saw a huge black spider down there when I did. A bad sign, a bad omen, and I've stayed away from cellars since. So even though I deserved some punishment for breaking the horse, time in the cellar seemed too severe.

I thought of the attic next, though I wasn't sure that this house had one. When I was afraid my father would find me in the cellar, I sometimes hid in the attic. Heavy and weighted down with alcohol as he usually was, I knew he couldn't bring himself to look for me upstairs.

"Don't be going up to the attic, boy, whatever you do," he'd say to me. "The attic is where hornets have their heaven."

He didn't say that just to scare me either. He didn't lie about that as he had so many other things. There were always three of four large hornets buzzing around up there. We didn't know why they kept coming. When my father was drinking once he said they must have smelled something sweet on my mother. Then he stared at her down there and started laughing while her face turned red. She never told him not to say such things (and he said a lot worse) in public. She was more scared of him than I was, I think.

You can't choose your parents the way you can your house. It would be a different world if you could. But when you stay in someone else's house you sometimes can imagine you've had a different life, which can be sweet for a while.

I get up from the La-Z-Boy realizing suddenly that I still had some of the broken horse chips in my hand while the rest were still on the floor. If I swept it up with the broom in the kitchen and emptied those pieces on the floor along with the pieces in my hand in one of their wastebaskets, they'd know for sure that someone was there while they were gone. Once they saw that, they'd install a security system, or worse, and it would become another place I could never visit again. A better solution would be to hide the pieces in some remote part of the house they might not visit or at the least not for a long time. Ironically, I thought of the attic then as a good burial place for the blue horse. But did they even have one?

I was up from the La-Z-Boy, next thing I knew, in search of the attic. Didn't think they had one but they did. It was small but large enough to stay in. Immediately, I emptied the blue horse chips in a wastebasket in the corner, all the while looking around for hornets, but I didn't see any. Saw no other bugs there either and so sat down on the one straight-back chair in the room.

The thing about attics is while they're the best place to hide because no one wants to climb the stairs (except as a last resort) they're also the hardest place to escape from. The benefits and disadvantages make going there a wash. If I stayed in the attic, even in a hornet-free attic like this one in Silver Place, could I hear the lady of the house if she returned? Or if I did hear, say, the key turning in the lock, would I have time to go down a flight of stairs to find a better place to hide? It would be a foolish risk—a kind of suicide. I'd have to stay in the attic till she fell asleep. Then I'd have to overcome my fear of the dark and of the hornets and wait till I thought she was asleep—an almost inhumane torture. Thank God she didn't have a dog, unlike so many other single women her age. The younger ones had roommates, for the most part, but the ones her age had dogs.

...

There must be a part of me that likes danger (or at least a manageable amount of it) because I decided to stay in the attic. I knew there was nothing much to see there—just some board games of Monopoly and Parcheesi and a collection of old dolls in various stages of decay, but I thought I could sit there in the chair by the small circular window, which let in the gray, cracked light—sit there and maybe sleep a few minutes. Why didn't I try to sleep on the bed in one of her bedrooms? Because I'm one of those with unpredictable sleeping habits. One time, not in this town but in a neighboring one, I fell asleep too long on one of the beds. When I woke up, I heard the downstairs door open. Worse still, I heard the voices of a man and woman. I'd wanted to smooth out the bedspread, and check for any silver or black hairs of mine (at thirty-five, alas, my hair is both graying and slowly falling out), but there was no time. Fortunately it was summer and the bedroom window had no screen. I was able to sliver snake-like through the window. I thought I heard the man shout as I ran through his backyard. Then I found an alley where I was soon able to get out to the street and run to my car I'd parked a quarter mile away.

The lesson I drew from what happened was: When you're doing a house visit, never lie down on a bed. They're too comfortable, too easy to fall deeply asleep on, whereas no one could sleep more than five or ten minutes on an attic chair. I sat down on it with that in mind and shut my eyes.

But the cab memory opened them. It was like the voices and visions were hiding in me waiting for the right chance to pounce and once I settled in the attic they saw their chance to come out.

"What's really the matter?" wolf/fox said, once more trying his kind tone with me. I was still on the highway, though he kept trying to persuade me to get onto the soft shoulder and talk there.

I didn't answer him. I was going fast—lights flashed by. Then I realized it was snowing—the snowflakes were huge too, some of them the size of eyes.

"Look how big the snowflakes are," I said, or meant to. It was like I was on another planet, where it was snowing white eyes. But it was still earth, I knew that, it's more like sometimes this planet seems like another one.

"You can tell me about what's bothering you," he said. "I'll really listen this time," he said, still not talking about snow but about what he wanted to.

I said nothing. I couldn't understand why the snow made no impression on him. But that's often happened to me. The things that impressed me didn't impress others and vice versa. Another reason why I like to visit houses—there is no one there to impress but me, and I can always find something to be impressed by.

"What's the matter? You're speeding again. You said you'd slow down."

Did I? I didn't remember saying that.

"Come on, slow down and tell me what happened. Can't you see I'm trying to help you?"

"You're trying to help yourself, I think."

"What's wrong with trying to help both of us? Really, tell me what's wrong with that? Come on, it's the only way."

"I did something bad to someone," I finally said. "And now I don't know what to do about it," I blurted.

"What do you mean, 'what to do about it'?"

"Don't know if I have the right . . ."

"The right to what?"

"To live, I don't know that."

I saw his face go extra white, like a field of snow.

"Listen, you don't want to kill me, do you? What would that accomplish? You know I had nothing to do with whatever you did, don't you? Huh? Don't you?"

"I hit him in the cellar from behind with a shovel," I said. "He used to beat me there when I was young, but this time I came back and hid and then hit him 'til he fell down and then I ran out and left him there by the clothesline."

"You said he fell down, didn't you? Well, falling down isn't dying, right?"

"I know that. I heard that he didn't die, just went to the hospital, but I think that's a trick to draw me out. I think that he did die. That's why I don't know what to do."

"I didn't hear of anything like that. You would have known if he died."

"How?"

"You would have been arrested. That's how you'd find out if someone died. Or, you would have heard it on TV. The TV would have told you what you did, or the Internet."

"How do you know?" I said, I was slowing down a little and I could see him getting encouraged.

"That's why they're machines. They know these things. They don't get emotional and make mistakes like people do."

I thought of my father chasing me around the house while I ran from him like a rabbit he was hunting. I thought of the sting of his belt on my bare back. His hot alcohol breath near me as he screamed. Then I pulled over and opened the door.

"OK, you can get out."

He looked at me. He wanted to hit me with a shovel himself and then dig my grave. He was on my father's side. I could tell but I let him go. He ran off the soft shoulder into the woods like a dog or a wolf/fox as the cars whizzed by. I saw the woods swallow him. Later, in the first house I went to, I wondered if I'd planned the whole thing, driving fast and blabbing about my father, so I could get it off my chest to someone—just so I could confess. I wouldn't put it past me. Strange how we keep secrets from ourselves, like our mind is a house of endless rooms and the truth hides in just one of them.

Of course I didn't tell wolf/fox everything. Didn't tell him about my apartment—dishes rattling, like they were out in a hurricane, glasses singing the way a choir of lunatics would, meanwhile the phone waiting for me, always waiting like an assassin. I knew Sun Cabs would fire me, on the phone, knew the passenger would call and that would be the last straw, and my apartment knew it too. No time to pack even, just time to find my way to some houses (according to my information just two were available in the area, including the one on Silver Place, where I broke the blue horse then buried it in the attic and where I'm still sitting, trying to sleep).

My mother claimed she never slept. Said my father kept her from sleeping. There were a number of ways he could do that. I didn't like thinking about any of them. Somehow my mother had transferred her inability to sleep to me. It hid at first in the house in my mind—maybe in the attic, maybe in the cellar (I couldn't tell), until I got older and then it seeped into me. Yet sometimes I could sleep, even when I didn't want to. It's not as if our abilities are completely destroyed when we get older. They stay with us in diminished forms until we, ourselves, disappear.

I remember playing hide-and-seek with my father when I

was five. It's become my first memory. I remember him laughing and hugging me when he found me. I remember his holding my hand when we went in the ocean—one of the very few family vacations we ever took, so long ago. I remember him helping me fly a kite on the sand dunes. A few years later he burned the kite one time when he was chasing me. Did it with his cigarette lighter, screaming like a billy goat at first then like a dog left out in the cold. I remember these things . . .

Then I heard it—the door opening, like the sound of time ending. I came back to the present with a jolt. It was too late to run. Too late to even shift my weight. Since I could hear the sounds she was making I knew she could hear mine, if I made any.

I heard a toilet flush. I heard her walking—probably on the linoleum floor in the kitchen. I thought I even heard her sigh. What would I do if she climbed to the top floor? No sooner thought than it happened—heard her climbing to the second floor, one floor below me. What would happen if she went to her living room and saw the blue horse missing? Would she scream? Call the police? What if she walked into the attic? What would I do then? Put up a struggle or give myself up? It's the same question I always faced with my father whenever he was chasing me.

Time goes in a circle, I said to myself, over and over as I heard her walking just a floor below me. The past never leaves us—only hides for a while until it reappears. The odd thing is, we cling to it as to our fathers, and even call it Father Time.

How many deaths did I die awaiting my fate with him while I hid? And now I'm hiding again. My flesh ached but I was still afraid to even shift my weight. Like most intruders I'm a coward, or rather a coward who takes outrageous chances at times and then suffers.

. . . I grew hungry, I kept imagining what food she had in her kitchen and then imagined feeding myself with it. I had to urinate too but held it in.

It was hellish to stay so still. Like our planet, we're meant to be in motion, I think. Maybe I'm an alien—the one the Internet is preparing people to meet. I've certainly behaved like one. My home had even banished me it seems. So why not just run for it?

Still I waited like a nervous hornet guarding its nest, forcing itself not to fly 'til the dark finally came, when, holding my shoes and praying there were no alarms I didn't know about, I finally snuck out into the night thinking, "I must move to another town, I must move on to other houses."

The Group

It wasn't until he'd finished coloring his hair that he realized he really was going to the group's latest party. Throughout the afternoon, and for days before that, Summers had thought of various excuses he could make to Morton, who at this point hosted more parties per year than he wrote stories, yet he didn't make the call. But why? Was he simply a glutton for punishment? Did he want to once more return to his apartment after the party feeling his mediocrity again confirmed in a public setting (though his career and overall life was no more mediocre than most of the group's)? Perhaps it was a kind of programmed curiosity unconsciously motivating him. The fear that if he didn't go, this would be the one party where something noteworthy would really happen, something along the lines of meeting a smart, successful literary agent who would take a sudden interest in him, ask him to send his few books, and eventually take him on and radically turn around his floundering career. Rationally he knew it wouldn't happen, but apparently the irrational part of him was stronger. It was disappointing to have to once more realize this about himself, that he'd go to something like this party on a raw, rainy November night, having to take a cab from West Philly to Center City and then having to take another cab back when it was over (his soon to be ex-wife now had possession of their car), unless he could bring himself to ride back with someone from the group, probably Aaron—who would be self-promoting the whole ride or worse still, Lucas, the biggest, most self-deluded braggart in the group.

What contempt he felt for the group, albeit mixed with pity, as he pictured them "networking" at their latest party. He closed his eyes, took a deep breath, and finished applying a few dabs of cologne, realizing that he also harbored the secret hope of meeting an appealing woman there as well—something even more unlikely than his agent fantasy.

Another deep breath, followed by another closing and opening of his heavily lidded eyes. He felt calmer now. There was no point in thinking at all if he wasn't going to be honest with himself, and to be honest he had to admit he also somewhat liked the group as well, or some of the members, though at the same time he found them unbearable, of course.

There was Emir, who could be warm and witty, sometimes even generous in praising the work of his peers. But once he turned to the subject of his thwarted career he quickly became obnoxious. How he'd hold forth with his exasperating, elevated eyebrows, which always rose paternalistically as he'd expound on his latest theory about how a country's (by which he meant the United States) literary influence reflects its political influence and so dominates less powerful countries (by which he meant his native Argentina) in the literary marketplace. In reality, Summers thought, Emir's theory was but the most recent explanation to account for his lack of success. That was the only literary/political issue that really interested Emir—though he never considered any purely aesthetic reasons for it, such as the arcane, precious, tediously academic quality of his prose. As Emir grew older and his failure (though he'd published a few novels with second-rate university presses) became more solidified, his theories became more grand, comprehensive, and conspiratorial. For some years now Emir's true art form had, in fact, become his theories, always cloaked in international intrigue, not his writing, which he rarely attempted now.

With his pitifully transparent self-love and ill-disguised disappointment in his life, Emir was reason enough not to attend the party, Summers thought, but there were even more compelling reasons.

There would be at least five to ten other blowhards there, who were even more exasperating than Emir (Emir was capable, at least, in the midst of one of his tirades, of being intermittently amusing). There was, for instance, Aaron, the self-proclaimed literary avant-gardist, who would tell you with a straight face that his writing had forever altered human consciousness. He'd published only with tiny presses that Summers suspected were partially or wholly financed by Aaron himself. "I wear my rejection by the New York publishing houses as a badge of honor," Aaron would repeatedly say. "If they ever slipped up and accepted my work I'd know immediately that I'd lost it, that I was no longer cutting edge."

Aaron recently celebrated his fifty-fifth birthday by throwing a party for the group at his loft in South Philly. With great ambivalence, Summers attended, not quite ready to leave the group but vowing to do so to himself in the immediate, or at least near, future. Yet here he was, three months later, getting dressed for yet another group affair, this time celebrating the unlikely, indeed shocking, Pulitzer Prize for music criticism his former schoolmate, Howard Pike, had just won. Pike had actually left Philadelphia and the group for New York twenty years ago, to seek his fortune, which he'd clearly found as music critic for the *Times*. The fact that he'd consented to take a train to Philadelphia and attend a party in his honor was regarded as an act of great generosity on Pike's part. Yes, the news about the prize was like suddenly being mugged. "I won't forget it," Summers said to himself, "It will always go on hurting me, and yet I'll have to shake Pike's hand and congratulate him if I go to the party." But still he went.

···

It wasn't his imagination; almost everyone in the group (except Aaron, who always wore "avant-garde clothes" that he designed himself) was more dressed up than usual, and even most of the men wearing jeans also wore ties and jackets. The women also wore nicer than usual clothes and a full compliment of make up and jewelry, and all because of their mighty visitor from New York, Howard Pike, who stood in the approximate center of the loft-style apartment, a Cheshire cat smile on his face as he accepted congratulations from one obsequious well-wisher after another.

Summers had already had a few opportunities when he could have made his move and shaken Pike's hand, but despite two vodka punches was still hesitating, and while he stalled he found himself chatting with Emir and his American wife, Hanah.

"Big crowd tonight," Summers said to Emir, half gesturing with his free hand.

"You noticed," said Emir, in his dryly sarcastic mode, which Summers usually enjoyed, at least in small doses.

"And so well dressed," Summers said, feeling self-conscious, in spite of himself, for wearing his typical group party outfit of a sweater and jeans. Emir was wearing jeans too, but also a cleanly pressed white shirt and a navy blue tie and blazer.

"Of course," Emir said, "Americans, even American bohemians, like our group, must show the greatest respect to an American prize winner."

Summers forced a laugh and also forced himself not to remind Emir that he'd lived in the States since he was fourteen and had been an American citizen now for many years.

"In case you're wondering," Hanah said, "his better half made him wear the sports jacket."

"I commend you on your courage and good taste," he said to Hanah.

Hanah forced a smile. She didn't enjoy his or Emir's sarcastic, bantering side and now looked as if she was only a few seconds from crying.

"Well, did you do it yet?" Emir said, pointing his plastic cup, no longer filled with white wine, in Pike's direction.

"Do what?" Summers said.

"Make your pilgrimage to Pike's Peak and pay your proper respects."

"Alas, not yet."

"Don't worry, he's still just Howie Pike underneath it all, just a little less self-deprecating now, as one might expect, but not really insufferable about it yet, by any means."

"Coming from you that's a ringing endorsement."

Emir shrugged. "Life has finally forced me to be humble."

"Really?" Summers said, as if playing his part to set up another joke, but the punch line didn't come. Instead, of all things, Emir asked him about his ex-wife.

"Are you still in touch with Judy? Do you hear from her?"

"Sometimes. I talked to her on the phone a couple of weeks ago. Why do you ask?"

"I always liked her, and never understood why you two didn't get back together."

"Emir, you're embarrassing him," said Hanah.

"No, I'm not Hanah. Am I?" he said, looking directly into his eyes.

"No, of course not. Emir has put in enough hours listening to me whine about Judy that he can ask me more or less anything he wants to about her."

"So, what's your answer?" Emir said.

"Answer to what?"

"Are you getting back together? What else would I be asking?"

"Well there's a short answer and a long answer."

"The short answer is the only answer. Do we even have time now for anything else?"

"No, we're not. I don't think we ever will be either, I'm sorry to say."

Emir rubbed his eyes for a moment, as if Summers' answer had suddenly made him tired. It was amazing that he still didn't wear glasses.

"That's too bad. She's a lovely person."

Summers shrugged—a nonchalant response more typical of Emir, he thought, that he immediately regretted. Emir's atypical line of questioning and oddly earnest tone must be disorienting him, he thought.

"So what's the long answer?"

"An explanation of the short one."

"Which is?"

He caught himself trying to think of a pithy reply, as if his primary purpose was still to entertain Emir, who, in turn, was continuing to surprise him with his sudden sincerity. Finally he gave up.

"It's nothing you haven't heard before. It just didn't work out with our both being writers, I guess."

He hoped that Emir wouldn't point out that Judy had achieved considerably more literary success than him and that it was he who couldn't really handle it well. Instead, Emir looked preternaturally sad. It made Summers glance quickly at Hanah, who also looked sad, as if they both were attending his funeral.

"But don't you think that love is more important than writing?" Emir said.

"Whose writing?"

"Our writing, mine, yours, the group's. What writer's work is more important to them than a love they have for another person, for a wife or husband or for a child? Such a person, who lived such a life of illusion and escapism couldn't be a good writer, anyway. Don't you agree, Hanah?"

"I do agree, Emir, but I'm also staying out of this."

Now in addition to feeling nonplussed and vaguely disoriented, Summers felt wounded and began to look over at Pike, who was finally standing alone.

"Well, I appreciate your concern," Summers said. "I really do. I appreciate both of you and I will think seriously about everything you said, but now I think I need to pay my respects to the guest of honor. If I wait any longer it will be rude, don't you think?"

. . .

Pike didn't look as old as he should have, as if winning the prize somehow drained some of the age from his face. We're almost the same age, Summers thought as he shook his hand. He shouldn't look younger than me too. Isn't the prize enough?

It was neither a tepid nor a strong handshake but it was a long one, as if Pike wanted to convey enthusiasm without a hug or any quotable words being said on his part.

"Congratulations," Summers said. "The world has honored you, now let me join it," he added, realizing that what he said was awkward at best and might well also be confusing. He thought briefly about explaining what he meant to say (i.e., he was already in the world, of course, and not waiting to join it, though it was true he often felt alienated from the world) but, of course, it was too late to explain anything like that.

"How are you, Roger?" Pike said, finally looking at him briefly.

"Pretty well. Can't really complain, though I do," he said, with a little laugh, and probably to be polite, Pike managed a laugh as well.

"The real question is how are you holding up against the world's onslaught of attention?"

"The world barely knows, much less cares."

"How can you say that?"

"Come on, Rog, it's a newspaper prize. People don't read newspapers anymore. Half the time I'm there I feel like I'm working in a museum or a crematorium. Hey," Pike continued, "I didn't see you at the big high school reunion."

"You went?"

"Absolutely."

"It never occurred to me that you'd go."

"The fortieth reunion, how could I resist? You know I always suffered from terminal nostalgia."

More like terminal narcissism, Summers thought. Of course

Pike would go. How could he resist all the adulation from his fawning classmates, especially since he was such an inconspicuous, sometimes bullied, student back in high school.

"If I'd known you were coming I would have gone," Summers said, averting his eyes slightly. "So what's it like to see the old group?"

"Surprisingly emotional. I just recovered from the reunion; well, it was five months ago, and now this. I'm very touched really."

"I'm glad you like it," Summers muttered. As he feared, Pike then asked him about his writing, but in such a merely-to-be-polite, perfunctory way that it was relatively easy to exaggerate and even to tell a couple of lies. Lying was a standard, even expected, part of conversation by the group that rarely was even pointed out by anyone behind the liar's back. It was paradoxical—"literary lying" was accepted as a normal part of discourse, but so was the chronic kvetching about literary rejection and failure from the same people who'd apparently forgotten their brazen lies and bragging from a half hour before. He himself had been guilty of this (although he did it less often than most members). Come to think of it, only Emir, old world gentleman that he was, never lied, though he was certainly guilty of complaining.

There was little to say after the opening pleasantries. Too much time had passed and, more important, there was too big a gap in success between them. Summers felt like a drowning man vainly reaching for an illusory life preserver as he tried to think of things to talk about—a couple of mutual friends from high school, a former creative writing teacher. Pike answered him politely but with little animation. And then suddenly Summers gave up, shook Pike's hand a final time, congratulated him yet again, and turned his back, expecting to return to the safety of Emir and his wife. But he didn't see them. He felt an odd bit of panic, then headed for the table to refill his vodka punch cup.

Really, it wasn't so bad with Pike, he told himself as he quickly filled and then drank from his cup.

"Excuse me," a woman said, who was surprisingly attractive. "Are you Roger Summers?"

"Guilty as charged," he said, looking at her more closely now. She had surprisingly thick brown hair, but refined, almost elegant features. His memory, no longer as sharp as it once was, came up empty. But why wouldn't he remember a good-looking woman who was so young—no more than thirty-five by his count? And how did she know him?

"I'm Renee," she said, extending her hand, which he more than gladly shook. Was it possible that she'd read one of his books? Heard him read somewhere in Philadelphia once or was she perhaps one of his former students?

"Have we met?" he finally said.

"Not until now," she said with a laugh, and he found himself laughing along with her. How charming women in their thirties could be! Especially when they were so enthusiastic.

"May I ask how you know my name?" he said, bracing himself for a tribute of some kind.

"Oh, I asked that man over there," she said, pointing to Lucas, who was just now giving him a pricelessly jealous dirty look, which helped mitigate his disappointment. So she hadn't read him, but still she wanted to meet him. Was he perhaps more youthful looking tonight than he realized?

"So I'm glad . . ." Roger said. "How did you happen to come here tonight?"

"I came with the man who told me your name."

"With Lucas?" he said, incredulously.

"Yes."

"I see."

"I saw you talking with Howard Pike, who's one of my idols of music, well of criticism in general, and Luke told me you went to high school with him, with Howard Pike, so I wanted to ask you what it was like talking to him and maybe if you could introduce me. I want to interview him for a magazine but, of course, I have to meet him first."

"I'm sure Howie will be delighted. He loves any kind of . . . informed attention," he said with more sarcasm than he intended. He felt his face might well be red now and looked away from her, at Aaron and his wife holding hands. He should have invited Judy to this, even just as a friend. These parties were now too painful to attend alone. It was yet one more thing that had changed these last few years.

"Come with me," he said to Renee, "I'll introduce you to him now."

. . .

He came to a kind of rest stop by a window that was open a few inches. For ten or fifteen minutes he'd been walking in a circular pattern around the loft thinking of Pike and his new female admirer, among other thoughts. He looked out the window and felt the cool air. Often in his own apartment when he was pacing late at night he'd look out at the street and watch a man walking quickly (was he anxious about who he might encounter on the streets?) or see a car screeching to a halt, or a hooker smoking a cigarette while she waited for a client, and once a woman chasing a man down the sidewalk yelling at him. Had he stolen something from her or just broken her heart? Tonight he saw nothing but an occasional car, silently rolling by as if on felt. It occurred to him then that while he felt so interested and even drawn to them, he'd never written about the people he saw on the street at night, or during the day either, for that matter. Would it have made a difference? Was his whole approach to writing, like his whole approach to the rest of life, seriously off course? He'd been such a dutiful postmodernist, Summers suddenly thought, but had he ignored people in the process? He'd certainly drifted from his wife, who was now assiduously pursuing a divorce from him. Was it time to admit he was wrong about some things, certainly about the way he'd treated Judy? Perhaps it was too late to construct a new literary identity at this point, but was it too late to speak to his wife from his heart? Hadn't Emir said love is more important than writing, or at least words to that effect?

Where was Emir? He suddenly wanted to talk to him with an urgency that surprised him, but when he scanned the room he didn't see him. Instead, he saw Hanah standing fifteen feet from him smoking a cigarette by another window. She looked oddly upset, almost forlorn (he hadn't ever thought of her as a woman who thought dark thoughts), but he approached her anyway.

"Greetings!" he said, hoisting his empty cup in a mock celebratory gesture. Hanah looked at him, as if puzzled in her grief, and nodded.

"Where is that elusive husband of yours?"

"In the bathroom for the last ten minutes."

How typical of Emir! He himself could never go in someone else's home, certainly not at a party, but Emir had the gift of being uninhibited.

"He's not feeling well," Hanah added.

Summers looked at her, surprised that she was smoking a cigarette, something so frowned upon by the group.

"Oh, I'm sorry."

"It's been like that for awhile now, because of the treatments. I told him to expect this. I urged him not to come tonight but he insisted. He loves the group so much."

"Excuse me, Hanah, for asking, but what treatments? For what?"

"Oh, you don't know? The radiation treatments—Emir has stomach cancer."

Summers put his hand to his mouth.

"Oh my God, I'm sorry, I didn't know."

"I thought you did. I thought he told his friends a couple months ago."

"No, I didn't know," Summers mumbled.

She continued to tell him how they found out and then decided to tell their friends right away, but Summers could scarcely focus on what she was saying. He was remembering, with unfortunate clarity, a number of calls Emir made to him—probably three calls—about a couple of months ago that he let go to voicemail. In his depression—it was shortly after Judy moved out—he hadn't bothered to check Emir's messages.

"I'm so sorry," Summers heard himself saying again, and then when there was a brief silence he said it once more. He wanted to say something else, perhaps explain about the calls he didn't answer. In his own depression then, he couldn't bear to hear anymore group trivia. It was always the same, those phone calls, but now, of course, it was different.

"Is this party over now or is there some event coming?" Hanah asked.

"I think someone is going to introduce Pike, you know, the Pulitzer Prize winner, and then he's going to make a speech."

"Yes, the speech. That's what Emir wanted to hear. He's so

proud of Howard. I hope, if he still refuses to go home, that he at least comes back in time to hear it."

• • •

Emir only missed the opening minute of Aaron's embarrassingly long and overly florid introduction. Pike at least kept it short and sweet and came off as one of the group, which, Summers concluded, was at least a substantial part of what he probably was.

After the applause died down and the toasts ended, Hanah drew Emir a few feet away from him and began talking animatedly. She was trying to persuade him to leave, Summers thought, but apparently didn't succeed. When they returned she said, "He loves to torture me with his stubbornness. But since he won't leave, I'm going to stay out of it and let you two talk," she said, looking meaningfully at Summers. Then lighting another cigarette, she walked across the loft, apparently toward the punch bowl.

Summers looked uneasily away from Emir, wondering if Hannah had told him about their recent conversation.

"It never occurs to her that she's stubborn too," Emir said. "Still, I go on with her."

"You've been married a long time. She's your soul mate."

"Over forty years," Emir said, nodding. "At this point I think of her more as my tomb mate . . . in the future, of course. I can't explain why I love her so much but I do know that I want to die next to her. I even hope we share the same worms, if it comes to that," he said with a little laugh.

Summers watched him closely while he sipped from his new glass of wine.

"I didn't know about your . . ."

"Cancer? My cancer?"

"Yes, Hanah told me tonight. I'm so sorry. It must be hell."

Emir shrugged and smiled ironically.

"It's not a hopeless situation. It's not impossible. But I'll tell you, having done both, having cancer is even harder than writing an uncompromising novel!" Emir said with a laugh, and this time Summers forced a laugh himself.

"You know it's funny," Emir said. "When I was younger I thought that books could capture life, the sense of time passing, much better than films, because films are too short. Now that I have so little time left, whether I beat cancer or not, when I think of my past now it seems much more like a movie than a book, because it all seems so fast-moving and so short. Do you know what I mean?"

"Yes, I do know what you mean. I've felt it myself. I've been feeling it all the time lately."

"Anyway, I shouldn't be talking about such heavy things at a festive occasion like this."

"No, no, you should," Summers said, surprised for a moment by the passion in his voice. "It's the most interesting thing I've heard tonight by far, believe me."

"It's just that, well for example, when you've been reading a long book, *Don Quixote* or *Remembrance of Things Past*, and you're getting near the end of it you want to talk about the experience of reading it, don't you?"

"Of course."

"It's like that with my life now. Not that I want to talk about the particular things that happened to me, it's that I want to talk, at times about how time is passing differently, as my memory of it is. I want to talk at times about how that's all changed."

"It's changed for me too."

"Really? Then we can talk about it even at this party?"

"We just did," Summers said and both men laughed.

"We should talk more often, my dear Roger," Emir said with a smile. "You shouldn't steal yourself away and make yourself such a hermit."

"Well, I came to this event. It wasn't easy to make myself come but I did . . ."

He noticed that sad expression in Emir's eyes again, his eyebrows dropping like flags at half-mast.

"Of course, I wanted to see you," Summers added.

"And the others?" Emir said, gesturing with his arm. "They are your friends too, aren't they?"

"Some of them, yes, I suppose. You must admit things get repetitious here, I mean all the complaining and defensive bragging."

"Yes, of course, that is what people do. But they are your brothers also."

"My brothers?"

"You share a common fate. They all want to give something to the world, to express something, and they're all thwarted because their work has cancer and is going to die. They're just a group of patients whose writing has cancer. But we still come together to celebrate, right? We're still alive."

. . .

He didn't ask anyone for a ride, in part because he left early (a few minutes after talking with Emir) but mainly because he wanted to walk. He passed by the subway station without much of an internal debate and ignored a couple of cabs he could have taken. He was walking through Rittenhouse Square now, through the elegant lamplit park from which a strange half-purplish light seemed to emanate. Walking through the park late at night generally made him a little uneasy and he'd normally walk on the sidewalk by the clothes stores and restaurants, but with his head full of Emir's words he somehow wanted to be among trees and flowers. Although it wasn't always the case, he still believed he thought more clearly when he was close to nature.

He was trying to account for why he felt so energized that he was actually contemplating walking all the way home to West Philly. Why did he suddenly feel so awake instead of his usual nocturnal exhaustion? Almost everything at the party had been the way he'd anticipated—the awkward pain of seeing Pike, the fawning behavior of the group—which only thinly disguised their collective bitterness—his failure, despite three or four drinks, to call Judy. He'd met no new women, made no publishing contacts. It was his conversation with Emir, of course, that made the difference, though he had trouble acknowledging it in part because he'd learned tonight about Emir's cancer. Was it right that he should feel so inexplicably alive from a man who was probably fairly well along in the process of dying? He didn't know the answer, he would never know what was right or wrong about many things, he realized, but he did sense that Emir wanted his words to have impact. So then this would have pleased Emir too, he hoped.

Up ahead, at the edge of the park by a street lamp, Summers saw a woman in a short skirt. At first he thought she was unusually pretty, like a younger version of Judy, but as he got closer he saw the years on her heavily made up face. For an aging hooker, Rittenhouse Square was usually off limits. She's not only too old to hook, Summers thought, she's in the wrong place, too, almost as if she's an alien.

"Hey mister," she hissed at him as he walked past her, "You want a date?"

"No, thank you," Summers said, reaching into his pockets and withdrawing a fifty-dollar bill. "But I have something for you." The woman looked scared as if he were about to point a gun at her.

"Here," he said. "Enjoy it."

She looked startled but she took the money quickly.

"God bless you," she said as he moved past her. Summers waved in response and blew her a kiss before finally leaving the park.

The House

The only three forces on earth capable of conquering, and capti-
vating and making weak willed, rebellious man happy are miracle,
mystery and authority.   Dostoyevsky, *The Brothers Karamazov*

He wouldn't do that to himself again. He wouldn't think of his
dream last night where Melissa had been first a little girl and
then a woman. Where he'd held her hand while they'd jumped
the waves and she'd laughed a sound high and bell-like that
he'd heard as clearly as if he'd seen her. Painful enough to have
dreamt it, he needn't torture himself by repeating it, too, especially on his way to meet Serena for the first time. Instead, he'd
think of something both stimulating and unthreatening by reviewing once again the rudimentary information he planned for
the introduction to his book in progress on the hidden function
of towns.

There must be a government building within the town limits, Tyler thought, as he drove to the restaurant, although only
a small percentage of citizens would ever require any in-person
services. Still, if they did, there would have to be offices filled

with people who could perform them. And, of course, the town would also require a court well equipped enough so that judges, lawyers, and juries could function smoothly in it. On the other hand, there didn't need to be a jail inside the town limits as long as there was one within an hour of it. In fact, it might be preferable to not have a prison in the town since its mere presence would create a measure of anxiety.

Of course, there must be a good-sized food market with a drugstore nearby and at least two restaurants, the larger one where one could go for dates or special occasions. The town must also have a bar, a doctor who was a general practitioner, a K–8 school, and a high school that, if not in the town limits itself, was within a few miles of it. Every town needs to demonstrate its belief in the future and so must have a school with a library and some kind of playground since one wants to develop sound bodies as well as minds—the little time that both will last—Tyler thought, with a bitter little laugh. He would only deal with the archetypes, with the deep structure that lies beneath virtually every town, including Stockbridge, which he was walking through now on his way to meet Serena Hansborough for lunch at the Red Lion Inn, Stockbridge's place for special occasions.

Strange thoughts he was having today. Lately he'd noticed that any disruption in his routine (which having lunch with Serena definitely was) greatly increased the rate of his unsettling thoughts, especially about his daughter, Melissa, whom he longed to see but who was in California (where she'd essentially written him off) futilely trying to become an actress. He forced his thoughts to turn to his date again, his first one in years. He was glad that he'd seen what Serena looked like already (one had to provide a recent photograph for the dating service). Hers was a kindly face, though a small part of him was disappointed. In years past he wouldn't have chosen to meet her, but now it didn't seem to matter much since he thought that at his age a romantic relationship was no longer possible.

It would be stimulating enough just to talk to a new person whom he already knew was friendly in an unassuming way and was a good listener, too, because they'd talked on the phone three times at some length before finally deciding to meet. Perhaps he would even speak to her about his book. He could tell she was intelligent. She'd worked as a librarian and English teacher and said she was still interested in reading. He'd never told anyone his ideas about towns, so in addition there now loomed the possible satisfaction of being listened to and in some way understood.

...

Although it was already summer it was still too cold to eat outside. Instead, they sat next to the window, as if to keep in close touch with the outdoors. She was wearing a light blue dress (rather more dressed up than he'd imagined) that accentuated the blue in her hazel eyes. She was soft-spoken and did appear to listen just as well as she had on the phone.

"I've been thinking a lot about towns lately," he heard himself say, trying to control the rising excitement in his voice.

"About Stockbridge?" she said, looking at him directly in a more sustained way than she had before.

"Some, but not really about Stockbridge per se. I meant more about how towns operate in a general way, why they have the things in them they do and how they function to control our fears and anxieties."

She looked puzzled. He could see she was the kind of person on whose face feelings registered with an almost cartoon-like clarity. Such people, especially those who were, like Serena, shy by inclination, seemed to have a certain innocence, which at this point in his life he found quite touching.

"That's fascinating," she finally managed.

"I'm actually planning to write about it."

"Is this something you'd consider publishing?" she said, her eyes opened even more than they had before.

"I don't know about that," he said with a little laugh. "I don't think there's a big market out there for articles about collective denial of death, which I think is the chief function of towns."

She stared deeply at him almost as if she were being hypnotized—a feeling he found he enjoyed. Then suddenly her face was flushed with enthusiasm. "I know the most interesting woman who's starting a publication, a very unusual magazine, which I think will be terrific."

"Really?" he said, feeling both interested and oddly jealous that this woman had made such a strong impression on Serena. "What kind of magazine is it?"

"A magazine of 'ideas.'"

"That would be unusual," Tyler said sarcastically, but in spite of himself, he was intrigued. Though he'd been an engineer and then a contractor before he retired, he'd always suspected he had a way with words. "And how far along is this magazine? Is it just in the talking stage or is it definitely going to happen?"

"Oh, it's definitely going to happen. I feel sure about that."

"But these things cost money. There are all kinds of expenses just to get it produced. How is it going to be financed?"

"Greta, the woman I told you about, will take care of that. She'll be the publisher."

"Has she done this before? Does she have a clear sense of how much money is involved just to physically produce it?"

"I'm pretty sure she can take care of it."

For the first time he detected a touch of irony in Serena's voice, and he looked a bit surprised himself.

"Do you know that mansion in Interlaken?" she said, in an almost conspiratorial voice.

"Which mansion?"

"The biggest one. The one that you drive up a hill toward, that's twice as big as any other house in the area."

He shrugged. He had a vague recollection but didn't think he'd ever looked at it closely or ever considered it when he thought about archetypal towns.

"She lives there," Serena said simply and then smiled.

"By herself?"

"I'm not sure. She has lots of friends who visit, especially when Tanglewood starts. But I think that only Greta lives there now."

"Did she marry?" he found himself asking. "Is her husband still alive?"

"I didn't ask. They were divorced years ago."

"But her friends visit a lot. That must be a comfort," Tyler said, not without a trace of envy, as he hadn't seen his daughter in almost three years and then only when he flew to Los Angeles without being invited.

"I'm sure it is," Serena said.

"And does she have any children?"

"I'm not sure about that."

"So, how did you two meet?"

"Just a few months ago she hosted an event for our local philosophical society. She does quite a bit of that kind of thing."

"And so you two met at the society and became fast friends?"

"Something like that," she said, lowering her eyes and blushing a bit.

He did remember the house, now, how could he not? It was the biggest he'd ever seen, with an enormous sloping, flowered lawn. He'd even stopped once in his car to stare at it and counted over fifty windows before he grew tired and stopped counting. When he was a contractor he'd often dreamed about being an architect and designing a house like hers. He didn't know why he hadn't remembered it when Serena first asked him, but now it seemed he couldn't stop talking about it.

"So, is it magnificent inside?"

"Yes, it is magnificent but in a rather quiet way."

"How do you mean?"

"There's not a lot of furniture, though what there is, is very elegant, of course."

"I imagine."

"But the whole place or what I saw of it, which is far from the *whole* place, is very uncluttered, and . . ."

"Understated," he said.

"Yes, that's the word I was looking for."

He continued asking questions, first about the house, then about the grounds; how many and what kind of flowers were on her lawn? How large and what shape was the swimming pool—it *was* a swimming pool behind that high wooden fence, wasn't it? Yes, he thought so.

When he was finally done with his house questions (it was already past the time when lunch should have ended) he began asking about Greta's life again. He now saw with piercing lucidity that every town needed a mansion, which functioned as the living example of human aspiration achieved, human royalty accomplished.

"Do you know if Greta has much hired help?"

"I think she has a kind of butler and a part-time maid who does the cleaning, but that's it. They live in the guesthouse and help her with shopping too, but I don't know of anyone beyond them. Greta's a very unostentatious person, would you like to meet her?"

"I would," he said, pleasantly surprised to discover that he really meant it.

"Why don't we go over there now? Of course, I'll call her first."

"Wouldn't that be kind of sudden?" Tyler said. "I wouldn't want to impose."

"No, no, she's very spontaneous and informal. The truth is I was just over there before I came to see you so I know that she's home now. As a matter of fact she was asking me a lot of questions about you, so I know she'd like to meet you. Come on, let's do it. What do you say?"

...

Tyler didn't know whether to be flattered or insulted by the invitation. After all, he thought, why was she in such a hurry to introduce him to a wealthy, ostensibly single woman if she was interested in him, herself. Maybe she also thought a romantic relationship was no longer possible, or at least not one with him. Or perhaps she was so guileless she'd acted spontaneously out of simple enthusiasm, without thinking through all the consequences. In any case he hadn't hesitated to go, still feeling a strangely powerful desire to see the house.

The ride to the mansion was less than five miles. He followed Serena in his car and could see that she was making a call, presumably to Greta. Once they reached the iron gate it opened automatically and they drove another quarter mile or so, on a slightly winding driveway past a series of gardens and flowering trees to the front of a garage, where Serena finally stopped. On the way to the front door he counted six different types of flowers—the dominant colors being white and a kind of shocking pink. The last thing he saw was a glimpse of a pool surrounded by the unusual combination of pine trees and pink roses before the door was answered by a tall man with excellent posture but squinting blue eyes.

"Good afternoon, Ms. Hansborough. Miss Nadan is in the living room."

"Thank you, Andrew," she said.

"Thanks," Tyler said softly as he followed behind her.

Because of the dazzling floral arrangements he'd just seen outside he'd expected the inside of her home to be brighter and more fragrant. Instead it was somewhat dark, vast, and odorless, like a municipal history museum, though the living room was brighter—as if a mist had lifted in it. He noticed several oil paintings on the wall but thought it rude to examine them closely to see if any of the artists were notable.

Greta rose from her green velvet chair to embrace Serena. All the chairs in the living room were velvet and alternately green or pink, like the pine trees and flowers around the pool. Greta herself was attractive, with purplish eyes and delicate features, though her skin looked filmy, as if too much water had been poured over it. Yet, as she shook his hand and told him it was lovely to meet him that disconcerting effect quickly vanished. She had to be at least fifty, Tyler thought, but beyond that it was impossible to tell. The work that had probably been done on her face was world class, as one might have expected.

"I've heard such wonderful things about you, Mr. Green. I'm so glad you came by," Greta said.

For the first time in years Tyler felt something akin to a blush. "Thank you," he said, "I've heard the same about you."

"Please sit down."

He sank into a green velvet chair five feet from her. "Your home is magical," he said. He had meant to say magnificent, "magical" seeming to him too feminine a word, yet he'd said it for some reason and it seemed to please Greta, who was smiling even more broadly than before.

"Serena tells me you're an architect."

"I was a contractor for a number of years. I wanted to be an architect but one always wants more than one has," he said, looking away from Greta for a moment at the white curtains that framed the picture window. The color didn't match the scheme in the rest of the room yet it somehow seemed to work.

"He's writing a fascinating book about the nature of towns," Serena said. She was sitting to the left and slightly behind Greta and he reminded himself to occasionally look at her.

"Really?" Greta said. "Is it about Stockbridge?"

Here was his chance to talk about it, but now it no longer seemed to matter so much.

"It's more theoretical than practical, more about how certain features of towns function to fill our psychological needs, in general, than it is about a specific town, though I did use Stockbridge as a model."

"Did you happen to write anything about my house?" Greta said, looking at him without her smile for the first time, which made him feel momentarily nonplussed.

"I didn't know your house and so I didn't, but now that I've seen it I'd like to include it in what I'm writing very much, if that's all right."

"Of course, I'm flattered."

"I'll have to think about it first, though." He saw that both women looked a bit mystified. "I mean, I'll have to see how it fits into my theory of . . . towns."

"Can you tell me more about what your theory is?" Greta asked. For the next ten to fifteen minutes he did. He didn't falter this time, as he had other times when asked to articulate his ideas. The right words came to him easily, whole phrases emerging from him as if he were a practiced public speaker. When it was done he received still more compliments and felt as if in some way he'd conquered both women.

• • •

Serena had left, claiming she had an appointment in Lenox, and now he was alone with Greta. For a moment he had the feeling that he was being set up, that it had all been planned so that he'd be left alone with her. But a bigger part of him thought of Serena as too guileless to be part of a scheme like that. Besides, while he half-heartedly offered to go, too, and said something to Greta about not wanting to "monopolize her time," she all but insisted he stay, which he realized was what he wanted to do anyway. In fact, in an odd way he felt powerless to leave. It was not that he was attracted to her in a conventional way. Sexually, he couldn't picture it—yet some force seemed to keep him rooted to his chair, and to their conversation. Was there really such a thing as a compelling personality? All he knew was that he couldn't stop talking to her. So far she'd been asking him most, if not all, the questions, but he wanted to find out many things about her life. Such as what she did with her free time? How did she get to this point in life? What exactly had happened to her husband? Did she have any children? (He thought Serena told him she didn't but that her house was often filled with guests.) Perhaps, most of all, what was it like to inhabit such a huge house, one that he couldn't yet fit into his theoretical model of a town? It was as if her home was somehow larger, or at least more complicated, than the rest of Interlaken put together, and yet she didn't seem, sitting there so serenely, to have the energy and dedication to detail to make it all run smoothly.

He wanted to know all this with an urgency that surprised him yet found himself still answering questions that she apparently wanted to know about him. It wasn't unlike a game of tennis, he thought, where one player (in this case, Greta) keeps the other pinned to the backcourt with a barrage of hard, deep ground strokes, forcing the other player into a defensive posture, which he can only break out of by an extremely powerful and well-placed shot of his own.

Finally his moment came. He had just answered her question about where he lived before retiring and moving to Stockbridge, answered her so succinctly that she was still sipping from a glass of water. At that precise moment he heard a strange sound, both muted and persistent, that lasted perhaps two seconds. That's when he took his "shot" by asking if she had any guests staying with her.

"No, I'm afraid there's no one here but us, and Andrew, of course."

"Oh," he said, nodding. He couldn't speak about the sound again—it would be rude. "I only ask because Serena told me that you often have many visitors."

"Oh my," she said, smiling broadly—a blush even appearing on her very pale white cheeks, as if he'd just flattered her in an extraordinarily deft and satisfying way. "If that's true, it's only because I've stopped going out . . . as much as I should."

"Why so?"

"Oh, just laziness, I suppose."

"It must be quite challenging to maintain the quality of your home," he said, a little awkwardly, "much less entertain people in it."

"One gets used to it," she said, her smile oddly contracted now. "I've little else to do. I'm not writing a fascinating book like you are."

"But I understand you're editing a fascinating magazine."

At least he would find out something about that.

"I'm really just providing some support. They forced me to accept the title of publisher, but others are really doing the work."

He wouldn't let it end that quickly and continued to question her. She never precisely refused to answer his questions—rather was masterful in evading any connection between her answers or anything else that might reveal a sense of narrative about her life. He did confirm that she was indeed divorced (here she made it clear by her facial expression alone that she wouldn't welcome any follow-up questions). She also said that she had no children but showed no sign of regret when she told him. She had inherited the house—it had simply always been here. When she was younger she traveled through Europe and South America, but now she rarely left the house. Would he, perhaps, like to see more of it? And so began his house tour. Even before they finished seeing the first three adjoining rooms he thought, "she's married to the house and the rooms are her children."

He saw a music room, in which there was a harpsichord and a glockenspiel. He saw a large room she called the Visitors Art Gallery, which contained art given to or bought by her from her many guests over the years, a few of whom were quite prominent painters. The library was not as large as he thought or feared and yet the books, most of which had brown or dark green leather covers, seemed to multiply as he looked at them, creating the impression that the room itself was expanding while he examined it. He noticed that the mahogany shelves gave an outdoors look to the room, although, like all libraries, it was the quintessence of the indoors.

"May I look for a moment?" he said, approaching the shelves before she said, "Of course."

He saw *The Collected Stories and Poems of Edgar Allan Poe*, Unamuno's *The Tragic Sense of Life* next to P. D. Ouspensky's *Tertium Organum*, Sartre's *Being and Nothingness*, next to Norman O. Brown's *Life against Death*, and next to that, a bevy of books about various kinds of black magic. He realized now that all the books had been repackaged in their leather covers. The cost in labor as well as money must have been astronomical, yet clearly the books weren't in alphabetical order.

"Your library is extraordinary. Is it organized according to any principle?"

"The books have been here for generations. I've long ago given up trying to alphabetize them . . . as new books keep coming in."

Next they saw a seemingly endless procession of bedrooms, half of which were decorated in a more traditionally feminine way, half in a more masculine manner. Somewhere during the flow of rooms she spoke to someone in her kitchen via an intercom. Turning to Tyler she said, "Do you prefer fish or meat for dinner?"

"Meat," he said automatically, but surely it wasn't time for dinner yet? Before he could check his own unreliable watch, a grandfather clock he hadn't yet seen next to him in the hallway struck six times.

"Would you mind shortening our tour and ending it at the dining room?" she asked.

"It's terribly kind of you, but I feel I've already stayed too long . . . I simply lost track of time."

"Don't be silly, of course you'll stay, for dinner. Time is all in our minds anyway, don't you think?"

The dining room (or at least the one she took him to) was neither as large as he'd thought nor as ornate. The mahogany table had a white linen tablecloth and a bowl of freshly cut pink roses in its center. The lamps were dimly lit, but two tall black candles near each place setting helped create a semblance of light. He wondered why it wasn't brighter in this room—there should still have been light outside—and then realized the windows in the dining room were atypically small, if indeed they weren't faux windows. A single painting, a skillful copy of *The Last Supper*, dominated the wall he was facing. It was perhaps the first work of art he'd seen in the house with overtly religious allusions.

The conversation lessened as they sipped their red wine (he pretended to drink more of it than he really did because he didn't like its taste). It was as if the oddness of the room was inhibiting them, Tyler thought, or perhaps they'd just been talking to each other for too long. He was relieved when Andrew brought the food into the room on a rolling cart. It was fun to eat with real silverware, though vaguely unsettling, as Andrew served them, to notice how white Andrew's skin was and how dim his eyes. Why hadn't he noticed that when Andrew first opened the door? Maybe he was too excited about entering the house; excitement often undermined perception. Also unsettling, from an aesthetic point of view, was the reproduction of the last supper painting on their plates, but of this he planned to say nothing. He did praise the food and deservedly so (the squash and artichoke hearts were especially tasty), thinking that might loosen up her conversation. Instead she answered him softly with a minimum of words, keeping her eyes averted from him. It was as if he'd lost her, or that part of her that seemed so interested in him as they'd talked the afternoon away. It was a definite blow to his ego, as if it hadn't been dented enough already, ever since he retired a year ago and essentially stopped hearing from Melissa, who was out living the high life while trying to make it as an actress in Hollywood, a doomed plan if ever there was one. He was thinking then about just when and how he would leave the house when he heard the noise again.

"What's that?" he blurted, no longer worrying if his question was in poor taste or not.

"I didn't notice, but it must be Andrew, he's the only one here," she said, looking at him almost indifferently.

A tremor passed through him. A human noise had definitely occurred, and as soon as dinner was over (he prayed there would be no desert), and not a moment longer, he really would leave. In fact, he placed his knife and fork on his plate to indicate that he was already finished.

Meanwhile Greta had rung a bell he hadn't noticed and within seconds Andrew appeared, tall and whiter than ever, as he stooped over his plate like a birch tree slightly bent in the wind.

"Yes, Madam?" he said, eyes focused completely on her.

"You must have made a noise that disturbed Mr. Green. Are you feeling all right?"

"Sorry, Madam, I have a cough."

"Do take care of it."

"Yes, thank you. It won't happen again."

She smiled slightly at Tyler then as if to say, that settles that. But it wasn't settled for Tyler. What he heard definitely wasn't a coughing sound.

"You may clear now, Andrew, and then bring the dessert."

"Yes, Madam."

There was no expression on Andrew's face. Tyler waited until the table was cleared before telling Greta that he'd already eaten too much of her food and couldn't possibly eat dessert. She scarcely seemed to acknowledge his remark, as if, once again, as in the case of "Andrew's noise," she hadn't heard it.

"I'm afraid I really must go now," Tyler said. He realized that on top of everything else he was starting to feel a little queasy. "You've been such a wonderful hostess," he added, but again she didn't respond or even look at him.

"It's amazing how much sickness people will tolerate, and still cling to life," she finally said, gazing into space.

Was she referring to Andrew? This time Tyler didn't respond. He was flabbergasted and starting to feel both extremely tired and vaguely out of focus. Could it have been the wine or else something he ate?

"I can understand people clinging to life if they have some important project, as you do, that they want to complete," she said, "but otherwise, really, what are they clinging to? After all, we think nothing of killing insects, every one of us is a murderer in that respect, and to me a person without a project is little more than an insect."

"I'm afraid I really must leave now Greta, I . . ."

"How is your daughter, by the way, the one who lives in California?"

How did Greta know about her? Had Serena told her? He was going to ask her about this but his dizziness was increasing.

"I'm afraid I'm not feeling very well."

"Oh dear."

"I'm dizzy and . . . I . . ."

"Don't try to talk," Greta said, as she once more rang the bell. In a few seconds Andrew reappeared.

"Mr. Green isn't feeling well and needs to lie down. Take him to one of the guest rooms."

He remembered getting up from his chair. He wasn't sure he'd be able to walk but didn't want Andrew to help or even touch him. They seemed to be going in a different direction than he'd taken before with Greta, and while they walked he thought he heard a new strangely muted medley of sounds, part moan, part wind, part chorus of stifled crickets. Then the hall seemed to suddenly expand in front of him until he couldn't see the end of it. He was just about to ask Andrew about this or at any rate to tell him he really couldn't walk anymore when Andrew stopped in front of a room and started fishing for a key. Then Tyler saw it. Perhaps sixty feet in front of him two or three people dressed in black and flashing by like vampires but with fixated stares more like zombies. It could have been a hallucination, but he heard the sound they made on the floor. He couldn't have imagined or hallucinated that, could he?

"You can lie down in here," Andrew said, ostensibly as oblivious to the vampire/zombies as to the dark symphony of sounds that preceded them. Tyler was so grateful to see a bed that he simply walked into the room and lay down on it just as Andrew closed the door. Almost immediately he fell asleep.

* * *

He must have slept a long time, well into the night, because when he woke up, though there were once again no clocks in the room (and his watch was missing), a dim purplish light was filtering through the windows and he guessed it to be somewhere between four and five. He felt certain that he'd been poisoned last night and was surprised that he hadn't vomited. He did feel a slight headache and dizziness but still felt a good part of his strength had returned. He was also certain now that he hadn't imagined the "people" he saw in the hallway anymore than he'd imagined those wind-like moans. This is a huge house of madness, he thought, which may well have other prisoners like myself. But was he a prisoner? It would be difficult to prove in a court of law. No one had forced him to stay as late as he did, nor could he prove he was actually poisoned.

He got up from the bed and tried the door only to discover it was locked from the outside. He'd predicted it to himself, yet he was shocked. Now, he clearly was a prisoner as he'd feared and as such couldn't knock or yell or do anything to cause Andrew to come to the room. Instinctively he felt his best chance was to be compliant and play along with them while waiting for his opportunity.

Why had he come to this house? Why? It began with his blind date with Serena, but why had he wasted so much time on her and later Greta instead of calling Melissa or simply flying to L.A. to see her on his own? How foolish to wait to be asked. How foolish to have that kind of pride with his own daughter.

He ran to the window. It was locked from the outside and though it was immense, it was divided into eleven rows of six small squares with each window framed by a panel of wood. He could see at once that he couldn't fit through any of them and pounded the window in frustration. But it was unbreakable glass and his hand throbbed in pain. What were their plans for him? Yet how could he begin to figure out the plans of the mad? Hadn't Greta said last night that she thought of certain people as insects?

His door opened then and he shivered, expecting to see Andrew or perhaps some other guard that he knew must exist. Instead, he was astonished to see Serena slip into his room wearing a white dress.

"Hello Tyler," she said, looking at him with a kind of confidence combined with a dash of disdain he'd never seen from her before.

"What's going on here? I want to leave at once."

"I wouldn't try the windows again," she said in that same disconcerting tone of voice.

"How did you know I did?"

"We know many things here. If you stay with us, you will too."

And so began their conversations, which would occur two or three times a day for an hour or so for what he guessed was a week. At some point while he was passed out they'd taken his watch from him, so it was difficult to guess the time, or even what day it was, much less the sequence of conversations and what was said in which one. And yet, what else did he have to do to occupy his time but to try to organize time itself into some semblance of order? His memories of his former wife, who'd divorced him, then of Melissa, were at first often excruciating to think about, and his work on towns absurd. His "town" was now the house, as his "house" was now this room. His theory on the archetype of towns seemed as irrelevant as the windows in his room, which he could neither open nor break.

Information about the house came slowly, though it had to be remembered whenever he got some and then fit into some kind of context. He remembered that during his first meeting with Serena he was not as tactful as he should have been and had blurted out a number of questions such as, who were the people he saw in the hall, and were they some kind of zombies or vampires. He got no direct answer to that question (which only served to confirm their existence), merely a fleeting look of concern. In conversation Serena was almost as evasive as Greta, but her face was far more revealing, especially, he discovered, when she was taken by surprise.

In their next meeting he held off on any more direct questions and controlled his tone of voice. Serena was still his only link to the outside world, and he wanted to increase his chances of being visited by her again. He also realized that if he asked little of her, her own purpose, and ultimately Greta's, might eventually emerge. So far, all she'd done was heap praise on Greta and the house and reiterate how all the guests were always so grateful to Greta. He'd hoped to find a crack in her loyalty so that they might potentially become allies and perhaps escape together, but so far he hadn't spotted any ambivalence in her about either the house or its owner.

It was only halfway through her third visit, which seemed to take place much later in the day than the first two, that he said, "She collects people, doesn't she, and then she destroys them?"

For the first time he saw fire in Serena's eyes. "Sometimes you have to kill the old to bloom the new," she blurted. Then catching herself, which he clearly saw in her anxious regretful eyes, she said she wasn't speaking literally of course, just metaphorically.

"You recruited me, didn't you? You use the Internet to meet people so you can bring them here."

"No one has ever regretted visiting Greta's house that I know of."

"I more than regret it. I loathe every room of it. It's killing me, as I'm sure it's killed many others."

"You're speaking out of anger and therefore not making sense. Anger has blinded you."

"Being in prison has a way of trying my patience, and don't tell me that I'm not in prison—that you're taking care of me again."

"But of course we are. When your spirit is angry it's easy to mistake opportunity for prison. You were in prison a long time before you came to the house."

"What are you talking about?"

"You've had a lot of years to be happy your way and can you honestly say you ever really were? You forget your e-mails to me where you talked about your loneliness after your divorce, your sadness about aging, all your career disappointments—and then the cruelest blow of all, your daughter moving to California and all but cutting herself off from you."

"Don't talk about her," he said, sitting back down on his bed and waving his arm weakly. He saw an image of Melissa as a child and felt a jolt of pain.

"Exactly," she said. "You've lived a life that is too painful to talk about. That, in fact, is the kind of life you've lived."

• • •

It was still sometimes difficult to think about Melissa but thinking about her had become more pleasurable than not—in fact, it was now his only source of pleasure. He thought he had spent his working life trying to advance his career, and then his retirement thinking and (less often) writing about the functions of towns, but he didn't spend his time doing either now that he was profoundly uncertain how much time he had left. Instead, he saw a gallery of pictures from his past of his blue-eyed, auburn-haired daughter. A game of gin rummy they played on the front porch. A Boston Marathon they attended, then a game of hide-and-seek that took place both in their house and in their yard. How she squealed with delight when she jumped out at him from her hiding place in the forsythia. These memories, and some lines he still recalled from the few letters she'd sent him, were his only solace and, besides Serena's visits, his only company as well. Since he now looked forward to thinking about Melissa, in what sense was Melissa in the past?

Still, it was difficult to remember their fights. He saw clearly how he'd isolated himself in his work, when he knew she needed some more attention, that out of some kind of fear, perhaps of his own need for her, he used his work as an excuse to withdraw from her, fearing . . . what? The very closeness he longed for now? What a way he'd lived. Serena was right: he had mislived his life.

He was still possessed with these thoughts, which came and left and returned again, like persistent ghosts, the next time he saw Serena. He no longer hoped she might become his ally, nor was he even angry with her. While he followed the ghost of Melissa, she blindly followed the tyrannical Greta. It was not as if he couldn't understand. So while he continued to confront her, he did it almost diffidently now, as if recalling something with his wife that had happened to them many years ago. He'd said, for example, in a mild tone of voice, "There wasn't ever a magazine, was there?"

"We knew the magazine would appeal to you," Serena said, with a smile she now permitted herself in light of the new atmosphere between them. "We knew you'd like to have an outlet to publish your work."

"Yes, it was my vanity that led me to the house and to every other wrong decision I made in my life. I see that it was all an illusion, of course, now that it's too late."

To which Serena merely nodded almost imperceptibly, with her Mona Lisa kind of smile.

"I suppose you got other people through different ways. You'd find out what their dreams were and tell them they must meet this 'most interesting woman,' who could help them come true. Greta, the keeper of dreams. Yes, that was the way you described Greta, as 'the most interesting woman.'"

"Greta is much more than merely interesting."

"Do you think she's God?"

Serena hesitated, "Greta is unique, but it takes some time and a true effort to understand her vision."

"But she understands us, of course," he said, with his old sarcasm again creeping into his voice.

"Yes," Serena said, "she does."

· · ·

Every day Andrew, and then finally a younger, well-muscled "assistant" named George, brought him his food. The large room also contained an adjoining bathroom—all his essential needs were met. At first he was afraid to eat the food, but after Serena ate some in front of him, that, combined with his ravenous appetite, made him eat the quite appealing food of the house once again.

In her last visit Serena told him that he was improving and might soon be allowed to exercise.

"Outside?" he asked.

She smiled. "Didn't you know there's a fully equipped gymnasium in the house?"

His life continued like this, gradually learning things about the house, without ever grasping its central purpose—much like his earlier life, he realized. No wonder that in his work on towns he began with his thesis about their purpose and proceeded from that so he could always have his thesis confirmed, a thesis that now meant nothing more to him than any dozen other ideas. Ah, it was ironic to have to use his mind this way, to be tested like this at his age.

Serena continued to be nice to him, and he looked forward more and more intently to her visits. He no longer referred to the house as a cult and barely ever talked about it anymore.

On her last visit she walked into his room wearing only a thin white bathrobe and offered herself to him. He stepped back, feeling both nervous and aroused, grateful and angry.

"She picked me for you, didn't she?" he said.

"She knows many things."

"All things?"

"More than we can count. But I was happy with her choice because you were always kind to me in your e-mails and on the phone. Even before I met you I liked you."

He looked at her shapely, still mysteriously youthful body and didn't know what to say or do. Old age really is like a second kind of childhood, he thought. It had been so long since he'd done it, would he still know how?

"You're not ready yet," she said. "I just want you to know we can do this if you ever want to."

"I've grown very fond of you," he said in spite of himself. "But I still want my freedom."

"You're as free as you ever were. Freedom is an illusion—it doesn't grow in nature—nature isn't free. It grows in our minds like the idea of heaven or perfection, but it's all an illusion that we generate inside ourselves, really."

"Did Greta teach you that?"

"Yes, she did. We may have misled you about the magazine, but not about our philosophical society."

She turned to leave but just before she opened his door (outside it he knew George and some other guards were waiting) he blurted, "I want to see my daughter."

"I want you to also. You will."

"When?"

"Soon."

"But don't bring her here."

"Don't worry. She'll never be a guest here. I promise."

"Thank you," he said, "for everything."

The door opened and closed. He felt something melt in his mind or heart, he couldn't be sure which. Could it be he was falling in love with a cult member, a slave of the house? He felt his eyes and discovered they were wet.

He remembered little of that night and later imagined he must have fallen asleep early. It was a strange sleep, deep but full of bizarre dreams and visions. Just before morning he entered a net of mists. He was running toward the water that he couldn't see to catch up with his little daughter, who had gotten loose. "Melissa, Melissa! Come back," he called out as he ran. Finally the mist disappeared. In front of him the sun was shining on a dazzling, emerald blue lake. Melissa was walking beside him holding his hand, first as a little girl, than as an adult, as she'd looked just before she left for California. They were talking easily about nothing in particular, and he was filled with an intense sense of joy.

He didn't wake up from this dream right away as he would have in the past, but managed to luxuriate in it for a long time, as if it were a movie he was directing. When he woke up he thought immediately of Serena. Like a miracle, she'd made the dream happen. She kept her promise, he said to himself with a smile. Then he thought of his dream again. It was like a glimpse into paradise.

ACKNOWLEDGMENTS

My thanks to the editors of the following publications, in which these stories first appeared:

Antioch Review	"The Dealer"
Confrontation	"Memo and Oblivion"
The Hopkins Review	"Caesar"
	"Memorial Day"
	"The Group"
Notre Dame Review	"The House"
Per Contra	"The Dolphin"
Pleiades	"Single Occupant House"
River Styx	"Mission Beach"
	"The Justice Society"
Story Quarterly	"The Interview"
TriQuarterly	"'Do You Like This Room?'"

My special thanks to Chris Cefalu, Edmund de Chasca, Doreen Harrison, Kimberly F. Johnson, Delia King, Barbara Lamb, Kelly Leavitt, and Greg Nicholl for their invaluable help.